DANGEROUS STROKES

A DARK MAFIA ROMANCE

BY LILITH ROMAN

Lilith Roman Books

Dangerous Strokes
First Edition | July 2023

Editing by Mackenzie Letson www.nicegirlnaughtyedits.com
Proofreading by Michele Ficht
Photos licensed from depositphotos.com

ISBN 978 1 7394803 0 1 (eBook Edition)
ISBN 978 1 7394803 1 8 (Paperback Edition)
ISBN 978 1 7394803 2 5 (Alternate Paperback Edition)

To find out more about the author please visit lilithromanauthor.com

AUTHOR'S NOTE

They're feared. Powerful. Ruthless.
And they don't just love... they worship.

Welcome to The Sanctum Syndicate series of interconnected standalones. Dangerous Strokes started as a short story that refused to listen to me. So it became a novel and I'm incredibly thankful it did, because this hero and heroine needed all the time in the world. Happy reading!

Love,
Lilith

CONTENT WARNING

Due to recent publishing guidelines, the list couldn't be included here, however I would never want to put a reader in an uncomfortable situation. This dark mafia romance is a work of fiction, and it contains violent and sensitive situations which could be triggering for some.

Please go to https://lilithromanauthor.com/lilith/books/warnings/for a full list.

DANGEROUS STROKES

THE SANCTUM SYNDICATE BOOK 1

LILITH ROMAN

BLURB

**It was supposed to be my last con.
But I didn't expect *him* to be the client.**

Dangerous, powerful, and drop-dead gorgeous, Ronan Hennessey's sharp blue eyes drew me in, but it was his wicked tongue that kept me there.

As one of the leaders of his underworld, I should have been scared. Instead, I was mesmerized. Enthralled.

So I sent him an invitation made of brush strokes and riddles, tempting him to chase me. One last adventure before I vanished to my island paradise after years of crooked black-market deals.

He was only meant to be a thrill. But when he called me his *little witch*, casting his own spell on me, my heart was in trouble.

Only, I didn't know someone else was already hunting me, determined to get revenge and make me suffer for a past deceit. It was only a matter of time until this enemy found my new identity.

Meeting Ronan changed everything and mine wasn't the only life on the line anymore.

Who will get to me first? The man who makes my soul sing, or the monster who wants to burn it?

PLAYLIST

Werewolf Heart – Dead Man's Bones
God Complex – VIOLENT VIRA
Left Me for Dead – Rob Dougan
Hell or High Water – From Days Gone – Billy Raffoul
Wicked Game – Chris Isaak
Change (In the House of Flies) – Deftones
PLEASE – Omido, Ex Habit
Me & My Demons – Omido, Silent Child
Love Is a Bitch – Two Feet
Vengeance – Zack Hemsey
Come Undone – Duran Duran
The Road to Hell, pt. 1 & 2 – Chris Rea
Iron Sky – Paolo Nutini
Daylight – David Kushner
Two Face (Omido Remix) – Jake Daniels, Omido
West Coast – Lana Del Rey
Love Surrounds You – Ramsey
Waking Up – MJ Cole, Freya Ridings
Sweet Dreams (Slowed + Reverb) – Ravens Rock
Nikki – Worakls
Mine – Sleep Token

*To the ones who can't find the light at the end of the tunnel...
it's there, waiting for you. You just have to bear the darkness
a little longer. You're stronger than you think.
You can do this.*

CHAPTER 1

Ronan

ANY THINGS WENT THROUGH MY MIND the moment this woman stepped into the private garden. They're gone now, though. Replaced by one singular thought burning its way through my chest, stealing the air from my lungs—*she'll eat me alive.* Bit by bit, she'll chew me whole, spit me out, then devour me all over again.

The strange thing is that I might actually ask her to do it. Might even beg. Which is why I know she must be a witch. There's no other explanation for this paradox, this timid, delicate thing delivering such a visceral omen.

I should listen to the details of the business meeting taking place at this very moment. But her pure, deep-set eyes, trapped in a limbo between gray and blue, put a spell on me with their peculiar sparkle. Just like that porcelain skin that seems to glow in this twilight. It makes me wonder if I'm the only one seeing the creature before us, or if I'm bewitched.

There's something about her. The way she timidly peeks at me from under those thin bangs that don't fully cover her forehead. Something about the way her delicate curves stand before us. She reminds me of those precious ancient statues adorning museum halls.

Us...

My mind shifts into gear, trying to break free from this witch's charm. I focus on all the people around me—my business partners, hers, and both our security teams.

"Ronan..." My brother's tone doesn't hide the fact that he's trying to get my attention. "Meeting in two days to see the painting and close the deal sounds good to you too, yeah?"

He's going to give me a hard time after this, I just know it.

"It does. We have a warehouse in a secure location, toward the edge of the city, quiet, secluded. We can meet there." They're the first words I've spoken since the meeting started, but I only seem to direct them at *her*—Ingrid Thorp.

"Respectfully, no." The spell breaks further as Erika Brand, her business partner, replies, pulling my attention.

"No?" I question, narrowing my eyes on the brown-eyed woman.

"No offense, Mr. Hennessey, but I would prefer we meet in a place of our own choosing. Where we are a bit more... comfortable."

She means safe. She doesn't trust us, but then again, she has no reason to. We've never met before. This business deal was arranged through the dark corners of the web, where shady deals are struck, and most are for items that will never see anything but a crooked market.

Ingrid seems to share the sentiment, shifting her weight from one leg to the other, rubbing her fingers together. Her eyes nervously flash from the floor to me enough times that it gets me wondering—is it because of the meeting or... me?

A strange heat fills a part of me that has no business waking up right now.

"I believe we should all be *comfortable,* should we not?" I was expecting this. "Name the place. We'll tell you if it works for us."

Erika purses her lips and reluctantly agrees after her eyes drift briefly to my brother. "Rosenberg Hotel, in one of the private dining rooms of the restaurant. Eight in the evening, in two days—Friday."

I turn to my brother Finn, to my right, Maddox and Carter behind me, and Vincent to my left. They all nod.

"Very well. We will bring our own appraiser and continue the conversation there."

"Just a reminder, to ensure we are all on the same page. The price is no longer negotiable, and the sale will be final."

"Final? No."

"Yes," she insists.

Erika's back straightens further, her attitude grave, like until now she kept her guard low so she could offer us some sense of ease. Maybe under any other circumstances, I would be affected.

Not now. Not when my eyes drift once again to the porcelain witch standing quietly beside her, head tilted down ever so slightly. Not with that deceiving virtue painted on her lush lips, when her eyes scream of wickedness.

A bizarre desire grows inside of me, one that wants to crack her open and find out where that wickedness comes from.

"If you do not agree with the terms," Erika continues, unwavering, "we have a long list of buyers, as you well know, who would accept them in a heartbeat. Considering the...

dubious provenance of the painting, surely you understand why we have to wash our hands of it right away."

"And surely you understand why three million is a lot of money to gamble with," I argue.

"If you're looking to gamble, Mr. Hennessey, I suggest visiting The Royal Casino on third street. We are seeking a business deal here." I think the air is sucked out of the atmosphere as Ingrid speaks for the first time.

Her voice distracts me from the obvious bite of her words. She sounds like a birdsong filling a meadow on a warm summer day, and I crave to be right there with her.

"Careful now, that sharp tongue and those steel eyes will get you in trouble." I lower my voice, reveling in the shock painted vividly on her parted lips. For a split moment, I forget it's not just us.

"What my partner means to say..." Erika says quickly, "is that we do not wish to waste our time or yours. We are positive that you will be pleased with the piece."

"Friday. Eight o'clock. The Rosenberg," I almost rasp, my throat constricting, my lungs close to heaving.

I'm suffocating.

That woman... she's infusing the oxygen with her seemingly innocent black magic, and I need to break the damn spell.

I have to walk past her to leave, and I can't stop myself from glancing over my shoulder. She turns her head slightly, but our gazes never connect.

I'm not sure if it makes me feel better or worse, but she's trying hard not to look at me. As I am at her.

It doesn't matter. The heat of her body as I brush past her seems to have the same effect.

***

We've just passed through the gates of the garden, my steps heavy and quick, eager to get the fuck out of there, when my brother gives me a forceful nudge.

"What the hell was that, man?! Do you even know what happened in that meeting?"

I roll my eyes, heading toward the driver's side of the Range Rover parked across the street, Finn falling into step behind me.

"I think we all know what happened there," Vin says, to my dismay.

Most people have an irrational fear of Vincent Sinclair's attention on them. I am no exception. It's the darkness of his black eyes that I try to avoid when I look in the rearview mirror. I swear to the gods the man can look into your soul, peel all the layers until he finds the exact information he needs to hold against you. He's five or six years younger than my twenty-seven, yet his talent doesn't show his age. He gets better the more he practices, putting the fear of God into people. Only, those people have begun calling him *The Serpent*, and they don't think it's God they should fear when they fall under his gaze.

He's a good kid, though—all four of them are.

My brother, Finnigan, the pretty boy who has been turning heads with his baby blues and curly blond locks, long before he started filling those shoulders and pecs with muscle.

Maddox Severin, who has never looked his age, towers over all of us. His wide, muscled frame growing month by month, nurtured by his hunger for grueling workouts and fighting. He's the one who trains all our men and we've had to build him a gym so he can focus his brute force there, not on our guys.

Then there's Carter Pierce, the man with peculiar dark blue and hazel eyes, that are as beautiful as they are empty. He's always prim and proper, with his white shirts, sleeves rolled up to his elbows, tweed waistcoats, and impeccable slicked-back hair and undercut. He doesn't really look like he's from this time. He's quite something—different. A man of few words and the ones he sometimes chooses make me wonder about the skeletons in his closet. Or maybe severed heads in the fridge. Yet he's the one I gravitate toward the most, and even after all these years, I still don't understand why.

We started this organization more or less together, even though Carter and Finn were away at university for a portion of it. It worked to our benefit. All the connections they sought there have proved fruitful, while Vin, Madds, and I built the bases here.

"There he goes again. He's gone."

"Fuck you!" I spit at Madds, who kicks my seat from behind.

"Wouldn't mind being lost in that blue-eyed little thing either," Finn teases.

"Gray..." I whisper. But it comes out more like a grunt. A visceral need to smack my brother's head against the dashboard arises, and I can't make sense of it. Even aware that the asshole is just messing with me.

"What did you say?"

"Nothing."

The engine roars to life, covering the rest of the bullshit coming out of their mouths. But it does nothing against my intrusive thoughts about the woman who almost took my damn breath away. I don't even dare ask myself if they all noticed it. I already know they did.

Fuck!

I put my foot down, the streetlights of Queenscove blurring as I drive through the night, knowing full well I'm stupidly attracting the attention of both the residents and the tourists of this seaside city. The majority of them are currently out on the streets since it's Saturday night.

Does it really matter, when we have most of the police in our pocket anyway? They won't stop us.

With my fingers tightening around the steering wheel, my mind drifts to those prominent cheeks, her round eyes, silky brown hair, square, yet delicate jaw... that high cupid's bow that begs to be licked.

Jesus Christ, what is wrong with me?

More importantly, what the hell is going on with her? Who is she and what is she doing here? A woman like her, so delicate and soft, doesn't belong in this cruel world—our world. It's too harsh for her, but I have to admit... she stands out beautifully.

That wicked gaze she left me with haunts my mind, a touch of darkness weaving through her soul, and I want to reach in and grab it by the throat. Squeeze it just enough that my dick wakes up at the slight tremor of fear that will no doubt shake her flesh.

Annika

DID I THINK THE MAN I SAW IN A PHOTO WEEKS AGO WAS going to be like *that* in real life?

No.

Did I think my skin would hold a constant stream of goosebumps during the entirety of our meeting, like I was being shocked the whole time?

No.

Did I think the man I've been obsessing over would fixate on me to the point I kept forgetting there were other people in the room?

No. But he did.

I was in a state of disbelief, of unrelenting tension, and something else... something that was making me both want to run and never leave his scrutinizing gaze.

I'm not sure what I expected from this meeting. I know what I hoped for but was certain wasn't going to happen. Men don't notice me, not when my best friend and business partner is around. With her golden hair always neat and sleek, her light brown eyes enhanced by perfect make-up, her professional clothes clinging to every delicate curve. She's full of color, brightness, and confidence, and I'm the one who blends into the background—one with the shadows at times.

This time, though, it wasn't like that. Even when he addressed her, Ronan Hennessey was looking at me. And no matter how much I prepared myself, I still had no idea what to do with myself.

I would feel guilty for not paying full attention to the business deal we were making, but my part in this usually finishes before this type of meeting takes place. It's normal for me to be tucked away in a corner, only intervening if someone asks specifics about the paintings. Hanna, or Erika, as the men we just met know her as, is the brains behind it all. I, Annika, not Ingrid, as I told them, craves the adrenaline of this business, but not the leadership of it. So I keep to myself, observing everything, supporting her. This time around, it was different.

After their organization won the black-market auction we launched for the long-lost Dubois painting—The Lady in White—Hanna began her usual research into the buyers. It was then that the photo of Ronan Hennessey fell in my lap, and I had trouble forming words. My skin was damp in a second, my breathing went wild, and my lower belly was doing strange somersaults. Never in my twenty-three years have I had a reaction like this to a man. Let alone just a photo of one. Unbeknownst to her, I started forming my own plan.

My usual shyness went out the damn window in that meeting. I still can't believe how I talked back to him. Hanna couldn't either. She asked me afterwards what had gotten into me, but I couldn't respond. Not yet.

Before I met him, I had so many questions about the

wide-shouldered man with eyes as blue as the clear summer sky. Was he a hard man? Were his good looks deceiving? Like a carnivorous plant, attracting insects with its pretty flowers and sweet nectar? Was he a horrible man? A rapist? A murderer?

Now, after I met him, I've answered none of the above, but have so many more questions.

I know nothing beyond how strong his jaw is, how soft his slicked back dirty-blond hair looks, and how contrasting the kindness of his eyes is to his overall image. That's what trapped me, just like those carnivorous plants—his eyes.

Before the meeting, I started forming a plan, knowing full well I never had to put it in motion. Not until I met him, until I got a sense for him in real life. See if his voice stirred the same feeling in me as his looks did. Find out if his eyes were deceiving or if he really did have some kindness in him. Men who ran entire mafias, who bought black-market paintings worth millions on the dark web, who dealt in God knows what else, rarely were.

After the meeting, my decision was made. The way he spoke of my eyes cemented my plan. That and how he spit back at me about my sharp tongue, sending a shock all through my body, settling deep in my belly, and refusing to let go. I'm constantly squeezing my thighs together, failing to release whatever hold he has on me, and I would curse myself for being so damn weak. I would, but I won't. This is exactly what I want. What I need... What I crave.

I want to fuel this obsession.

Nurture it into a new life.

Because I knew from the way he watched me, like he wanted to devour me whole, that he would be my end and my new beginning.

CHAPTER 2
Annika

"ARE YOU READY?" HANNA ASKS, SMILING AT me before she climbs into the back seat of the car.

One of our security guys holds the door open so I can follow.

"I am."

I'm lying.

I know what her question means—*are you ready to close the last deal of our career and retire to the dream houses we bought in Falk Isle?*

I'm not.

I've lived more in the four years since starting this business than most people live in a lifetime. I've met some of the sweetest people and others who make my skin crawl to this day. I've had more identities than I have surviving family members. I've lived in more cities than I have fingers on both hands. And yet I'm not done.

She clasps my hand and squeezes it reassuringly.

"You're fidgeting. It's going to be fine, Anni. It's no different than all the other jobs."

I pull my hand out of her hold when I feel it getting clammy, wiping it on my dress before I grab onto the collar of it and make some room for air to go through.

"It's hot in here. Why didn't we cool the car before we left? The painting is going to melt."

"It's insulated and protected. It will be fine," she says, squeezing my hand again.

I won't.

Before every meeting, I ask myself, sometimes Hanna too, the same sort of questions. Will they know? Did I make a mistake? Did I miss something? It's funny how the same questions give me anxiety, only I'm looking for different answers now. I'll get them soon enough, if my plan goes well.

I slam back into the seat, catching the gaze of the driver in the rear-view mirror. He averts it quickly, but I don't miss the slight uneasiness.

"Is there something going on with..." I subtly point to him as I whisper to Hanna.

She's smirking. "I think you're a myth to them. They didn't have much proof of your existence until recently."

"What are you talking about?"

"We've had this team for months now, and up until two days ago, none have seen you properly. I think they've seen your shadow around the house, the blur of you as you quickly emerged for snacks before running back to your studio. But nothing more."

"Oh..."

I turn back in my seat and catch a glimpse of both the driver and the passenger trying to steal looks. It dawns on me that I don't even know their names. I'm awful. They'll think I don't care, that I'm some bitch who thinks nothing of them. But that's not the case at all. I just... disappear.

"Don't worry. I've explained to them that when you work, you retreat in your own little world, like a parallel dimension where you can live in the strokes of your paintings. They knew they wouldn't really get to see you, but they had to keep you safe wherever you were hiding. I think they're just getting their fill of your beautiful face while they have you."

I can't help but roll my eyes.

"Sure. Stop talking like I'm some fair maiden living in a tower with princes lining up to catch a glimpse."

"You may as well be."

I scoff, ending that subject then and there. I'm a weird recluse, not some freaking fair maiden.

The period buildings of Queenscove's old center make an appearance outside the car windows, distracting me. They're imposing in their beauty, not their size, the ocean acting as their background on the left side.

We've been here for a little longer than we usually settle in one place. Although we've been fairly hidden, since this last deal has taken so much longer to complete. But I would be lying if I didn't admit that I've stalled slightly too. One day, after I was cooped up in my studio for just over four weeks, frustrations running high, anxiety beginning to cripple me, I needed air. I had to get away from that space, the house. It happens rarely, but this particular job has been different. It's the end of our journey, and there's something about this Laurent Dubois painting that gave me so much trouble.

Maybe it's the meaning of it.

Either way, that night I ran out of my studio, out of the house, and lost myself in Queenscove's streets. Before I knew it, I was here, in the old center, and the ocean at the end of all these streets made me fall in love hard. There's something about this city that speaks to a different side of me than the one who wants to live in a cottage, in a small fishing village.

So, I stalled. Just a little bit.

"We're here." Hanna startles me out of my thoughts.

The car stops and out her window, the private back entrance of the Rosenberg Hotel greets us. It's been one day, twenty-three hours, and thirty-five minutes since I laid eyes on Ronan Hennessey for the first time. In person.

My heartbeats seem to echo in my chest, like the cavity is entirely hollow, this anticipation excruciating. I almost jump when one of the guys opens my car door.

"Here we go." I whisper to myself.

It will be the last deal we strike together... and the first I strike on my own.

Ronan

IT'S JUST LIKE ANY OTHER BUSINESS MEETING—WE MEET, we see the asset, we pay, we shake hands, and we leave.

But this is not like any other business meeting at all... is it? This one is with *her*.

It's been forty-eight fucking hours of those blue-gray eyes haunting every single moment of my day, and every second of my nights. She creeped into my thoughts at the most inconvenient of times, distracting me, keeping me awake, filling my dreams. Last night I could barely sleep because I knew those eyes would be staring at me today. Reinforcing their hold, along with the spell she must have put on me.

Even now, as I sit at this table in one of Rosenberg's private dining rooms, her eyes cloud my mind. Enticing, entirely too fucking mesmerizing.

And suddenly, they're real. Staring right at me.

"Gentlemen. Good evening."

I rise from the chair at the same time as the guys, and inhale so fucking deep, I think my lungs will rip at the seams. I need all the oxygen I can muster to get through being in this small room with her. But a faint wildflower scent fills me, and all that air gets knocked right out of me. *Shit.* My cock twitches—I don't think it got the memo that this is a business meeting. Who can blame it? She looks like a siren, that black dress hugging her perky tits and small waist before falling off her delicate hips, revealing nothing more than her slender arms and perfect legs below the knees.

We all greet them, shaking hands over the table. When I touch *hers*, she pulls away so damn fast, you'd think I burned her. But she's the one who seared my skin.

"Please. Have a seat," Carter says, pointing to the chairs on the other side of the table.

Another deep breath fills my lungs and I steady myself. I need to be present this time around. I can't have a repeat of the first meeting.

Only, my eyes betray me, and when I catch her gaze already on me, it feels stolen. She turns immediately, running over all the faces in the room, and it's not hard to notice that she's forcing her composure. I cock my head just as her eyes land back on mine, grinning just enough that it throws her off her game and her alabaster cheeks flush pink.

Either she's just as affected by me as I am by her, or... it's the meeting making her uneasy. Which is another reason why I need to focus.

"Gentlemen, I hope you understand that Ingrid and I don't want to linger too long, so if you don't mind, we would like to go straight to business." Erika, the prim and polished one my brother wouldn't shut up about yesterday, speaks.

But that's not what I want; I want this meeting to last as long as it takes me to get my fill of Ingrid.

"Just a moment," I say, lifting a finger.

She frowns, but a knock sounds at the door.

"Come in."

The women and their security stiffen, but Finn lets them know the waiter is here. We quickly order our drinks and refuse food, anxious to get to the important part of the evening.

"Apologies. You see that horizontal thin strip of glass about a third way up the common wall with the corridor?" Finn explains. "It was Rosenberg's delicate way of ensuring you can see if someone's coming so you can halt the conversation."

"This place was built with a purpose, I see," Erika says, brightening a shade as she looks at my brother.

I turn to him, and the man is the same. What the fuck is it with these women? We spoke three words, yet somehow, we seem wrapped around their little fingers.

"I suggest we wait until the waiter returns with the drinks before you show us the painting. In the meantime, we wouldn't mind learning more of its provenance, especially since it has been lost for... almost a hundred years now, is it?"

I try to distract them from each other.

"Over." Ingrid speaks just above a whisper, and her voice sends a rush of shivers through my chest.

I'm back in that meadow again.

"*Over* a hundred years," she clarifies more boldly.

I nod and rest my elbows on the table, clutching my hands together, a grin slowly pulling at my lips.

"So how did you come across it after it's been lost for *over* a hundred years?"

"I'm afraid the story is as anticlimactic as we've shared before. It was found hidden in an attic," Erika replies instead.

"Just like that, The Lady in White, the long-lost Dubois, forgotten in an attic." I direct my response to Erika, but my eyes never leave the steel-eyed witch.

"It was my attic. Well, my grandfather's, actually." Ingrid speaks, that revelation making me straighten my back.

But her partner seems to have followed too. Once again, I

think the woman is doing something out of character.

Is this an insight into her life? Why did she willingly share it? Is she trying to make the information more believable? Because, to be honest, the fact that it is a piece of her makes it all that more unbelievable since she's sharing it with us, of all people.

"My great-grandfather worked at Venator Castle. He was there in 1931 when the fire broke out, and he was so deeply attached to the painting, that he had to rescue it before the flames took it. According to my grandfather, The Lady in White was the spitting image of my great-grandmother. She was already dead. She died in childbirth and was the absolute love of great-grandpa's life. He refused to take another woman after her, and the only photo he had of her was misplaced. He was left with only The Lady in White. So, the official story was that it was charred in the fire."

Fuck...

She's not lying. I have no idea how I can tell, but she's not. Maybe it's the slight sparkle in her eyes or her flushed cheeks, but the woman before me has just bared a part of herself.

For what purpose?

I look at the guys and they all match my stare, even the stern Vin and the emotionless Carter—her story is true.

The waiter knocks before entering with our drinks, holding us all in a strangely uncomfortable silence, more questions lingering in the air. I'm not sure what it was about that story, but it held emotions, and this transaction has suddenly become more personal.

Or more dangerous.

"Please," I say, gesturing to the painting as soon as the waiter closes the door behind him.

Erika rises and gently unwraps it, the tension sizzling in the windowless room, and as soon as the last of the covering comes off, I suck in a breath.

It's her.

Spitting goddamn image of the woman sitting across from me. Sure, her lips are thinner, her nose just a bit larger, her hair more on the blond side than Ingrid's, but... the resemblance is there.

Am I imagining it? I turn to my right and catch Vin's eyes going between Ingrid and the woman in the painting at rapid speed. No, I'm not imagining it.

Carter rises at the same time as Anthony and Jonathan, the appraisers we brought with us, and they circle the piece of art like hawks.

Technically, Jonathan is far from an appraiser, but the man was born, raised, and bred in galleries, auctions, and museums. It's his love for art that made him dive into the stealing and selling of it too. Even though now he's moved up and he runs a criminal organization which facilitates smuggling and other endeavors. But art is how he met his partner in both crime and life, Anthony. He's the appraiser. That was his job when they met. He investigated the authenticity of paintings and sculptures. From what we've heard from Carter, who put us in contact with Jonathan—his father's best friend—Anthony almost called the police on him when he realized he was authenticating a stolen painting. They've been together ever since. Quite romantic, really.

In our underworld, not many stories have happy beginnings. Or ends, for that matter.

"Fascinating," Anthony mutters to himself.

They pull out a series of rare old photographs which were digitized and blown up, to attempt to compare the two. They are the same age as Ingrid's great-grandfather, so they work more as general guidelines, unfortunately. But even in that poor quality, you can see the tinge of a resemblance with the woman before us.

The final confirmation of authenticity will be in the chemical analysis. And it better check out, because the only way we can order that whole lot of tests, is by buying the piece.

We're hoping Anthony and Jonathan's eyes can spot any inconsistencies, if there are any.

"And you mentioned some restoration has happened?"

"Yes. Unfortunately, there was some smoke damage, so it has been cleaned, and some small areas restored," Ingrid replies to Anthony.

He nods, returning to his inspection while Jonathan steps back, looking intently at the work of art, his gaze flashing to Ingrid every few minutes.

This lasts for the better part of an hour. The two men even step out twice to discuss in private, and when they return for the second time, even though Jonathan seems more reserved, they declare their satisfaction. Much to the pleasure of my partners, Madds doing a very bad job at hiding his restlessness.

I can't blame him, especially since the conversation was strained. Finn couldn't take his eyes off Erika, and Ingrid and I appeared to be looking anywhere but at each other. It didn't ease the tension, though, constantly being drawn to the woman before me.

"Well, gentlemen, it was a pleasure doing business with you." Erika firmly shakes our hands after the money transfer is confirmed, lingering a moment longer on Finn. Ingrid, steps back, nodding her goodbye. She's either eager to leave this room or is avoiding touching us. Or me.

At this point, I'm eager to get the fuck out of here too, my body so tightly wound, my back damp from the strangeness of this interaction. I haven't touched a cigarette since I was in school, but I'll be damned if I wouldn't smoke a whole pack of them right now.

Nah, I need to hit the gym. Maybe jump into the ring with Madds. Either way, I need to blow off some steam as soon as possible. Beat the image of Ingrid out of my damn mind and erase her brief touch from my body.

It's not like I'm ever going to see her again anyway.

Then why is that thought making me even more antsy?

CHAPTER 3
Ronan

"**S**O DID IT CHECK OUT?"

My brother enters the office of our latest business venture. A legal one this time—Midnight, our speakeasy. Carter and I were looking through some new membership applications who have gone through our vetting, since the clientèle has to be very carefully chosen. It was his idea to open something like this. A place inspired by the roaring twenties, private, comfortable, an interesting space for all sorts of people to meet, whether for business or pleasure.

It's also the safest place for the painting until we wash our hands of it and make a small fortune too.

"It did," I say, my brows furrowing. "Why exactly do you look disappointed?"

"What? No, I'm glad. I'm happy... so happy," he trails off.

"For fuck's sake, man. Don't tell me; you wanted to see Erika again."

His eyes widen for a moment—I fucking caught the bastard.

"You know you could just ask her out, right? You don't need an excuse like a fake painting to see her again."

"Nah, man, you're so off. I'm not interested."

If only I hadn't known him since he was born. I roll my eyes and turn to one of the documents Carter pushes my way.

"So, it's all good, we can move forward with this deal?" he continues.

"Yeah, we can. There was a little bit of doubt with one of the colors, apparently. Back in those days, they used plants and natural sources or substances to obtain them. One of the shades of blue posed some uncertainty, but not enough to warrant it being fake. The margin of error is way beyond that," Carter explains.

"Right, right..." Finn drifts off again before he finally walks out, a bit deflated.

He's going to drive me mad until he meets this woman again. I've never seen him like this. It's been over a week, and every time we're outside, or in a bar, or restaurant, or goddamn anywhere, for that matter, he's on edge. Constantly looking around, just in case he sees her again.

But... fuck, I've been looking right along with him.

Maybe because of the masked sinfulness in Ingrid's gaze, or the softness of her. Of the way she looks, like she belongs in those times when this painting was done, draped in fine silks, with a crown of flowers on her head.

"Do you guys need me tonight?"

Madds all but bursts through the office door.

"Christ, man, one of these days we'll fucking shoot you by accident if you keep barging in like you're about to kill us all."

He scrunches his eyebrows like he has no clue what I'm referring to.

"So, do you?" he asks again.

"I don't think so. Why? What the hell did you do?" I walk around the desk and take a better look at him—red cheek, faint bruise under his left eye, his knuckles banged up.

The man simply shrugs.

"Just blew off some steam."

"I hope you kept it under wraps."

I'm getting a headache.

"Umm... yeah. Sure."

He straightens, and I can't help but laugh. Our friendly giant isn't even trying to hide the fact that he's lying.

"It was for a good cause. I was helping a lady in need," he explains.

"You know... ladies?"

"I know one for sure."

I want to ask more, so much more, but his grip on the door handle and frame threatens to break them both if he doesn't leave.

"I swear, we might as well build a damn bare-knuckle boxing establishment in our basement. At least you can make some money out of all this pent-up energy of yours."

He cocks his head, scrunching his eyebrows like he's genuinely considering the idea.

"I mean..." I hear Carter behind me, and I turn my head to him as he crosses his arms. "It could certainly be interesting. We've been trying to find a better solution for the money laundering side of things."

I can see the wheels turning in his head, but Madds pulls me back to him.

"Sounds good to me. I'm gonna go now. Call me if you need me."

Where the fuck is he running to?

"Just... take it easy," I tell him, knowing full well that is not what he's going to do.

I want to touch the painting and feel Ingrid's skin against mine. That one searing touch when we shook hands was nowhere near enough. Never in my fucking life have I been so wrapped up in a woman. Yet so reluctant to seek her.

What am I afraid of?

"She's perfect, isn't she?" Carter asks, appearing next to me.

"She is..."

"She would look quite perfect out in the bar if we didn't have to sell her."

Sell her?!

Fucking hell, he's talking about the painting... of course. I rub my temples and sit in the leather chair behind the desk, clearly needing some space from the image of *her*.

She is spellbinding, and the sooner I get rid of that steely gaze following me around this room, the sooner I can go back to business as usual.

Wait... I quickly go back to the canvas, leaning over to take a closer look at her eyes. The painting itself is only about twenty inches in height and fifteen in width, but it's not a close-up portrait. It's the full image of her sitting in a chair. So even though the details are quite clear, like her facial features, the texture of the various fabrics and surfaces, the scale of the woman itself is quite small.

A tiny detail like her eyes could be missed, especially when there aren't many records of it.

I might be mistaken. I may be remembering this wrong... but if I'm right, we're fucked. Erika and Ingrid even more so.

"Carter, I seem to remember there is an old tale about Venator. It briefly mentions Lady Bournwell. Can you please do some research, find it, and call me as soon as you do," I tell him as I quickly walk around the desk, grabbing my phone and shooting a quick text before I grab my car keys too.

"Will do. What are you seeing, Ronan?"

"I'm not sure, but if I'm right..."

"Yeah, I'm still here. Why?" Finn startles us when he slams through the door, in response to my text.

"I think you might get your wish and see your darling Erika once more. But I'm not sure either of you will enjoy this meeting."

I can't pinpoint the look in his eyes—confusion, excitement, anger? Either way, I have a hunch that it matches mine.

"Ronan," Carter warns. "What are you seeing?"

I turn to The Lady in White aka Lady Bournwell, making sure once again that my eyes aren't playing tricks on me. They're not.

"The color of her eyes..."

Annika

MY DAMP SKIN BURNS UNDER HIS PALM AS HE DRAGS his hand down over my breast, without pausing to give it the attention it needs. Only a gentle squeeze, not enough before he moves down my middle, pushing his front against my back, steadying me with his firm touch on my lower belly. My body melts against him when he reaches my wet pussy, sliding a finger between my folds, spreading that wetness over my clit. Knees threatening to buckle, I don't have time to steady myself before I'm bent over the table in front of me and he's down on his knees behind me.

I grab onto the edge of the wood, just as he spreads my legs and grabs my ass cheeks, opening me up to him. I'm shaking for different reasons now. When he blows against my center, my whole body shudders and the dirty sound that escapes my parted lips makes him growl. I know it's coming, his tongue is so close to my clit, I can almost feel it, and...

"*Anni...*"

"Ronan..." I moan.

"Anni!"

Huh?

"Babe, wake up. We have to go soon."

My eyes snap open, and I look around me like the house is on fire. But it's only Hanna here, watching me with a strangely suggestive look. Heat grows in my cheeks, but I turn and quickly jump out of bed, heading toward the bathroom.

"So... did you sleep well?"

"Yes, fine," I mumble before shutting the bathroom door behind me.

"Just fine. Interesting." I hear her muffled chuckling.

Fuck's sake.

Was I moaning in my sleep? Oh God, this is mortifying.

Bracing myself against the sink, I'm met with the most serene face in the mirror. I'm not sure who that woman is, but she doesn't quite look like me. The gray-blue eyes resemble a gemstone instead of the usual muted steel. She's... glowing.

"It must be the humidity." I roll my eyes at myself and turn the faucet on cold, before splashing enough water on my face to erase the lingering touches from that dream.

By the time I'm done, I know it's not enough. It's changed nothing, because every time I close my eyes, I can see his hand on my breast, sliding down my body, even the shock of the moment I'm slammed against the wood, bent over the table.

"Shower. I just need a shower. A cold one."

I quickly turn it on, undressing as fast as I can, and jump straight in. Instant goosebumps rush over me, the water becomes like ice against my hot skin and, unfortunately those chills have the opposite effect on my pussy. It constricts so tightly around nothing but the memory of those fingers sliding between my folds, frustrated that I woke up before it got further.

"Focus, Annika. Focus!"

But how can I when this fantasy is fueled by adrenaline of my own creation?

Is he going to find me? Find us?

I need to get away from Hanna. She shouldn't be involved in any of this. She's going to kill me when she finds out what I've done. She's going to ask me why and I have no concise answer.

* * *

Leaning against the open front door, I watch as the last of our belongings are loaded into the moving truck. My paintings are there, most of my supplies, some of Hanna's favorite pieces of furniture, irreplaceable antiques, most sourced through questionable means. Only a select few are there, and they're all going into storage for now, before they'll be loaded in a container and shipped home.

Home.

What a strange word... after all these years of being nomads, of being different people, we will finally have everything we worked for.

Then why do I feel so utterly incomplete?

The doors to the truck close with a loud, metallic bang, then the movers walk over to Hanna, and I watch them have a brief discussion. One of them looks besotted as he listens to her speak, the other glances my way, nodding once. That's it. No one ever lingers, no one ever watches me with that yearning look, with hunger.

Except...

No. Not now. You need to focus!

But then again, there is a reason why I'm going off plan, and he has far too much to do with it all.

"It's strange, isn't it?"

Hanna startles me. When did she finish talking with the movers? When did she walk next to me? I swear, I'm losing it.

"What is?"

The two guys wave at us before they climb into their truck. I wave back, then turn my attention to her.

"This... it's over. Everything in the house is gone. The charity called to say thank you, by the way. The rest of our prized possessions are on their way to our forever homes. I don't know, this whole adventure we've been on for the last few years is finally done and somehow it feels..."

"Bittersweet." I fill the pause.

She nods, her gaze on the truck disappearing behind the hedgerow at the edge of the property.

"Most people could only dream of retiring before they hit thirty... or forty, or fifty, for that matter. And we now have that," she says, turning to me with a sheepish smile on her red lips. "The adventure is over."

"And you're okay with that. Right?" I question, lightly narrowing my eyes.

She nods again, pausing a bit longer than necessary.

"Hanna, are you alright?"

"I am, yes, sorry. It's just strange. All these business deals, the risks, the rush... I'm so used to them. Don't get me wrong, I'm looking forward to the cocktails on the beach, the nights swimming in the ocean or my pool, the books, all the projects I have planned. I was even thinking of opening a charity of my own, doing something more with all this money. But it will just be a bit of an adjustment, I guess."

Only, I'm not ready to adjust. She seems to be. Which is why what I'm about to tell her might fuck with all that peace.

I sigh and take a seat on the first step.

"I'm looking forward to all of that too, but... not just yet."

She climbs down the few stairs until she stands in front of me, her eyes wide, expectant.

"What do you mean, Annika?"

Shit, she only ever calls me by my full first name when she's serious. I rub my hands over my face, thankful to be make-up free right now.

"I... shit, I don't know how to tell you this."

"You better try. Fast."

"Before I say anything, I just want you to know that I did this for me and me alone. I don't want this to mess with you, your dream, the peace and quiet in your new life. I would actually prefer you to be as far away as possible, because I need you safe. I'm only telling you this because you deserve to know."

"Anni, you're freaking me out. What the hell is going on?!" she snaps, crossing her arms and tightening them around herself.

"I'm not ready to be done."

I let that sink in. I could have sworn I saw a glimmer of understanding in her eyes.

"I'm not talking about the business. I'm done with the deals, forging, etc. That chapter is very much closed. But... it's the thrill I'm not done with. I guess... shit, I don't know. I don't know why, I can't explain it. I'm fooling myself by justifying it with the fact that I was cooped up in the studio for a lot of this time and I somehow didn't get my fill. But I'm only using that excuse because I can't explain it otherwise."

She narrows her eyes, clearly trying hard to be patient with me.

"I made a mistake, Hanna. An intentional one. The painting we sold to R... The Lady in White—I gave her my eyes."

"You did what?!" she shouts, hands going to her hips as her mouth falls open.

"Slightly. It's not obvious. It's not at all common knowledge what color her eyes were, and due to the size of the painting and the size of her head, it's not easy to tell, unless the person who looks at it knows…"

"The color of yours. Oh my God! You did it for…"

"Myself, Hanna!" I interrupt, my tone growing higher. "I did it for myself. I'm ready to give them the money back. I put it aside specifically for this, but I need… fuck! It's hard to explain, okay? I can't even fully explain it to myself."

"Don't lie to me. This is about Ronan."

"The craving was there before he showed up in the picture. But I don't think I would have acted on it and set the plan in motion if it wasn't for Ronan," I admit.

"Annika, what the fuck!? They're gonna fucking kill you! What were you thinking?! You want the thrill of the chase?! Where? To your death?! Because this is where it's headed! Jesus Christ, they're a goddamn crime syndicate, for God's sakes! What are you gonna do when he finds out?! Seriously, what are you going to do? Run, let him chase you for bit, let him catch you? Then tell him it's okay, you'll give them the money back, and expect him to be like… *yeah, sure Annika, you fucked us over, but now all is well, and we'll fuck and live happily ever after*. Goddamn it!" She whips around, stomping away toward the corner of the house.

I get up to go after her, but she spins around, pointing at me.

"No! You better not follow me."

Shit.

I stop, frozen in place like a puppy who just got scolded, because I know this mood, that look from her eyes— I need to let her go process.

* * *

Forty-something minutes have passed and I'm navigating nervously through my phone, scrolling aimlessly from clip to clip on the addictive app I'd discovered a few months ago. Numerous funny dog videos later, and people lip-syncing, and I can't take it anymore. The tension is too much. Even the cool AC of the car is not doing anything to soothe me.

When I look around, I finally see Hanna coming from the house, somehow more relaxed. I climb out of the SUV and walk over to meet her.

"I want in."

I stop dead in my tracks, taken aback by the confidence of the words she just spoke before she even reached me.

"No. This has nothing to do with you, and I don't need you to babysit me. You're not responsible for me." I'm quite aggravated by this sudden change.

"I'm not gonna lie and tell you that there isn't a part of me that wants in because I'm scared something will happen to you. You're my best friend; I will not say you're like my sister, because if I ever had one, I probably would have hated her, but you're my family, and I cannot fuck off to my dream island home and sit there, worrying about you. But... I get it, Anni. One last adventure, and what better people to choose to chase you, than the Hennessey's."

I can't process her words. I refuse to. I shake my head until she stops talking, because this is not how this is supposed to go.

"This is my plan, my idea, my infatuation, the risk *I* am taking. I cannot drag you into this. God forbid anything happens, it will be on me, my fault. I can't let you join me."

"It may have been your idea, but you're not forcing me

to join."

"But if it wasn't for me, this insane scenario wouldn't have even existed. You wouldn't have had any danger to put yourself in. Shit... I should have just told you I'm going on holiday alone," I grumble, running my hands through my hair as I begin pacing around the brick driveway.

"Oh yeah, because lying to me is a much better idea. I get it, Anni, I do, but I'm a consenting adult. I can choose for myself if I wish to put myself in danger or not, and if I didn't want to do this. If I thought it was truly a horrid idea, then not only would I not choose to join you, but I would convince you not to do it either."

Taking a breath, I pause and weigh her words. She cocks her head, crossing her arms, knowing full well I'm just about to come to the same conclusion as her; if she wanted to convince me not to go through with this plan, I would be in the car on our way to Falk Isle right now. She could sell ice to an Eskimo, as cliche as it sounds. She's the best salesperson I know, and convincing me to drop this plan would be child's play.

Damn it.

"I need it too, honey." She comes to me and gently grabs my shoulders before pulling me into a warm hug.

When she releases me, everything about her has softened, but her eyes sparkle in that same way they do before we're about to strike a new deal and meet our next clients.

"I've been preparing myself for this for a while, psyching myself up, planning. You've been thinking about it for half an hour," I tell her in a gentle tone.

"The adventures we've had in the last few years have come with a different kind of pressure. It was thrilling, no denying that, but this is... unlike it. It's personal. Exhilarating in a whole new way I cannot possibly pass on."

I know what she means. There's a heat growing inside my chest the closer I'm getting to the moment it will truly happen. I want to scream at the top of my lungs, scream with joy in anticipation of the little chase I planned and the unknown it will bring.

"Okay, but, Hanna, I'm not messing around with your safety. You have to be really, really sure. It could go terribly wrong."

"It could. But so could everything else. Everything about this life could go terribly wrong at every single moment and turn. And just like you... I need this. I feel like I'm not done."

"If you're sure..."

She might be able to convince me to go her way, but there's no way I'm changing her mind when she's set on something. And who am I to tell her it's wrong when she's doing it for the same sort of reasons I am.

"I'm sure. Now, walk me through the plan."

CHAPTER 4
Ronan

WE BURST INTO THEIR HOUSE LIKE WE thought they'd actually still be in here. Rushing through its empty corridors like we didn't already know it would be devoid of furniture, no speckle of dust, no life. I bet my left arm that if we check every inch of this villa, even the fingerprints will be wiped clean. They're gone. Fled to yet another city, dumped yet another identity. We knew it was unlikely that Ingrid Thorp and Erika Brand were their real names, but Carter confirmed it today. No trace of their real ones yet, though.

But the villa they called home during their stay in Queenscove is not entirely empty. Even in my wildest dreams, I couldn't have fathomed finding *this*.

She's right here, steel eyes sparkling through the brush strokes painted on this canvas, innocence staring back at me as Vin re-reads the handwritten text we found on the back of it.

By the old cottage, deep into the woods,
Where the water runs warm from the hills above,
One night a year they all gather,
Filling the forest with their songs and laughter.

I'm joining them just this once,
Hiding amongst their sways and their songs.
I will give back all that you seek,
I only wish to know if your cravings run just as deep.

A taunt. That's exactly what this is—a taunt, sitting neatly on a wooden pedestal in the middle of this large room.

It took my fucking breath away when we opened the double doors and found it.

There is no Lady in White here, though. This is Ingrid. Her nose, her defined jawline, her high cheeks, perfectly supple lips. But it's her eyes that draw you in, because beyond all that innocence, something new looks back at you from the canvas's surface—need. A challenge.

I can't make sense of this. She's painted in the same style, in clothes from the same era, she's just closer in the frame. Close enough to see every beauty mark, the faint freckles that dust her nose, yet these brush strokes look like they were painted centuries ago.

It might as well have been done by Dubois himself.

How the...

"Fuck...?" I trail off as the puzzle pieces don't fall, but crash into place. One by one, they shake my very core, and I don't know if I should be angry or impressed.

"What?" Vin questions, raising an eyebrow.

"This, it's a self-portrait. They're not just selling forged paintings."

I look to Finn, who's now standing beside me, and I can see the exact moment realization strikes. They're making them. *She* is making them. I just fucking know it!

She paints.

I knew she was fucking special, but this is way beyond anything I imagined. And the surprises seem to keep coming. I can't wait to tell Anthony that the painting he appraised and concluded it's the real deal, not only is fake, but it was painted by the woman who stood right before him the whole time he was analyzing it.

What now, though? My partners expect me to shove this information away and focus on business, on... payback. How can I when my need for this woman has just reached different heights? I have to know so much more about her. Discover her. Her name. Find out what else she can do with her delicate, talented hands and her beautiful brain.

I can't take my eyes off of her. I'm drawn in like a moth to a flame, and even though I know I'm going to burn, I can't choose to stop flying. This is how I know she's a witch. Otherwise, I can't explain why I have it in my mind that if I touch her painted cheek, I will feel the softness of her skin under my fingertips instead of the surface of the canvas. I'm almost certain that if I get close enough, I'll even smell her perfume.

Her natural one, seeped in wildflowers and rain.

There's no denying this—I'm fucked. Slowly and painfully, I'm being ripped apart, split in two; one side has to fulfill a duty, treat them... her, like any other person we've done business with. The other side, though, it needs to chase her, take this challenge, and find out just where she'll lead me. It's aimed at me, there's no denying that.

She quite literally propped herself on a pedestal for me.

"I'm slightly confused. They're mocking us, but why like this? Why a portrait of herself? I don't get it," Vin says, crossing his arms over his chest.

"I think I do. If I'm right, it has nothing to do with *us*," I say, raising my gaze for a moment, enough to see him cocking his head and an eyebrow.

I thought it was a mistake at first, those blue-gray eyes replacing The Lady in White. It was all deliberate. Perfectly planned. If not for me, then for whom?

There's a tint of jealousy springing up inside of me. It's fueled by the knowledge that there's no way she painted this self-portrait so quickly... since the moment we met until now. No way.

Maybe, maybe it wasn't for me after all.

When I realized the painting they sold to us was forged, it wasn't the prospect of getting back what we are owed that thrilled me. No. It was seeing her again. An excuse for more time. I know I'm supposed to get some sort of revenge for her deceit, but the only punishment I can think of executing will make her beg for more.

Somewhere not that deep inside, I have already decided— *she's mine*. At least until this chase is over.

"Wait. Can you read that again?" Finn asks.

"*By the old cottage, deep into the woods, where the water runs warm from the hills above, one night a year they...*"

"I know what it means! Fuck, we all do!"

Vin looks at him like he's lost the plot.

"Midsummer night!" I continue, the ball dropping.

"The Falls!" he hollers.

The younger residents of Queenscove have a party once a year in the woods, next to a natural pool fed by a waterfall. It's a keg party, but amongst the ancient trees that surround the clearing, dancing under the fairy-lights they drape in their branches, it feels different. I haven't been in a few years.

"When is it?" I ask, sounding much too eager.

"Tomorrow," Vin replies.

When I look at him, I'm met with a grave expression.

"We'll get the money back." I straighten myself, wiping whatever trace of enthusiasm off my face.

"If they were men, would we spare them with just a *refund*? What about the damage to the reputation we're so carefully trying to curate for our organization?"

I fucking hate when Vin is right, but goddamn it, this is not about him. I'm frustrated, confused, fucking excited. Not pursuing this causes a sensation of dread to seep inside of me and I can't allow it. But I'm not against Vin or the others. The little witch dared to cross us, fool us, steal from us.

Right now, I both want to make her pay for her deceit, and punish her for her wickedness.

Which one will I enjoy more?

Annika

I'M ON MY THIRD BEER, AND EVEN THOUGH I KNOW I should stop, keep a level head, I can't help myself. I'm guided by the sound of the waterfall blending in with the music, by the smell of the trees, of the warm water where some people swim, the twinkling lights draped in the trees. I haven't danced like this in so long. To be fair, I've *never* danced like this, pirouetting around the trees, while others use them as their little corners, to laugh, talk, get more... intimate.

Mixed with the anxious anticipation, the atmosphere is electric.

Hanna's a few yards away from me, lost in dance like I've never seen her lost before. She looks relaxed, so welcomed, considering how she's always had to be the serious one. Always level-headed, since she's the reason why the business worked flawlessly all these years. We've had breaks between jobs, but her part never truly stopped. She had to be on the ball and constantly aware of what was going on before and after a business deal. Seeing her like this, carefree, is quite a wonderful sight.

Smiling, I move with the music, turning my back on her as I take another swig of my drink. But I almost choke on it when prickles rush down my back. I whip around to the sight of none other than Finnigan Hennessey startling Hanna as he wraps his arms around her and pulls her back to his front.

They got our message.

A smile creeps on her lips, but it falls before it settles, her eyes widening instead as she looks past me.

This is it. This is the moment.

The prickles have found their way back up my spine, converging on the nape of my neck, wrapping around my throat like ribbons. They tighten, seeping down my chest, over my breasts... down over my abdomen. Right where an arm suddenly circles me, holding me in place as another comes around my arm and chest.

It's... different.

Hanna attempts to step my way, eyes wide with concern, but Finnigan keeps her in place.

I swallow an invisible lump lodged in my throat and reluctantly look up behind me. The eyes that stare down into mine freeze me in place—Carter Pierce, one of Ronan's partners.

But the prickles that mark my skin aren't for him. They're still here... like the predator still lurks.

Carter turns me around, sliding his hand on my lower back, the other gripping my free hand.

"Don't spill, please." He signals to the cup I'm holding.

His politeness is sincere, but chilling.

He leads me into a slow dance around the trees, taking control with such security. Not once have we caught our feet on a branch or a root, yet his eyes have never left mine.

"You got the message," I dare say, but speaking to him gives me the impression that I should ask for permission first.

"*We* did, yes. It wasn't meant for all of us, though."

His palm on my lower back presses just a bit harder, but he doesn't pull me closer. He keeps this interaction strangely appropriate.

"Did you all come?" I finally ask in a shaky voice.

He nods. "I found you first."

There it is, a grin pulling at his lips and, my God, I want to scream and run. I'm suddenly a fucking rabbit circled by a wolf pack foaming at the mouth, only it's just one of them. Only Carter.

"Please, I…"

"Don't beg. Just dance."

I don't even want to protest. I can't explain it. His will is somehow my command and self-preservation tells me I have to follow.

Hanna's back in my line of sight as Carter spins us around gently. That expression still haunts her features and Finnigan notices. He pulls her, slightly forcefully, into a dance, but once he leans over, whispering something into her ear, she calms, giving me a reassuring smile that makes me slightly confused. But it works, it calms me too.

Until I look back up into Carter's cold gaze.

"Will you hurt me?"

It's then that I see through a small crack, beyond this shell.

"Only if you ask nicely."

I accidentally step on him, caught off guard by the answer that makes me blush instantly, and I know he's being sincere again. Too sincere, my mind jumping to all sorts of ideas. But he doesn't dwell.

"I looked into you. So many identities, so many successful

jobs, no hiccups. All these risks and never any issues, as far as I found. Why this, why now?"

"What do you mean?"

His only response to that is a *don't insult me* kind of expression.

"I saw the way you looked at him." He pauses, his gaze flickering somewhere behind me. I try to follow it, but he continues. "The way he looked at you too, *Annika Backstrom.*"

He knows my name.

"So, you found out our real identities."

"I did."

"Well, I guess the cat's out of the bag, then."

"No, not really. I only peeked into it. Nothing's out yet."

Wait.

"So, you're telling me that Ronan doesn't...?" I'm shell-shocked.

"No, he doesn't. I didn't want to take that pleasure away from you."

"Oh..." How interesting.

He grabs the cup from my hand and sets it on a small table, then pulls me into him, guiding me into a dance that's definitely more intimate than I'm comfortable.

"You're playing a game." He delicately grips my hand, spinning me, before he pulls me back into his body. "I like games." He spins me once more, but this time he stops me with my back to his front, his hand on my middle as he sways us slowly. "Let's hope he likes them too."

It's then that I see him, maybe seven or eight feet away, leaning against a tree, his arms crossed, his expression dangerously close to anger. That one single look makes me question this whole plan, my infatuation with him. The worst thing is that it fuels it too.

Carter brushes the hair off one of my shoulders, exposing

my neck, and leans in to whisper in my ear. At that same time, Ronan pushes away from the tree, his gaze murderous, explosive. It's impossible, but I swear that his heavy steps are sending vibrations into the ground, right into my chest, gripping my lungs and squeezing all the air out of them.

"I'm only here to prove a point. He's all yours now," Carter whispers. Then he's gone.

But Ronan's pace never slows, and I take quick steps backwards as he closes in. My back hits the harsh bark of a tree at the same time the man himself reaches me, caging me in as his hands slam on either side of my head.

The strained rise and fall of his chest sends a hot breeze coasting against my own. No part of him is touching me, yet every bit of my skin responds all the same.

"The moment I first laid eyes on you, I knew you were a witch. But I didn't quite know the magnitude of it. You're the one who's been putting spells on all these people... for so many years. Bewitching us with your brush strokes that cover all sorts of lies."

I've heard that warm voice in my dreams every night for almost two weeks now. Sometimes I hear it when I'm awake too. It reaches a dangerous level in its haunting, and it's breaching a boundary too close to obsession.

"The spell wore off now, little witch, and all that's left is you, me, and The Lady... with steely eyes. Or should I say, ladies."

That boundary is turning to smoke with each word he speaks in that menacing voice, with its slight gravel laced with fury. It fuels my self-destructive need that has gained a new life in the last few weeks. It craved a challenge, and the challenge is right here in front of me, stealing my air and giving me pure fire in return.

"It warms me, knowing that you remembered the

color of my eyes... and recognized it. How delightful, Mr. Hennessey." I say with a smirk, yet I'm surprised at my boldness.

"That sharp tongue of yours begs for punishment yet again."

I stop breathing at that moment. Blinking too. But I manage to keep my back straight, my gaze on his as I retort.

"Maybe yours deserves a taste of it too."

I don't miss how his eyes flicker to my lips. How his breathing is so much heavier. How he's so much closer now. Is he aware?

"Carter's working on finding all there is to know about yours and your partner's business. Learning all about the different names, cities, all those lost paintings suddenly uncovered, and a hell of a lot of money you made."

He's talking slow, emphasizing his words in a way that makes me wonder what else he can do with that slithering tongue. I can barely focus on what he's actually saying.

"And they all have one rather important thing in common—not one of them was discovered as a fake. Not a single person was able to identify any inconsistencies, not even in the chemical analysis. You've never. Ever. Made a mistake, little witch."

"Surprised?" I ask, cocking an eyebrow as I straighten my posture, pushing away from the tree, just about touching him.

He doesn't play, though. One hand goes straight to my chest, pressed right at the base of my throat as he shoves me back against the rough bark, taking my breath away with a slight ache.

"I am. Because we both know this was no mistake. Why?"

Jesus Christ.

His searing touch spreads fire over every inch of my skin, settling deep between my legs, forcing them to press together for some sort of relief.

"I'll answer. If you do something for me."

"More than let you live for deceiving us? Stealing from us?"

I smile, and I don't know why, but his hard gaze falters for a moment.

"Smaller scale than that."

He watches me for a few moments, his gaze caressing my jaw, my cheeks, studying every bit of my face as his hand moves up around my throat. He doesn't squeeze, though, just holds it there in this possessive grip, my pulse bouncing off his skin.

I take the silence as my cue to go on.

"Dance with me, Ronan Hennessey."

CHAPTER 5
Ronan

ANCE?

Her small hands reach for my waist, her touch startling me even over this t-shirt, and they move up until they wrap around the sides of my neck.

She holds me there and, for some reason, I let her. I'm afraid to move. I can't explain it. It's like I've just met a bear on a walk and I have to stay completely still so I don't get eaten alive. And at the same time, I know that if I take just one step, if I let go of her throat and grip her waist instead, my reality will change. I will no longer be skirting on the edge between business and pleasure... the line will be gone completely, and the purpose will change.

Was it ever about business?

My life will change too.

I keep that hold on her throat, squeezing slightly, enjoying how her lips part, feeling her life pulsate against my palm. I think that maybe if I squeeze just a little harder, she'll give up.

Only the little witch slides those hands until she grips my short hair between her long fingers, pulling just enough that an image flashes through my mind. Not a memory—*a fantasy*. Her soft skin beneath me, damp with sweat as I drive my cock into her, her legs around my waist, those fingers tight in my hair, holding on. It's a goddamn beautiful image and I want to turn it from fantasy to premonition.

My dick seems to want the same thing as it grows stiffer than it should at a public party. Even here, in the shadows of these trees.

Moving my grip to the nape of her neck, I pull her to me with one hand on the middle of her back.

She's got me so deep under her spell, breaking my reality and replacing it with illusions I crave to materialize.

"One dance," I say as I look down at her. She's so fucking close, I struggle to keep my half-hard cock away from her.

Only, she shakes her head slowly.

"Two dances," I try again.

The softest of smiles pulls at her lips before she shakes her head again. I spin her around in a pirouette, watching that smile turn from shock into gentle laughter, her hair a flowing veil as it whips around her face. If her voice sounds like birdsong, her laughter is a whole flock making up their own melody.

"Three is my limit, little witch. Besides, I'm not here to dance. I'm here to get what we are owed. Including your punishment."

Her cheeks flush the brightest red, her lips part in shock, and her eyes... they're showing her wickedness in such bright shades. Clearly, we're not thinking of the same type of punishment, but when she pulls a bit of her bottom lip between her teeth, I forget what punishment I had in mind.

I'm trying to change the mood, to stop from losing myself into the night with her. What the hell does she want from me? Why did she bring me here?

She circles one arm around my neck and pulls herself up until her lips hover too close to my ear.

"I can fix The Lady's eyes and you can still sell it as the original. No one will ever know."

I shake my head as she comes back to face me. Closer than she was before.

"We're not in the business of selling fakes."

"Only contraband and stolen antiquities, then?" she taunts, cocking her head, but the smile never leaves her lips.

"Is that what you think we do?"

"Amongst other things. Is my painting not good enough for you? You'll make millions on it. So many more than the ones you gave us."

I narrow my eyes and grip her hand, pushing her into another pirouette, before I slam her body in mine, taking her breath away and enjoying it.

"There's no guarantee that whoever buys it won't find out. Besides, I would rather have the money back, for the inconvenience. For the deceit. For dragging us here in your little game."

I lean in closer and closer as I say those words, almost brushing her lips before I move to her ear.

I'm so tempted to get a taste... just a small one.

But as the song ends, I completely let go of her and take a step back, putting much needed distance between us.

She looks momentarily lost at the move, and I can't ignore how that innocence seems to settle back on her features, in her body language. I think the alcohol is fueling her courage, and she might need more to hold on to this audacious façade.

She's so fucking delicate, I want to scoop her up in my arms and wrap her in silks and soft furs, keep her on a pedestal and feed her grapes.

God-fucking-damnit!

I need to step away. I'll tell Carter to take over and get our money back, but knowing the bastard, he'll probably tie her to a chair and torture her until she returns it with interest.

I whip around and walk away.

Two… four… six steps…

I try not to look back to check if she's still there, watching me, or maybe following. But I fail… and what I see when I turn, stops me dead in my tracks. She's walking around the left-hand side of the large, natural pool, casually stripping her top off.

"What the actual fuck?"

All these people, all these fucking men around, and she's taking her top off! I can already see a couple of guys sizing her up as she bends over to slide her shorts down her legs and pull off her Converse.

Only when I've crossed half the distance do I realize I've started heading her way.

I'm not sure what annoys me more, the fact that she's so careless in front of other men when she's all alone, or the fact that all those assholes are fucking drooling over her sweet little body in that skimpy swimsuit. In her retro-style bikini she's covered more than others, but I don't give a fuck.

She doesn't even look my way. The damn woman already knew I was going to return. That in itself gets me even more annoyed, but this time at myself.

How can I not be predictable when she just added fuel to the fire of the already enticing game she's playing. She looks devastatingly breathtaking as she walks up a high boulder, the waterfall acting like her background in this cinematic image.

She dives in just as I get there, barely making a splash before she emerges a few yards away. And I'm just standing here, like an idiot, unable to peel my eyes away.

Fuck!

Her gaze falls on me as she smooths her wet hair back, and I'm trying very hard to find reasons not to jump in with her. Vin will fucking kill me. We're here for a reason—business, or better yet, payback. They crossed us, and they have to suffer the consequence.

But they're women, Ronan... we don't fucking hurt women.

No, that we don't. Plus, in that little riddle she so carefully crafted for me on the back of her painting, she already said she's returning the money. This... all of this is not about that—it's about cravings, desires, deep needs we both seem to want to settle.

I managed to peel my eyes away from her and catch a glimpse of Finn. The man is completely lost in Erika, dancing like they're the only people in this forest. He's given up the whole purpose of this, if he even took it seriously in the first instance. My bet is on *no*. In a way, he's a better man than I am. He knew what he wanted and went straight for it, no beating around the bush.

Suddenly, I'm distracted.

"I'm definitely tapping that tonight."

"Fuck you, man. You only like blondes anyway. This one's mine. She has my name written all over that sweet ass."

I'm not sure how many shades of red exist, but I know for a fact that I'm seeing all of them right now. I turn to find somewhere to my left the same assholes that were watching her before she dove in.

"One more word about *my* woman and I'll slice off your tongue and shove it down *his* throat."

"Who the fuck do you—" he spits out, a smug look on his face.

His wide-eyed friend interrupts him, whispering something in his ear. The next moment, the color drains from his face at the same time his shoulders tense and he averts his gaze from me.

I don't have time for this.

"You have five seconds to apologize and fuck off out of here. Three... Four..."

"I'm sorry, Mr. Hennessey. I—It won't ha—happen again."

I've never seen anyone walk that fast. They didn't even pick up their clothes.

A sharp pain draws my attention to my palm, and I realize I've been squeezing my fist hard enough that I left red marks with my short nails.

If I wasn't sure what I wanted before, this whole interaction pretty much sums it up. I can't deny myself. I won't. I want to play her game. I want to sink into this spell of hers.

I realize that, in this moment, I'm able to predict my own future. When I look back at her, this will be it. I'll be lost. Maybe for a night, maybe for two, maybe a month, or forever. I'll be lost in her, and climbing back out of whatever abyss I'll be caught in will be close to impossible.

It can change my life. Scar me permanently...

So, I turn and meet her gaze, falling straight into the void, as I lose my clothes down to my boxer briefs, and dive into the chilly water.

When I emerge close to her, she's almost expressionless. There's a completely different intensity in those eyes and it creeps up my spine. Like she knows something I don't, in on some sort of secret about my life that only she can reveal.

"What did you think, little witch? That you can tease me? Make me chase you around our city? Get me to play your games, just so you can expose your pretty ass and tits in front of all these men, showing them what's so... clearly... *mine?*"

Her eyes widen, lips parting as she focuses on me, my words crashing down on her harder than this waterfall that drowns out the party raging beyond the pool. I grab Ingrid's hand, pulling her with me as I begin swimming toward the waterfall without waiting for her reaction or response. She struggles to break free, screaming in vain, so I pull her in front of me so fast, she swallows water, and it shuts her up. I keep swimming forward with her facing me, the sound of the falls deafening as the spray becomes much thicker.

"Hold your breath!" I yell.

"What?"

She barely has a moment to take a gulp of air, before I dive underwater, pushing us through the weight of the falls smashing us.

When we come up for air, we're on the other side, the thundering of the waterfall softening in this narrow cavern. She barely takes a shallow breath and she's yelling at me, brushing her hair away from her face. But once she's finally wiped her eyes, she stops mid protest, looking around us in awe.

I pull her up a step naturally formed in the rock, beyond it creating a calm pool the size of a large jacuzzi tub, where the water reaches the middle of my thighs. She follows blindly.

"Oh my God..." her whisper echoes softly.

The waterfall still splashes us, but I press us against the eroded rock, as far as we can go. We're utterly isolated here. Alone in this atmosphere broken out of fairytales, moss, and low plants clinging against the rock.

"I believe I promised you punishment. This feels like the

perfect place to start," I tell her.

Disbelief laced with uneasiness falls on her features and she turns around, pretending to admire the space.

Oh, so that's how it is.

Grabbing her shoulders, I whip her around, and press her back against the hard, rock wall.

"I've done my part. I came here, played your game, danced with you, now it's your turn. You have a debt to pay, little witch."

Her eyes widen as I strengthen my hold on her. She looks between us, her body stiffening as she weighs the implications of my words, twisting them in her mind.

"L—Like, now?!"

"Now, later, tomorrow, many days after. You crossed us, cheated us, and stole from us. Did you think you would get away with a dance?"

"I have your money," she says, her voice losing its courage.

"And we have a reputation that won't be built on leniency."

Her lips part, but she's stunned into silence.

"You wanted to be in control, paint me to your liking, and wield my shadows. But our world is built on the shadows of yours, and no amount of color will pull it out of darkness. You need to learn that these things do not go unpunished."

Fear falls over her gaze, but her expression transitions seamlessly to brazenness.

"Teach me, then."

It takes me a couple of seconds for my brain to fall back into its place. *What did she just say?*

Instinctively my hand goes straight to her throat, squeezing lightly until her pulse vibrates against my skin, and with parted lips and doe eyes, she awaits her punishment.

I should... I really should make her pay. But I knew from the moment I saw her face painted so beautifully on that canvas that I was lying to myself—it was never going to happen. Not in the way men like us are expected to do it. Our mafia will not be built on her shadow, there are plenty of others out there who will be part of the ground we step on.

"What's your real name, little witch?"

"Annika." She doesn't even hesitate.

"Annika..." I drag the sound through my throat and fuck me if it doesn't belong.

Leaning in, I brace my forearm on the rock wall.

"Tell me why."

My hand on her throat is just a touch now, brushing my thumb against her pulse as I cock my head and wait for her words to come.

"Umm... why what?"

She swallows, slow and hard, her pulse quickening as I drag my palm up her throat.

"Why—" Pressing my thumb against her jaw, I turn her head to the left—"did you decide to"—I lean in, dragging my nose up the length of her throat, drawing in her scent—"play this game with me?"

A shudder shakes her flesh as my breath caresses the sensitive skin under her ear.

"Because... uhm..."

Her chest rises and falls in rapid successions, pressing against me.

"Because why, little witch?" I punctuate the question with my teeth around her lobe, and she swallows a whimper that puts a smile on my face.

"Because I haven't been able..." She pauses as I flick my tongue over the bite, then swipe up the contour of her ear. "To stop thinking about you."

Me neither, but I'm more interested in her side of things

now. "That's all it took? A meeting with me and..."

"No."

Her hand presses on my waist, holding me in place, as she takes a slow breath in.

"It was more. We look into all our potential clients, Ronan."

Goddamn my name on her lips when she's so breathless. It's not fair that it sounds enthralling, like goddamn black magic. I pull away just barely, and when I turn her head to face me, our breaths turn into one.

"So, you looked into me."

"Yes. Well, Hanna did... or Erika, as you know her. I saw your photo."

She's covered in goosebumps, beautifully flushed, and I'm not sure she's conscious of the slight roll of her hips into me. So, I press myself into her in return, reveling in that sweet moment she realizes, her lips parting with a gasp. My hard fucking cock might have something to do with that too.

I grip her jaw and can't help myself from dragging my index over that soft lip, and dipping in her mouth for one delicious moment that makes her pause.

"Go on," I coax her.

"This was our last business deal. We were supposed to leave it all behind after this. But I just... I could not pry you out of my mind. I needed more." She takes a deep breath as I brush my thumb on her lower lip, before dragging my hand down her throat, my hand now a pretty necklace as it presses against the base of it, on her chest.

"What did you need more of?"

"I can't explain it. I knew something was missing, but only after I saw your photo did I understand. I needed a... particular thrill."

"A thrill?!" I push on her chest, pressing her harder against the wet rock, slightly offended. "Is that what I am, then? One last adventure before you retire?"

I don't miss the slight hurt in her eyes, but fuck it, I'm no one's plaything. She wraps her hands around my arm, pulling me to her.

"You were a feeling, Ronan. I knew nothing of you, couldn't assume anything, including if it would be returned. I just... craved. Until I met you. Then it became impossible to stop fant—thinking of you."

Fantasizing?

I can't help the slight grin pulling at my lips, nor the sudden roll in my hips, grinding against her.

"I know I sound like a crazy stalker. I just can't help—"

"You've haunted me since the moment I laid eyes on you," I interrupt her, and she sucks in a breath.

"Have I?"

"Every day. Even when I thought I should kill you for how you crossed us." I drag my hand down her chest, between her breasts, across her stomach until I grip her hip harshly. "Even when I dream. Especially when I dream."

Are these confessions too much? Too soon? Somehow, it seems bad that it doesn't feel soon at all, but just right.

"It's only fair. You've been taking over my dreams too." She smiles and goddamn her lips and those wicked eyes.

Her hips move in an enticing, slow grind against mine, but her eyes are so focused on me, I don't think she knows how fucking crazy she's making me right now. My cock is bursting to feel her properly, my hands itch to stroke her soft breasts, her ass, and fuck me if I don't want to fall on my knees right here, right now, so I can taste her little pussy too. She's maddening and she's not even trying.

"Tell me, little witch..." My thumb circles that soft skin around her hip bone. "Through all those fantasies, did you make yourself come thinking of me?"

Her eyes widen, slight shock filling them as she pulls the side of her bottom lip between her teeth, her smile turning sinful. "I couldn't."

"Was I not enough? Was the thought of my tongue on your skin not enough to get you off?" I dip into that sensitive spot where her neck meets her ear and swipe it with my tongue. "Or my hands stroking every inch of you?"

She shakes her head, rubbing her cheek against mine.

"I refused to give myself that—an orgasm to a fantasy of you."

I almost freeze, but I meet her gaze, so close, our lips almost touch. Almost.

"Why, Annika?"

"I felt like... like I was stealing it away from you. The real you. This first orgasm had to be yours. It *has* to be yours."

Sweet Mary mother of God.

The world stops spinning, time on pause. I can't even hear the waterfall anymore. Life seems to have ceased. Apart from ours. Just as our lips gravitate closer, with no space left for even a breath, annoying fucking screeches split our silence and the whole moment crashes around us.

I exhale as I pull back, turning to the people who just passed through the waterfall—one girl, two guys.

The spell is broken.

"Oooh, looks like we have a party on our hands! Who's this little lady?" A lanky, smug looking asshole smirks toward Annika, and I feel her wince under my tightening grip. "She looks positively delicious, perfect for a sandwich. Willing to share?"

The dead man wiggles his fucking eyebrows at me, and it takes but a second for my hand to wrap around his throat, slamming his back against the wall, his fingers clawing on my arm. Someone gasps behind me, then I feel a hand on my back, but this is not the fucking time.

"I usually enjoy teaching dickheads like you a lesson," I seethe. "But you wiped off the line when you crossed it, and I need to redraw it in your goddamn blood."

He's writhing against the cave wall, smashing his hand onto my arm, trying to pull it off as he repeatedly attempts to gasp for air but fails. He sounds like a dying cat, and I squeeze his throat harder to silence him. Turning purple, his eyes bulge as more hands slam against my back, and an arm wraps around my throat, trying to pull me off of him. I throw my head back and a sharp pain splits up the nape of my neck as a screeching woman shouts abuse at me.

"Shut the fuck up!" I yell and whip my gaze to the side, my eyes landing on the woman who freezes in place, next to an idiot who's holding onto his bleeding nose.

"Ro—Ronan?"

A sweet, meek voice pulls my attention, and I look to my right where Annika stands, wide-eyed, hands pressed against her chest. Fear is painted in her eyes, but more vivid than that is something else—realization. This is her first-hand experience of what she's gotten herself into.

When the man suddenly gasps against my hand, I throw him into the other two, watching them fall like dominos.

"Next time, you're all fucking dead," I grunt.

"You asshole! Wait until I tell my fucking father! You'll be in jail before the end of the fucking week!" the one who's supposed to be dead yells between gasps.

"Good. Go tell him. Tell him that Ronan Hennessey strangled you for propositioning *his woman* in front of him."

He scrunches his eyebrows, calculating my words like there's a familiarity to them. I don't wait for the ball to drop, but I hear their whispers after I turn around.

I ignore Annika's stunned expression, grab her hand, and pull her away with me, disappearing through the thick curtain of water, back into the real world.

CHAPTER 6
Annika

HE PULLS ME THROUGH THE VIOLENT SPRAY threatening to catch me in its underwater whirlpool. My hand is still in his as he guides me away from the waterfall, and with the other one, I'm frantically pushing off the hair clinging to my face. The world seems to explode around us all at once. Music and laughter, incessant background noise mixing with the cascade, and it's almost too much, too soon.

I turn my gaze to the falls, even as Ronan still moves us away from it. I want back... back in that moment where he kept me on the precipice of pleasure and longing. His touch on my skin, the electric bursts rushing from head to toe, his breath against my pulse, those hungry eyes on me.

Then the fury came, the violence, and I should be terrified. It should make me scream and run. But it was the protective look in his eyes that keeps me here.

I'm screwed.

Is he what I expected?

No.

He is more, so much more. He's the promise of everything I fantasized about and everything a man like him would never give a woman like me. I'm not falling, I can't fall. I'm leaving soon.

But he called me *his woman.*

No! Goddamn it, Annika! It was the heat of the moment and he was just proving a point. Focus!

"Ronan, stop." I pull my hand from his and break free.

He turns to me, the look in his eyes filled with a desperation that takes me aback. It's... feral. Raw. Angry.

"I'm not using you." I have no idea why I just said that. I could smack myself right now.

He cocks his head as he treads water, his gaze unchanged.

"Then what are you doing?"

"It's already set. Your money will be returned tonight. If it's not already in your account."

He scoffs and shakes his head.

"So that's it? You had your little fun. You brought me here so you can see how I fit against you, and now you quite literally paid me for it?"

"What?! No!" I almost shout, in shock at the sudden switch in him.

"Then what do you want, Annika? You said you came after me because you crave more. What do you crave, little witch? It's not just my hands on you, my tongue on your skin, my thick cock inside that tight little pussy. It's not just that orgasm you saved for me."

The water I'm submerged in has nothing to do with the sleekness between my folds or the shudder that turns the fabric of my bra into sandpaper against my peaked nipples. I shake myself mentally, because the answer to his question seems harder to put together than I thought.

"You felt like... you would notice me in the background, see me in the shadows. You felt like, if I ran, you would actually chase me."

I drop my gaze, shaking my head.

Pathetic—this is how it feels—fucking pathetic. A ball of self-pity and insecurities thrown in this goddamn pond for a man I've known for a couple of weeks and seen three times. I have no idea what the hell is going on with me, how a simple image of him on a screen sent me down this rabbit hole of cravings and potential destruction. Hanna was right. All of this is a stupid fantasy that could go sideways.

I don't know this man. He could be anything... he could be all kinds of wrong.

A shudder explodes up my spine, prickles spreading all over my skin when I look back up at him. Because his gaze spells words I couldn't possibly say out loud. *Desire* wouldn't be a good enough word. *Craving* is not quite right. But there's a blaze spreading in the blue of his irises, and it envelops me in its heat.

"It would be impossible not to see you in the shadows. You don't blend, Annika, you fucking shine."

Ronan

I MAY BE GOING INSANE, BUT FUCK IF I CARE RIGHT now.

A piece of her looks broken, and I yearn to mend it. She thinks she's invisible. Jesus, she doesn't notice all the people who can't take their eyes off of her.

Maybe she only notices the right ones.

I'm swimming closer, pulled toward that abyss filled with nothing but her, enjoying the way her features brighten as my words sink in. The silence between us is intense, begging for no interruption, nothing but exchanged gazes. It makes me want to sink into that abyss all on my own.

So, I do.

I let the water swallow me, pushing through the sting in my eyes so I can see as I grip her waist and pull her down with me. She fights me for a few moments before I stop her right in front of me, and by God... she's a nymph, dangerously beautiful with her soft hair flowing around her.

I grab the back of her head, wrap my arm around her

middle, and press her against me as the water seems to be pulling us deeper. All of a sudden, she seems to awaken from the spell, looking around her frantically and pushing against my shoulders, panic for air starting to settle in.

I should go back up, I know that. But that's not why I'm here with her, and that's not what I'm about to do.

My lips meet hers, and I kiss her almost desperately, forcing her to me as the pressure of the water threatens to pull us apart. I sink into the softness of her lips, demanding more, pushing my way into her sweet mouth, and taking my fill of her. Nothing could have stopped this kiss after that broken moment behind the waterfall.

She writhes against me, both in attempts to break up to the surface for air, and to get closer to me. She slams her fist against my shoulder, but to no avail. And there's one moment, one sweet fucking moment, when the tension in her muscles gives in. Submitting to the fear, the adrenaline, to my tongue fighting her own, to my touch too, and I grin against her as I blow air into her mouth through the kiss.

She stills, eyes widening as she realizes what I teased. There's no hesitation when she grabs the sides of my head and kisses me like her life depends on it. Ironically, it does.

But her famine is not just for air. She swipes her tongue through my mouth, tasting me as wildly as I was tasting her. Then she sucks against me like she's trying to pull the air right out of my lungs. I give her nothing. Only a grin.

She stuns me, though, wrapping her legs around my middle, catching me in a strong grip and jerking me once, like she wants to force the air out of me.

The effort is useless, but I commend it with a smirk as I press my hand harder against her head and decide to reward her. I slowly blow air into her mouth, and she sucks it in greedily. When my lungs empty... all that's left is us, our kiss. Slow now, dragged out, our tongues drawing lazy circles around one another. Even here she tastes of honey and dreams, wrapped into everything that's good in this world. Like she was made just for me. So, I savor her some more, until I think she forgot she was drowning just seconds ago, forgot she's underwater, because she's confused when we break the surface and the world screams to life around us.

"You son of a bitch!" Slamming her fist against me, she gasps for air. "You could have killed me!" she yells, the sharp sound almost unnatural coming from her. The noise of the waterfall drowns it, and others can't hear her panic... or anger.

I catch her wrist as she attempts to slap me, but let the other one land against my cheek, just so I can grab the back of her head and crash my lips to hers all over again. She squeals against my mouth, but she can't hide the lust that shudders through her when I bite her bottom lip.

"I could have, yes," I say as I break the kiss.

Her expression falls. Reality gently settling in.

"No. You wouldn't do that."

"Why are you so convinced?"

She stills, slowly sinking. I pull her close, her ear near my lips.

"You said you craved more. I'm giving you... *more*," I whisper.

Pulling away enough that she can look at me, her eyes flash somewhere behind me for a split second. A peculiar smile tugs at her lips, but it vanishes as fast as it appeared.

"How much more can you give?"

That wickedness is back in her eyes, and it sends a quake straight through me. I didn't realize I released her wrists, not until she lets herself sink and disappears underwater.

I shake my head, and the spell of her gaze along with it, letting out a short cackle, then I follow her beneath the surface.

I can only see a few feet in front of me, if that, but she's not here.

What the fuck?

How is that even possible? I whip around, trying to distinguish something through this darkness, but it's futile. Did she sink too far? I let myself go, swimming farther, but the pool is not actually that deep. Where the hell is she?

I rise back to the surface, frantically searching for a trace of her, before I take a deep breath, ready to dive back under. But the witch is perfectly fucking fine. The water runs over her smooth skin as she walks out of the pool, right next to the boulder from where she dove in. I was right, she is a nymph, because how the hell did she swim so fast? She grabs her clothes and pulls her shoes on in a hurry, before joining her friend who's waiting for her.

This is not fucking happening! Goddamn this woman!

I'm already swimming toward the shore, but she's at the edge of the forest already. Then the little witch stops, turns to me, and even from this distance, I can't miss the paradox of a smile she throws at me—both devilish and timid—before she disappears into the darkness of the trees.

I'm out, pulling my clothes on as quickly as I can, uncomfortable with how they stick to my damp skin, then look around for my brother. I finally see him coming back from the opposite direction the girls ran to and meet him halfway.

"They're gone."

"What?!" he questions, frowning.

"Just now. They grabbed their stuff and disappeared into the forest. Where's Carter?"

"He left not long after you found Ingrid."

"Annika," I correct him.

He raises his eyebrows and laughs.

"What did we get ourselves into?"

I rake a hand through my wet hair, sighing.

"Fuck if I know. But let's face it, it's all because of me and... *her*."

"Yeah, we're just willing collateral damage," he says, laughing again, completely unbothered. "Come on, show me where they went."

***

"What the hell just happened, brother?"

After they sped away from the parking lot from the edge of the forest, we just about managed to catch up with them.

Far too late though.

We didn't stand a chance.

Now, we're on the floating dock, watching them wave dramatically at us from the boat that speeds away. They had everything ready for their theatrical exit. There's no time for us to prep our boat. They'll be out of sigh before we finish.

"They played us, that's what happened," I say, wiping a hand over my face.

"Nah, we're players too. This is just our official invitation." Finn turns his back on the calm sea, tapping my shoulder as he walks away with a great big smile on his face. "Let the games begin, brother."

I'm powered by adrenaline, desire, and frustration, but they seem to go hand in hand. Somehow fueling each other and putting more kindling to this obsession that grows for this woman.

Maybe it's that pure, naive look that makes me so damn hard, or maybe it's the fact that underneath it all, there's probably not an ounce of innocence about her. She's a witch in disguise, stirring a potion that drags me closer and closer to her. But her potion smells of wildflowers in bloom and she might as well douse me in it because I'm coming for her.

Wherever the woman is, she's already mine.

But I'll play her game. Relinquish the control. Because she's been doing a damn good job so far with the rules.

* * *

"You guys are fucked, aren't you?" Madds smirks.

He cocks his head as I take a seat on the couch across from him and Vin. We've gathered in Midnight, as we always seem to do since we opened this place. I look up at my brother and he just shrugs, turning to head to the bar.

"Don't answer that," Madds continues, shaking his head as he leans back. "I'm not gonna sit here and tell you that you shouldn't. You're big boys, you know yourselves you shouldn't. But... the dick wants what the dick wants, and sometimes the heart agrees with it too."

"Damn, you're a veritable poet, man." Finn places a drink in front of me before he takes a seat on the free armchair to my right. "Realistically, it's not common knowledge who they chose to strike the deal with. The people who would try undermining us theoretically don't know, and even if the information would get out, it's information we can control. How much damage can it really do to our reputation?"

"Just get our money back and we'll be good," Vin grumbles, shaking his head in some sort of acceptance. But I can see the shadow of a smirk there.

"We will. As of now, we're the only ones who know the painting isn't real, so it's all under wraps."

"Actually..." Carter walks into the barroom from the corridor that leads to the office. "Our money has been returned, and that second part isn't entirely true."

She really did send the money back. I didn't fully believe her when she said it, yet now this seems like some sort of test. Technically, I got what I was chasing her for. *Technically*.

"Explain," Vin says, cocking his head, and my shoulders suddenly tense up.

"I kept an ear out since we found out the painting was a fake. Someone's been knocking on some doors for information, very low key around the underground art world. I did a bit of digging and one very angry man who bought a disturbingly expensive painting from two women, found out a couple of months ago that a fake had been sitting behind his alarmed glass display in his mansion."

My chest tightens, and Finn is suddenly still. So damn still, I'm afraid he'll shatter if I touch him. I have no idea what's going through his head. I don't even know what's going through mine. Varying emotions that amount to one that dominates them all—confusion.

I'm fucking confused. Am I scared this man will go after her? Am I scared she'll get hurt or killed? Am I reserved because I just met the woman mere weeks ago and caring about her fate is fucking ridiculous?

Bewilderment... this is exactly what clouds my mind.

If she was any other woman, she would be long gone from my radar. I wouldn't care. I would barely remember her name.

"Fuck," I sigh, shaking my head at myself—she's not any other woman. This one I like. Really fucking like. Like I'm goddamn hypnotized. "Who is he, and does he know who he's looking for? I wonder if the girls know."

"There're feelers out there, placed by people who work for him. However, he seems to have deep pockets. I have my men working on identity. For now, it might be okay. They seem to be based far away in the northeast."

"We can handle deep pockets. Hanna mentioned that she keeps an eye on the people they sold to, so they might know," Finn says as he rises.

"We can," Carter agrees, nodding calmly, "but just because I haven't found his name, it doesn't mean he's a nobody. It means the exact opposite; he's a somebody big enough that his identity is effortlessly hidden, and anyone but him does the work."

"See what else you can find," Finn adds.

"Carter..." My voice seems to simmer angrily. "Did you find them? They didn't disappear into thin air. It's been three days. Where are they?"

He raises one eyebrow at me, and I swear I can see my maddened expression reflecting in his own. I want to rein it in, but I can't seem to manage. It's all too much. Stealing my oxygen and weighing me down. I need to get the fuck out of here.

I need air.

I need to think.

Shit.

I step around the coffee table, ready to jump over the damn thing, and head toward the door.

"I did find them."

His words stop me dead in my tracks. I don't turn to face him.

"Bovely Island."

CHAPTER 7
Ronan

WE'RE SNEAKING THROUGH THE FERNS, making our way up on the slight slope of the small laurel forest, the last of the sunshine lighting our way. We strayed from the path when we heard something that sounded a lot like a voice out in the distance, as we headed up to the villa that sits at the top of this hill.

There's little chance that Annika and Hanna didn't see the speedboat Finn and I came in. Despite the dark clouds that followed us here and whatever violence was brewing at sea, the position of the house gives you quite an advantage. Which means that we definitely didn't imagine the voices we heard—it's them.

Out of all the islands in this archipelago, they chose Bovely, the smallest one. Fifteen minutes is all it takes to walk from one end to the other. It's privately owned, with just one house, and a clear neon sign pointed at our targets, just for us.

I've never been here, but our parents were invited a few times. Back when old man Bovely still had his stamina and health, he used to throw some fancy, weekend-long parties. He can't come here anymore, even if it's only thirty-forty minutes away by speedboat, but he lends it over to his closest friends whenever they want an escape. I doubt there're many of them left, though. Once you become old and frail, people seem to abandon you. You become too easy to forget. It begs the question—how did Annika and her friend manage to get their slender fingers on it? I'll add it to the list of things I want to find out about the witch.

It gets my blood boiling, knowing this foolish woman not only challenged me, but she fucking lured me, a damn stranger to her, to a private, isolated island, where she's utterly defenseless. Fortunately, it's also what gets me both intrigued and painfully hard.

Not far ahead, rustling of leaves catches my attention, my adrenaline spiking almost instantly, and I signal the direction to Finn, who's about six feet away.

The wind picks up, and the whole forest becomes alive in seconds. It's the strangest thing, like the trees begin to sing, covering our steps as we hurry cautiously.

The sun must have hidden behind some clouds because it's much darker here now. Even more of an advantage for us. It's exhilarating. Stalking through the shadows, hoping I'll catch her at a vulnerable moment, then... pounce.

And just like that, I catch a glimpse of them, scurrying around the trees, peeking around themselves... looking for us, and it puts a great big grin on my face. Finn's too. He's not even paying attention to me anymore. He's found his target, and he's going for it. The whole ride here, he wouldn't shut up about Hanna, how amazing she was, how smart, all the things he wanted to do to her. I shut my ears at that part—no brother should hear about the places the other's tongue wants to reach.

I share the sentiment, but I don't need to share the mental image.

It's only been three days, but seeing her again does something peculiar to my insides. For the first time in my life, I have to wonder... is this what everyone means by *butterflies*?

"It's gonna hammer down in a minute!" one of them, maybe Hanna, shouts over the loud wind in an urgent tone.

Raindrops have started to fall, no trace of the warm light from the setting sun anymore, the forest much darker than it should be at this time of day. Its song much more violent.

They pick up the pace, but we're right there with them, and I'm focused on the woman who clouds my judgment with the need for her. Her brown hair, black in this lack of light, flowing as she begins to run. She's practically goddamn floating. This is one of those moments that would be shown in slow motion in movies... it feels like it is.

They stop, catching their breath, and carefully look around before they exchange a knowing gaze, probably realizing that all this rustling of leaves might not be just from the wind. Finn and I made sure to hide, stalking behind trees and dense bushes, getting closer and closer to the creatures who lured us here.

Suddenly, lightning bathes the forest in an eerie light, just as the first thunder of this brewing storm cracks, and my witch jumps into a sprint with a loud yelp.

I don't hesitate. I run after her, the adrenaline and excitement pulling at my lips, the roaring anticipation of getting my hands on her, something I've never experienced. My cock is already hard—too hard—rubbing uncomfortably against my jeans. I want her more than I've ever wanted any other woman. Every other desire I've had before her pales in comparison. I almost regret not taking her behind that waterfall. Almost.

The smell of her skin, the taste of her, the way she fit against me, it was so goddamn intoxicating. I was close... but I couldn't. Even without the interruption, I didn't want to take it further in that place. I fooled myself by reasoning that teasing her was my retaliation for pulling me into her game, but in reality, I wanted more for her. She deserves better than a quick fuck.

But after three nights of dreams haunted by her, as I watch her sweet body move through this thickening rain, I don't think I can give her better. I don't think I can wait. I can't fucking help myself. I need her.

My flesh feels wrong without her body wrapped around me, my fucking lungs won't stop heaving unless she's swallowing my breaths, and my heart won't stop racing unless she's there to soothe it. I almost hate myself for these thoughts... they taste slightly bitter, like weakness. But maybe it's because she's not officially mine yet.

Then, it's time to make her.

Lightning splashes our whole world in shades of blue, and she turns her head right at that moment, stumbling as she sees me running not that far behind her. She yelps as I grin, and I could have sworn I caught a glimpse of a smile before she turned back around, quickening her steps.

I could try so much harder, run so much faster. I could catch her in the next few seconds. But why spoil the fun? Especially seeing how hard she's pushing herself, knowing full well goosebumps mar her skin because of me. Even better, knowing that she still hasn't touched her pussy, made herself come without me.

I can guarantee she's getting slicker by the second

between those sweet thighs. It's not even wishful thinking. It's a fact.

And I'm about to prove it.

"Such an easy game you're playing, little witch?" I shout.

We must be nearing the house now, but as I finish that taunt, the damn woman takes a sharp right through some tall ferns and bushes, and I lose her. Clearly, this is not all she has. This rain is falling harder now, and as I stop to wipe it from my eyes, I listen to the forest. Listen for her.

I think she stopped too.

Walking slowly in the direction she disappeared in, I use the wind to cover my movements. I catch a glimpse of her signaling something to her friend still in the distance, as she moves fluidly from the shadow of a tall bush to hide behind a large tree.

Then I'm there, on the other side of that tree, and before I can do anything, I see Finn stalk behind Hanna, suddenly wrapping a hand around her middle while covering her face and pulling her back behind some tall foliage, the wind drowning her muffled yelp.

"Hanna?" Annika calls for her friend, forgetting about her cover, and turns to find her gone. "Hanna?!" Her breathing picks up, forcing herself to control the panic. "This is not funny! Hanna!"

She's distracted, and just like that, I round the tree and I'm right behind her. She's dripping wet from the rain, as am I, yet the heat of her body warms me, even though we're not touching. Her muscles still all at once, her shoulders frozen in place. The tension is palpable. I could do it. Take her right here, right now.

I could flip her around and sink into her against this tree. I could do so much more.

But I like this game.

"Run," I growl in her ear.

"Aaah!" she yelps and sprints away, not even daring to look back.

I take off after her, a great big fucking grin making my cheeks hurt, reveling in her quick step, her nerves, her growing sense of dread as she stumbles, caught by various roots and plants.

Even if it's already raining, somehow I can sense the moment the skies break open all at once, and the water that falls on us is so dense, I can barely see a few yards in front of me and the ground becomes a slippery mess. It makes this hunt even more rousing.

"You wanted a chase, Annika! But you don't seem to be running fast enough! Almost like you don't want it as bad as I thought you did."

I let the words drift through the trees, and they seem to fuel her as she picks up the pace.

It's no use. I'm determined. More than that, this is making me ravenous. I'm right behind her now, just as thunder shatters the atmosphere once more. She yelps and stumbles, and I watch her dive forward, almost in slow motion. I'm not sure how I got here, but I'm suddenly next to her, throwing myself as far forward as I can to catch her and break her fall.

She screams as she lands on top of me, but we roll on the ground, caking ourselves in mud and broken leaves, as I hold her to me. Beneath me, she's caged in, breathing frantically.

The predator caught the prey. And my, my, what delicious prey.

Before she can even think of running, I grab her arms, stretching them above her head, and grip her wrists in one hand, pinning her down. Her gaze fixes on me, her chest pushing against me with every ragged breath, but when her lips part, I'm done. Mine crash against hers, kissing like the world is about to end with this raging storm and this is the last chance I'll ever get to taste her. She moans into my mouth, her body softening beneath me, her hips pushing up into me, before she wraps one leg around my waist and holds me against her. Her tongue in my mouth is frantic, licking every bit of me she can reach, and I realize how much I'm loving her game. I'd play it every day for the rest of my life if the chase would end with a moment like this one, nestled between her legs, with her sweet tongue in my mouth, desperate to have me.

We're sinking into the wet ground, the storm turning from bad to worse, but I can't possibly stop. I won't. Only for a moment do I break the kiss to admire her. Wet, muddy, red cheeks—she's a goddamn vision. She's a deity dropped on this ruthless earth just for me to taste, to worship, to own. She's fucking mine. There's no other option. No way out.

Not for her, and definitely not for me.

"Are you hurt?" It dawns on me that we rolled a few times.

She shakes her head as she bites her lip, and my eyes almost roll in the back of my head as she grinds her hips against my hard on.

"Goddamn witch, you'll be the death of me."

My lips find hers again, this kiss turning into a violent affair, the waves of rain our melody, and the trees thrashing in the wind our song.

I'm leaning on my forearm next to her head, running my other hand all over her body, no regard to the mud as I reach underneath her top, straight for those pretty tits of hers. She feels so fucking good in my hand, her hard nipples screaming for attention, and I couldn't possibly deny them. I squeeze lightly, enough that she whimpers into my mouth, pushing her hips into me with another needy grind, begging for more.

So, I do, I give her more, pressing my dick against the

warmth of her center, cursing every single layer of clothes covering us right now. But I keep going, dry humping her into the mud, kneading her tits, and biting her lips and tongue until we're a fucking mess of greed and lust.

I can't wait anymore. I probably should. I should stop. Take her to the house and sink into the heat of her properly, in a soft bed, beneath clean linens like she fucking deserves.

"I'm sorry...." I plead against her lips as I rise on my knees. Dragging my palms down her inner thighs, I grip the thin fabric of her leggings, pausing for a moment. Waiting for a reaction, a plea to stop. But her pretty face is caught somewhere between shock and desire, lips forming a perfect O as she stares between her legs. I pull sharply, splitting her leggings at the seams so I can get exactly what I ache for.

Jesus Christ, she's not wearing panties.

It's a fucking sign, and by God, what a pretty sign it is.

I fumble with my jeans, almost ripping them open, desperate to sink into that beautiful cunt of hers, and by the time my cock is aligned with her slit, I'm caging her in once more, and she wraps her arms around me.

Enticing whimpers fill my ears as I push in between her sleek lips, my thick cock strangled by the tightening pulses. It's a cruel form of torture, because I'm not sure how I'm supposed to last beyond three pumps when she feels so flawless wrapped around me. I have to. I have to stretch this insane sensation for as long as I can, just as I'm stretching her right now, pressing farther until I meet the end of her. We're both panting. Her eyes sparkle, looking at me like I splattered the sky with stars myself. I hold that gaze as I slide back, then immediately pound into her, watching those steel irises explode as her whimpers turn into sharp, echoing moans.

So, I do it again, slowly sliding out, before slamming back in, just to savor that explosion in her eyes again, the pleasure rippling through her features, her brows pulling together, her cheeks flushed as she bites her bottom lip.

We're soaking wet. The rain is so heavy, we might as well be fucking underwater. But I couldn't care less. This is exhilarating! I just cage her in, shielding her as much as I can from the onslaught of the downpour. Then I dive in, pressing my lips to hers as I fall into a delirious rhythm, fucking her frantically until I swear we've made a little nest within the soaked soil.

She mewls into my mouth, forcing me to swallow my own name as it spills off her lips, and it makes me buck my hips harder into her, grinding after each thrust so I can rub against her clit, reveling in how her pussy clenches when I do.

"You're perfect, little witch, and you're mine. You're fucking mine!" I all but roar.

She moans louder, the sweetest of smiles painted in lust, the perfect answer to my confession.

I pick up the pace until I can't tell if she's crying or moaning, and just when I think I can't possibly hold back anymore, her soaked cunt clutches my shaft, rippling as she screams. My name falling in waves of euphoria off her lips does something to me. Maybe even more than the tremble of her whole body with the violent orgasm that triggers mine in a split fucking second. I roar as I come inside of her so fucking hard, she spasms with each burst that fills her.

My brain is in pieces; I'm not quite sure what the hell just happened. All I know is that it's never been like this for me. I've never screamed my release. Or felt this animalistic need to take... I'm not even sure I've sated it yet.

"Ronan..."

"Yes, baby."

"I... wow..."

I smile, dropping small kisses all over her face.

"I know," I tell her.

"I feel like I need to thank you."

"I think I'm supposed to do the thanking, little witch. And the apologizing."

I slowly pull out of her, do up my jeans and rise, before I pull her up to her feet.

"You already said you were sorry, before…" she says with a confused smile, "but I'm not sure why."

"Because I couldn't wait. I didn't give you something better, softer, at least in a house."

She laughs, that damn birdsong filling my ears again.

"You gave me exactly what I wanted. Everything I needed."

Those words would get me hard again if I wasn't still halfway there. But suddenly it dawns on me what an idiot I've just been.

"Oh, Annika. Shit, I… fuck! In the heat of the moment, I completely forgot about a condom. I promise I'm clean, but… I'm so sorry."

She raises her eyebrows with a thoughtful look.

"I forgot too. Don't worry, I have an IUD, and considering I haven't had sex in over eight months, I'm clean too."

She laughs, but in typical man style, all I focus on is that she hasn't touched a man in that long. It strangely makes me feel good that I was the one to break her dry spell. Like she chose me specifically. How peculiar.

"But now that you said that… umm… your c—you are dripping down my legs. And this storm is getting a bit scary now."

It's my turn to laugh, but knowing that my cum is rubbing between her thighs makes me want to do some dirty things that might delay us even further.

But we're *actually* dirty, our clothes caked in mud.

"Let's go to the house."

She takes the lead, and we walk through the thick storm, and I can't help but wonder what's happening with my small boat right now. I can hear the waves from here, even though we're almost in the middle of the island. I didn't even think to have a look at the weather forecast. It might have been a mistake, but I guess we'll find out.

When the house comes into view between the trees, I thank the gods, because I've been walking behind this woman, watching her ass cheeks peek from between the rip in her leggings, and I need to be close to her. I want to wash myself and touch every single bit of her body, stroke, and lick, I want it all.

We burst through the door, shutting it behind us as the rain threatens to soak the inside. I don't know where my brother and Hanna are. They might already be inside, so we need to hurry before they see Annika with her ripped clothes.

"Bathroom." I can't seem to form any other words.

I follow as she leads me through the house, and I'm learning what tunnel vision is, because I could be anywhere right now, in a crowd, in a damn dungeon, literally anywhere, and I wouldn't even notice.

All I see is her.

When the resemblance of a shower enclosure blurs behind her, I reach for the door I just passed through and slam it behind me. I don't wait. I lean in slightly, wrapping an arm under her ass, lifting her to me as she wraps her legs around me, and presses her lips to mine.

I walk in the shower, blindly reaching for something to turn on the water. When I finally find it, the first spray comes out cold, but it doesn't deter us. We only break the kiss when our muddy, soaked clothes are too much of a barrier, and we all but rip them off each other. Then we wash the mud off our bodies with such speed, you'd think we were about to win a damn prize.

I guess we are.

"I played your game, little witch," I say, pausing as I take a hard, deep breath. "Now it's your turn to play mine."

She smiles at me, but the sheepish expression turns wicked as she drops to her knees before me, and I don't have time to process before her hand is at the base of my cock and the tip of me hits the back of her throat. I'm seeing stars and almost choke on my own spit.

"Fuck... Annika."

Who am I kidding? This is still her game. And I don't think I'll ever stop playing it.

She sucks me slow and deep, her small hand following her lips as her tongue licks the underside of my cock. I'm going to burst right here. It's torture. Slow, grueling, delicious torture, and I would take it to the very end if I didn't want to be deep inside of her.

I grab her under the arms and haul her up, my cock falling with a sloppy pop from between her lips. Gripping her head in my hands, I kiss her so fucking roughly her teeth split my lip. But fuck if I care. My goal is clear—sink inside her cunt until she screams my name again and wipes the memory of all other women from my mind.

Spinning her around, I bend her over, and hold her in place with a hand on the middle of her arched back. I can't help but pump my shaft a few times at the view of her eagerly awaiting my cock, as she braces her hands against the wall.

Her cunt is far too inviting to keep her waiting.

I press between her folds, parting her as I rub over her slit, reveling in the shudder that shakes her body. She pulses around me, and I take it as my cue, wrapping my hand around her hip, fingers digging into her flesh, and push through her tightening walls.

Dear God, how am I going to last when she does this to me?

I slam home with one hard thrust, and she yelps, almost slipping against the wet shower wall.

"I dreamed of this. Your little cunt wrapped around my cock, your steel eyes filled with need... I thought I knew what to expect. Turns out, I'm a clueless bastard and thank the gods I am."

This is different from what happened in the forest. The hunger is still here, but I'm fucking feasting on her now, sinking into her cunt like it's Nirvana itself and I'm building my own home inside of it.

"Ronan..." She rolls my name off her tongue like a lustful prayer, threatening to make me come dangerously fast.

Then I wrap one hand around her neck, holding her in place as my thrusts threaten to topple her, and with the other, I reach around her middle, until her clit is beneath the tips of my fingers. The moment I roll them over her swollen bundle, her legs begin to shake, her cunt pulses around me, and her walls milk me thoroughly from the inside out.

"Ro—Ronan... I—I'm coming!" she cries so sweetly as she shatters around me. But it breaks me too. Making me come like never before.

Christ, what have I done?

Her spell is complete.

There will be no one else.

CHAPTER 8

Annika

WE EMERGED FROM THE SHOWER much later. I didn't want to leave. It felt like a sanctuary, sheltering us in a bubble of sex and desperation. Such sweet desperation. Keeping our hands off each other to wash ourselves was torture. The shower gel pouring too slow, the mud not washing off fast enough, and I couldn't wait any longer to get my hands on him and mouth around his cock. After he fucked me so damn well, we still weren't fully sated, and my hair was taking too long to wash. So he dropped to his knees, stopping my efforts, threw my leg over his shoulder, and ate my pussy like it was the richest feast after being starved. He made me come so intensely, I couldn't hold myself up and slid against the wet wall until my ass hit the floor. But he saw me there, all shattered and powerless and he pulled me under him, my leg still hooked over his shoulder, and slid inside me until I was utterly full. Begging for more was futile. He fucked me as the shower rained over us, caging me in with his ridiculous body, muscles flexing above me, sinew making him look like a raging beast, and all I could do was moan and smile.

I couldn't stop smiling...

I still can't. And it's been three days.

Three days of fucking, although one of those times I could have almost described it as *making love*. Three days of his hands constantly on me. Three days wrapped up in a cocoon, prisoners of this seemingly never-ending storm. I would thank the gods for the opportunity, but this was supposed to be one night. Would we have been the same if we weren't stuck here together? Would the hunger be the same? Would this need to constantly touch each other still be here?

The weather has been merciless, the pouring rain an understatement to what has been bashing against our windows. The sea is a torment, ruthless waves smashing against this small island with such force, there have been a couple of times when Ronan has had to hold me, soothe me when my anxiety got a bit out of hand at the thought of this storm worsening. But waking up because of shattering thunder has been strangely comforting, because even in his sleep, this man wrapped an arm around me and pulled me to him, sheltering me in his comfort.

Our life inside this house is like a strange fairytale. Such a brutal contrast to the harsh tempest fracturing the world outside. We're trapped in our bubble of decadence, watching it like a movie through our windows.

I've only been out of the bedroom two or three times since he arrived. We've barely seen Finnigan and Hanna, especially since they're on the other side of the villa. Which in hindsight is a good thing, because I've passed way too close to their side of the house when they were in the middle of some... interesting action... and distance is exactly what we need in those situations.

When I did have a bit of alone time with Hanna, she looked happy in a satisfied, content kind of way. I've never seen her like this. Disheveled, beautifully broken. I wonder if I look the same. I feel it.

"Tell me then, was it your dad who inspired you to paint?" Ronan walks into the bedroom with a tray of finger foods for us. I'm starving.

I grab a cherry tomato and a piece of mozzarella, stuffing them in my mouth before I answer. Mmm... Thank God we stocked up the kitchen before this storm hit.

"Yeah." I give a partial answer with my mouth full.

"I'm not sure you look quite that happy when I make you come."

I stuff a piece of bread in my mouth too.

"It's not your fault. Nothing will ever compare to food."

This time he laughs, and it makes me pause. He's a beautiful man, but when his eyes crinkle from laughter and smile lines crease his cheeks, he's godlike.

"Go on, tell me," he pushes.

"Both my parents are artists." I take little bites of the delicious food, so I can still talk. "My mother is a free soul. Always painting these extravagant modern pieces that most people don't quite understand. My father is the lover of the ancients, the classics, the renaissance... everything that stopped being painted two hundred years ago. He dedicated his life to restoring art, traveling the world, and sometimes taking us with him. I learned everything from him."

"Is he as successful as you are?"

I give him a knowing look.

"Definitely not in the same way. As far as I am aware, my

father doesn't forge famous and lost paintings for a living."

"You certainly do have quite a talent. You fooled so many appraisers, so many people..." he trails off with a look on his face that looks a lot like pride. "I'm not sure I've ever heard of anyone like you. You're a genius with a paintbrush, little witch."

My cheeks burn, and I bow my head, stuffing another cherry tomato in my mouth to keep from saying something stupid. I appreciate compliments, but there is something about them that makes me want to run and hide while shouting *thank you, but I don't deserve it, or maybe just a little bit.* I wish my mind would make sense.

"Out of curiosity, was it true? The story you told us about the *original* Lady in White painting."

"That great-grandpa took it?"

He nods.

"Yup. All true. Only it wasn't exactly saved. About a third of it was burnt. I have it in storage, which is why I was so sure I could forge this one with minimal risk. I studied it thoroughly over the years and there was never a risk of anyone finding the original."

"It's ironic that this is the one you decided to screw up intentionally." He smiles, shaking his head.

"None of this situation has made any logical sense to me." I admit.

"Weren't you worried that your dad would find out that this painting was on the market?"

"No. He doesn't know about the painting. Grandpa told me that my dad's a bit too honorable and would end up returning it if he knew. Why he thought I wouldn't do the same... I don't know. Plus, black-markets are not my dad's playground."

"Your grandpa must have seen something in you. Where

are your parents now?" he asks.

"West Coast. In a small fishing village, living in this crazy split-personality cottage, that literally looks like they built it at the same time, but separately. Half the house is all mom, colors splashed everywhere, almost psychedelic with a touch of bohemian, while the other half is neat, in elegant, neutral colors and fine antiques. Somehow, it works... just like them."

He laughs lightly, the way that emotion once again pulls at his lips and crinkles his eyes, making me melt. I've seen plenty of beautiful men before, but none hold a torch to Ronan. He wears his looks with such nonchalance, like he's barely aware of how stunningly attractive he is, yet he's utterly comfortable in his own skin.

"With their combined lifestyles, it sounds like it could get intense between them," he jokes.

"It does. They've been together for almost thirty years, so they're used to each other. But it also means that they love getting on each other's nerves. They're a weirdly beautiful couple," I say, rolling my eyes at the memory of their house and life together. But I catch a tinge of longing in Ronan's eyes. For a moment there he loses himself.

"What do your parents think you do for work? Especially with all this traveling?"

"The same thing as dad—restoration—which is great since it's normal to travel a lot in this job. However, I told them I work for private collections, so they can never to see my work out there. Unlike my dad's work, which is public since he works on monuments, churches, and other public buildings."

"That's quite interesting, straightforward, since you didn't have to put too much effort into the cover."

He has this sparkle in his eyes that looks a lot like respect.

"Considering that neither he nor your mom know

of your job," he continues, "do they actually know how talented you are? Or the fact that you probably surpassed your father's skills?"

I shrug, swallowing another bit of food.

"I never thought about that, to be honest. Proving myself to them was never really on my mind, and they were quite relaxed in their parenting. They didn't make my talent a competition. And in terms of my dad, I would never say I surpassed him. Our talents have just been specialized differently. He restores, and I like recreating. I've been doing it since I was young enough to hold a paintbrush."

"What made you start?" he asks as he grabs another piece of salami, pushing my way the mozzarella he can see I'm obsessing over.

"Emotions. I looked at a painting, and I could see the expression of the subject. Even in those posed portraits, you could see how they clutched the fingers, the tension in the shoulders, or the love in the eyes. But recreating it... it makes me experience it myself. The first time I did it well, I cried. I was painting loss, a mother holding her dead son draped limply in her arms, as she stared at the sky, begging God for a miracle. When I look at a painting, I can admire how it depicts the emotions we're all supposed to see, but when I paint it myself, I can feel them."

"Damn... that's not what I was expecting, if I was expecting anything at all."

"I'm sorry. I know it sounds a bit... crazy." Can I hide under the covers now?

I keep wondering when this man is going to realize his mistake and run far away from me.

"It sounds beautiful." He pulls the tray away, setting it on the nightstand, before crawling on top of me, pushing my legs apart with his and nestling between them, as he swipes the stray strands of hair from my face. "And there's nothing wrong with a little crazy."

"Hey!"

I smack his shoulder, but he catches my wrist, pinning it above my head, a grave, mildly amused rumble vibrating through his chest.

"Careful, little witch, or I might punish you for that."

"Promises, promises."

Ronan

I REACH OVER NEXT TO ME BEFORE I EVEN OPEN MY eyes, frowning when I fail to find what I need—Annika. Blinking a few times, I attempt to focus on the world around me and the empty bed. I lift my head and look toward the en-suite bathroom, but the door is open, light off. She's not there.

My head sinks back into the pillow and I rub my eyes in an attempt to wake up quicker. We went to sleep so late last night, and we didn't even end in sex. We were talking for hours. About life, her wants, needs, dreams, and everything in between. It was surreal. Like I was living in some chick flick movie where they played a montage as the couple kept shifting in bed in all sorts of awkward positions while telling stories and laughing. This wasn't a movie, though; this was real life... my life. This woman has turned me upside down. If this isn't black magic, I don't know what is.

I throw off the covers, looking for my phone to check the time, since this damn storm is keeping us in a constant state of darkness and we never know if it's morning or afternoon. I track it down—seven twenty-three a.m. Damn, she got up early.

I'm about to head out the door when it dawns on me that I'm stark-fucking-naked, and I'm sure if Hanna is out there, she would prefer not to see quite this much of me. I washed my boxers last night and my jeans a couple of nights ago, since the very few things we brought with us we stupidly left on the boat. We're not even sure if it's still there on the shore, let alone our clothes. I go to the bathroom, thankful when I find my clothes dry on the heated towel rail, then I quickly wash my face and brush my teeth.

Now it's time to find my woman.

When I enter the living area, it's quiet, the sounds of the storm playing on repeat in the background, bashing at the windows in hectic waves. It seems to be easing down, but not enough that we could leave this house. Let alone this island. But fuck if I care that I'm stuck here. If I left, I wouldn't be able to enjoy this incredible view—Annika sitting at the round breakfast table in the bay window, chair turned toward the ocean, a small canvas in front of her, lost in her brush strokes as she paints, completely oblivious to my presence. Her hair is wrapped in a loose bun at the crown of her head, messy strands fallen around her slender neck and soft face, and I'm not sure if I want to make myself known. There's something about this image, the serenity of her against the tumultuous storm in the background. There's so much perfection in this paradox.

I lean against the kitchen island, arms crossed over my chest, watching her delicate fingers swirl a brush in a small color palette, before moving it with ease on the canvas that's no longer white.

I want this—her—for more than just now. I want her

when the storm is over. I want her back in Queenscove. I want her for as long as she'll want me. Only, I fear I'll keep her even after that.

My bare feet start moving before I made the decision, and her shoulders jerk ever so slightly when she realizes she's no longer alone.

"Morning, baby."

My voice comes out croakier than it should, my throat dry. Dehydration or thirst for her... not sure which. The bare skin of her neck and shoulders comes alive with goosebumps.

"Morning, baby." She matches my words with sweetness in her voice I want to taste.

I lean in, wrapping my arm around her chest, careful not to disturb her right arm that she paints with, and kiss the nape of her neck, before moving to that sweet spot where it meets the shoulder. She sinks into me, but doesn't stop painting. So I sneak a peek at the canvas. It's almost the complete opposite of her other works I have seen so far. She showed me quite a few photos on her phone, and this is nothing like them. The strokes are rough, almost chaotic, yet there's a hidden order in all that chaos, because I can see it as clear as it looks out the window... the storm.

She painted it all; the waves, the thrashing trees, the broken skies, and the rush of the rain.

Only the feeling it gives me is not of turmoil, but of calm. A strange sense of elation. It feels as ethereal as what her and I are experiencing inside this house, even if the strokes depict the anarchy outside of it.

"It's beautiful, Annika."

"Thank you. I wanted to capture this moment... and maybe someday, if I want to remember what it was like, I can feel it all over again."

I don't realize I'm squeezing her until she stops painting.

I'm jealous. I wish I could do that, find a way to experience something all over again, almost like it's the first time. I release her and rise, standing behind her.

"You'll have to tell me what it's like."

She tips her head back, and I lean in, pressing a kiss to her forehead. But when I rise again, she looks back at me with wide eyes.

"What?"

"You're saying it like you—like you're going to be next to me years from now," she says on a shaky breath that both confuses me and makes me fear its implications.

"Annika, I—"

"Morning!" Hanna's voice interrupts me, and I'm slightly annoyed. But at the same time, a little thankful.

We haven't known each other for that long. I have no idea if what I'm feeling is the result of our forced proximity, cooped up in this—granted, large—villa, or if it's all real. There's this sense inside me like I want her for the rest of my life, but is it real? What about her, does she share the sentiment? Can she trust it? Or is she going through the same erratic trains of thought as I am?

"Morning." I turn to Hanna, swallowing my worries for now.

She's wearing what is clearly my brother's t-shirt, and he shows up right behind her, in nothing but his joggers. Thank God I take care of myself and have a fairly fit body, because otherwise I would have quite a complex next to him looking like a damn surfer-boy with his sun-kissed, toned form, and wild blond curls. I am a little jealous that Annika is witnessing this.

I look down and catch her gaze on him, lingering after she says good morning, before she turns her attention back to the painting. Okay, maybe I'm a bit more than a little jealous.

Hanna takes a seat on the other side of the table, and I join Finn in the kitchen, fiddling with a pot of coffee as he pulls some ingredients out of the fridge.

"This storm better be easing soon, because we're quite low on food. These are the last ones." He places a half empty carton of eggs on the gray granite countertop.

"I'll just have some granola and yogurt. There's still plenty of that," I say.

"Actually, I could go for some of that as well," Annika says without turning her head from the canvas, and Hanna signals that she would like that too.

"Three to one, I guess. Enjoy your eggs." I turn to Finn, and he seems pleased. He's always been well taken care of, not that he doesn't know the value of money, but he's never really been in a situation where food was running low and there was no indication of when the next meal would be.

I hope he will never be.

I take bowls, yogurt, and granola to the table, while Finn makes an omelet for himself, and brings the coffee over.

"Any news on when this storm is supposed to finish?" Hanna asks.

"Why? Are you in a hurry to run away from me, darling?" Finn slides in the seat next to her, pinching her chin and pulling her to him.

"Yup."

He laughs, and she playfully rolls her eyes. I'm not sure what to make of this, but my brother's eyes are awfully sparkly.

"Forecast said that it should have eased off today. Obviously, that's not the case. So hopefully in max two or three days, it will be over. We'll have to check if our boat is still whole, but honestly, I doubt it."

"I'm not gonna cry about it," Finn adds. "It was a fairly

cheap speedboat."

"You'll give us a ride back to Queenscove, right?" I nudge Annika, and she smiles.

"Can I think about it?"

"No."

She laughs and shakes her head.

"Ours—well, our rental, is in the boathouse. So hopefully there's no damage," Hanna says.

"One of the other guys will come and get us if not. No worries there," Finn reassures them.

"You're coming with us after the storm anyway," I add, watching as Annika turns to face me with a lifted brow.

"Are we now?" She asks in a high tone, dropping her canvas and paintbrush on the table.

"Well, you're no longer in your house, you're running out of supplies here, and I... umm... I want you there."

"You don't sound very convincing, brother."

I feel the need to eradicate that amusement with a punch. Maybe a kick in the teeth to wipe that pretty smile off his face.

"Fuck you!"

"We can temporarily rent our own place," Annika says, laughing at us.

"Waste of money. Especially since you've had to refund us for that painting," I joke.

"Funny. But I have plenty left." She smirks.

Does she not want to spend more time with me? I can't figure out if she thinks she's imposing, or we really aren't on the same wavelength.

"We'll talk about it later."

Even if this discussion affects her friend, this is between Annika sand me. There's this feral need I'm having an inner fight with, one that wants to throw her over my shoulder, haul her ass into my penthouse, and keep her there. But at the same time I have to remind myself I'm not a caveman, and I have to let this be her choice. None of those sides are winning right now, so I would rather wait to have this talk when it's just us two.

"Anni, your painting is gorgeous! So different." Hanna finally looks at her friend's work of art.

"Yeah, real different, actually. At least from the one you left for my brother," Finn adds, winking at her.

I really will punch him.

"I've been meaning to ask actually" Finn continues. "Did you just randomly haul around a self-portrait of yourself, or did you paint it in that short week?"

"I started it a while ago, but never felt the need to finish it. It felt a bit narcissistic to randomly have a portrait of myself in my house. This... situation..." she says as her haze flickers to me, "gave me the incentive to finish it."

"How convenient." My brother snickers, and I feel the need to move on. Talking about me or us feels oddly uncomfortable.

"How did you end up doing what you do?" I finally begin eating my yogurt, waiting for one of them to start.

"Well, we're done now. Your job was the last one. Although considering Annika's change of plans, the previous one was technically the last one." Hanna speaks first. "Starting it just kind of happened. It was one of those crazy ideas, like when you get drunk with your friends, and you start saying that you should all open a bar or something. It was kind of like that. I was watching Hanna in her restoration classes, and I was joking that she would be an amazing forger."

"I think we can relate, since we did exactly that—opened a bar with our friends." Finn laughs.

"You have a bar?" Annika turns to me, and I realize that all this time, we've been talking about us and her, not much about me. She's far more intriguing to talk about, though.

"You didn't pay full attention to the background check I showed you, Anni, did you?" Hanna crosses her arms over her chest, leaning back into her chair as she watches her friend with a quirked eyebrow.

"Umm... yes, sure I did. I guess I forgot."

"Or I made the mistake of showing you a photo of Ronan before I showed you all the important bits."

Well, damn if I don't feel good knowing that I was such a distraction for her.

"We both went to the Hardwin Institute of Art. She was a year older than me, but I don't know, we just clicked. I was in Restoration, and she was in Art History," Annika tries changing the subject.

"Yeah, Carter uncovered as much." I nod.

"I guess we just saw potential in one another. A different purpose than all the future starving artists channeling their inner DaVinci around us."

"It's quite a leap, though, isn't it? The life of a painter to a life of crime?" I ask. It's not necessarily that, but the fact that Annika's personality is a contrast to this type of life.

"It was a leap, but I gladly made it. I don't know how to explain it. I didn't know back then either. There was this need inside of me that kept screaming for more. I was the shy one, not because I don't have courage, but because the opportunities around me didn't seem to fit what I truly wanted. The moment I was presented with the prospect of forging a painting for our first deal, I ate up that adrenaline like it was my first meal after starvation."

"You were restless," Hanna says, nodding. "For days at the time, you weren't sleeping. All you wanted to do was paint."

"I really was. I've always been introverted, never put myself in any uncomfortable or simply different situations.

The idea that I had to stand quietly during a shady business deal, watch someone analyze my painting, then get away with the con, gave me a sensation like no other. Obviously bypassing the whole starving artist phase of my career was a bonus too," Annika says with a giggle, and it pulls a strange reaction out of me. An endearing smile... and isn't that just a little bit too close for comfort.

"You craved the thrill..." I comment, remembering our conversation from the waterfall.

"I did. It felt like a different persona. I craved to bring her forth—me... you know what I mean. It was like sliding over a mask over my usual shyness."

Seeing her blush, I tug her to me, and she nestles into my side. As she melts into my comfort, I drop a quick kiss to her forehead. I'm just glad that whole journey brought her to me.

Only this seems to be a slippery slope. I keep sliding down further and the rabbit hole is in my sight. I'm losing myself and it's only been a few days. Well... technically, it's been a few days trapped in the same house, in the same bedroom with her. But she's been haunting my dreams and crawling under my skin since the moment I laid eyes on her.

Being in this house, unable to even go out for a walk, completely glued to one another, is both incredible and terrifying.

Is this real? This weird warmth spreading like liquid fire between my ribs, pulsing with every beat of my heart whenever she simply smiles at me? Or the ache that makes my hands tingle whenever she's out of reach?

I want her more than I've wanted anything in my whole goddamn life. Even when she's right next to me, she's not close enough. I ache with the need to crawl under her skin, feel her every moment of every day. Have her steel gaze on me, enjoy that wicked smile. I want my cock inside of her at all times, her tongue in my mouth, her soft hands caressing my skin. She redefines addiction and it fucking scares me.

Four days brought me to this point. God knows what will happen to me by the time this storm ends.

CHAPTER 9
Annika

FTER A WHOLE WEEK TRAPPED IN THE storm, the background noise of the seaside city of Queenscove is like a sweet lullaby. We arrived yesterday afternoon on the boat Hanna and I rented, which luckily survived the storm. Ronan's speedboat didn't. It was shattered, laying all sad a bit too far from the shore.

The island seemed to be in fairly good condition, and we left a lot of our stuff there since, technically, our visit to the city is only temporary. I tell myself that I plan on staying just a bit longer than needed to refill our supplies, only to appease Ronan. I'm kidding myself. I know it's not true. I want more time with him, but there's this nagging voice in my head reminding me this is temporary—I'm leaving soon.

Although as I watch Ronan shift all the clothes in his walk-in wardrobe to make room for mine, then empty two drawers, I have a feeling he has something different in mind.

"I don't need that much space, Ronan. I barely have any clothes with me. A drawer will be fine."

But the man simply turns his head, gives me a smile that appeases my obvious delusion, and carries on with his task. He finishes and comes to me, sliding his hands over my hips until they settle on my ass and pulls me to him.

"Are you sure you're okay with me being out all day? I feel bad. It's your first proper day here, with me, and I get pulled away for business. I just... I need to catch up with the guys, and we have some meetings I can't miss."

"It's okay, Ronan, I survived just fine without you, you know."

In reality, I'm not so sure I'm okay with it. Not because I want him with me, but because staying with him in his lavish penthouse, sleeping in his bedroom while he goes to work, seems far too close to real life. Our island bubble burst; we're no longer trapped in this fever dream. This is real life... and he's welcomed me right into it.

I know I signed up for this thing with Ronan but, honestly, I didn't think past the chase, past the adventure, past the thrill of it all. It never crossed my mind that this could be more than sex.

But here I am, standing in this ravishing man's walk-in closet, my smell all over his sheets, the painting of myself that I left for him leaned against the wall of his bedroom, and my future doesn't seem to be in my hands anymore.

"You're doing that thing where you get lost in your thoughts," he says, bringing me back to the now.

I scrunch my eyebrows. *Thing?*

"What thing?!"

"You look right through me, narrowing your eyes like you're calculating the world's most difficult physics formula."

"Oh."

He cocks his head, and I can tell he wants to ask more. Obviously, he's noticed this expression on me before, and I wonder if I do it every time I think about the future. Is that what he wants to ask me?

"So you'll be gone all day?"

He pulls his lower lip between his teeth, sighing almost silently before he finally answers.

"I'll pick you up at seven. We have a reservation."

"Oh, that sounds nice. Restaurant?"

"Yeah, nice one, up on the hill."

"Sounds like it will be our first date." I feel the heat in my cheeks. Why, though? We've already slept together—many, many times.

"We could do a movie too, if you want to keep it classic." He laughs, his features brightening up all at once as he gazes at me from under his low eyebrows, the uptilt toward the temples giving him a mischievous quality. Even with the slight crook of his otherwise straight nose, the godlike beauty of this man makes me weak in the knees.

"Next time." I wrap my hands around his neck, pulling him down to me and pressing a long, soft kiss to his full lips.

We sink into ourselves, deep enough that his hands are now kneading my ass, rolling my cheeks and making me a whole mess between my thighs. His brother's voice startles us into reality, calling him. Ronan swears against my lips, nibbling at my lips as I start laughing.

His erection is now blatantly visible against the dark blue suit trousers, and he gives me a menacing look when I shrug and start backing away into the bedroom.

"Work is calling, baby," I tease.

"I might let it *ring* a little longer."

He's about to pounce on me, when a knock sounds on the

door and Finn's voice comes through.

"Did you hear me? We got to go, Carter just called."

"Coming! Give me a minute!" he shouts back.

He's readjusting his cock, and I didn't realize I was licking my lips until his eyes turned hungry on them.

"Okay. So, I'm going to go to the bathroom, because at this rate, you will never leave this bedroom," I say, going to him to press a quick peck on his cheek before I scurry away. "See you at seven."

I shut the door behind me, locking it before I flatten my back to it, exhaling so loudly I'm sure he heard me from the other side.

What did I get myself into?

* * *

Hanna looks at me with an inquisitive gaze as she holds the straw of her cocktail between her slender fingers.

It's already our fourth day here and we're still nowhere close to doing what we came here for—restocking our supplies for Bovely Island. We've been out on a couple of dates, a few times with the rest of the guys too, and today, Hanna and I have been exploring more of Queenscove. Still, neither of us has mentioned even once anything about when our time here will end.

We've done a great job of avoiding our reality.

After stopping at the penthouse to change into something a bit more stylish, we decided to go to an outdoor cocktail lounge, close to the beach so we can enjoy the salty breeze of the early evening. Being here outside the context of work is different. With no security with us either. Our guys are gone; we relieved them of their duties when we decided we were going to do this crazy thing... taunt the men of a damn criminal organization.

"You're different, you know," my best friend says, a strange smile on her lips.

"What are you talking about?"

"You look more... settled within yourself. Like your skin fits you better now."

What a strange thing to say.

All I can do is narrow my eyes as I try to understand her words.

She shakes her head and grins.

"I'm excited for Midnight tonight. I've never been to a speakeasy before," she says, her tone turning giddy.

"It will be interesting."

"You seem unsure."

"I guess I am. All the places we've been to with them, apart from the penthouse, have been either chosen by us or have been in public. We've never actually been in their world. This will be different. It will be our first real taste of the men we've been living with for almost two weeks now."

"Anni, it's just a bar," she shakes her head, smirking. "What do you think they'll have there? Thugs and guns everywhere, shady business deals in every corner, piles of cash on every table?"

I smack her forearm and cross my arms.

"Hanna, you know exactly what I mean. Everything we've been experiencing so far was skirting at the edge of it all."

"Well, you better get ready to dive in, because Finn just texted me that they're outside."

I take a deep breath, then down the rest of my Espresso Martini.

"Let's go, then."

I rise, heading through the indoor area of the lounge, Hanna in tow, already catching a glimpse of my man leaning against his sleek black Mercedes, strong arms crossed over his suit-covered chest, watching me from beyond the glass doors.

Jesus fuck, he's sexy.

I don't miss the two women who slowed down right in front of me as they were walking on the sidewalk, their eyes fixed on Ronan, their short, tight dresses suddenly riding just a bit higher. But the man cocks his head to look right past them, a wicked smile on his lips as he extends his hand to me. Only I seem to notice how the women look at me in mild shock, flip their hair over their shoulders, and quicken their steps.

"Hello, stranger."

Placing my hand in his, I let him pull me against him, his other hand sinking into my hair, crushing me onto his lips, devouring me like he's been hungry all day.

When we break apart, I look over to my right, to where Finn opens the door to his own car for Hanna, and I can't help but catch a glimpse of the two women who passed by. They look positively sour, as they quickly turn back around and keep walking.

It feels good, being the woman others envy. I've never experienced this before.

"What are you snickering about?"

Was I?

"Oh, nothing."

"Shall we go, then?"

I nod as we pull away from each other, and once again he opens the door for me. He's been doing this every time we go somewhere—always opening the door for me. I can't help but wonder if this is a honeymoon phase thing, or if it's simply Ronan.

He slides in the driver's seat, turning on the purring engine of his car, then pulls onto the street after Finn.

"How come you didn't come with only one car?" I ask him.

"We weren't together. I had a meeting, and he was closing a deal out of town."

"Out of town?"

"Yeah, Levane, a city about an hour and a half away. He only just came back now, so we ended up synchronizing."

"I'm still not fully sure I understand how your organization operates."

I look at him, trying to see in his expression if by any chance I crossed a line by asking.

"What do you want to know?" He reaches over, wrapping his large palm around my leg, giving it a slight squeeze.

Focus, Annika, focus.

But his fingers tickling my inner thigh in his possessive hold are replacing all my thoughts with filthy fantasies.

It's just a hand, Annika. Pull yourself together, for God's sake.

Tell that to my pussy. She didn't get the message.

"Little witch?" He glances over when I don't respond, trying to keep his eyes on the road.

"So, it's you, Finnigan, Vincent, Carter, and Maddox, but who's the actual leader?"

"None of us. That was the whole point when this all came together. We didn't exactly plan it this way, but it was a natural progression. Obviously they're five-six years younger than me, so we didn't start at the same time, but we lead together. Each with our own set of skills."

"Were you the first?"

"Kind of, but not in the way you think. I decided not to go to university, and I went into the family business instead. Not because I wanted to follow in my parents' footsteps, but because I wanted to learn. Then a few years ago, I took over a strip club that sort of landed in their laps when they purchased a building here in the city. I pitched an idea, asked for a small investment from them with a promise of a return with interest. Not that they needed the money, but it was for my ego. I transformed it into a luxury gentlemen's club that turned very profitable, from more points of view than one."

He pauses for a moment as he takes a turn away from the main boulevard we were on.

"More points of view?" I ask, curiosity spiking.

"First, I started getting into the black market, using every bit of profit from the club, after paying back my parents, and with time, we were dealing in more and more expensive pieces. Finn and the guys were always around. I'm not sure how they found each other, but I swear menace attracts menace, because they compliment each other so fucking well. Finn wanted in before he was even eighteen. I refused, but he didn't give a shit. I wanted something better, legal, for his future, but I couldn't get rid of him. The compromise was that he had to at least try and go to university. So he followed Carter there. Madds and Vin stayed here. Two businesses evolved from the club—an escort service, that's run by an associate, and information. Vincent was most attracted to the former. Anyway, it all went from there, and here we are, still early in the journey, but fuck, we've been through some shit."

"I didn't know you owned an escort service."

We're driving behind a building, still close to the city center, and we seem to be slowing down in a parking lot that doesn't really look like anything special.

"Some cards we keep very close to our chests and the escort service is one of them. Nobody knows it's ours. We try to keep it way in the background, because the escort service is a front. They're all basically trained to extract information.

People get stupid and reckless when they see a pretty thing or they're horny. So we take advantage of that. Whoever sees us with one of the girls and recognizes her, they just think we hired them for the night just as they do."

"What do you do with all that information?"

He presses on the breaks as he swiftly pulls into a space, his eyes fixed on me, the look in them darker than I've known it.

"We use it."

This is where the insight ends—on a chilling note that leaves me with even more questions. Only, I think I should stay ignorant to the answers, because I have a suspicion this is where the violent side of their business begins.

He gives my thigh another squeeze, then captures my chin between his thumb and index fingers, then pulls me to him until his lips meet mine. He kisses me breathless, and before he lets me go, he swipes his tongue over my top lip, like he's getting one more taste. I'm not sure what this man does to me, but I would spread myself open on a platter for him so he can keep going.

He slides out of the car, walks over to my side, and helps me out of my seat, guiding me toward a metal door that looks like the entrance to the building's boiler room, not a fancy bar. Another car pulls into the parking lot and Finn and Hanna come out, heading our way with great big smiles on their faces. She looks so damn happy.

"I was expecting one of those tiny sliding doors and a thug looking through it," I tell Ronan.

He laughs and scans a card against a panel I didn't notice, then presses his finger to it.

"This is the back entrance."

"So you have that at the front?!"

"Something like that."

I follow him through a corridor, then another, then through a door to what feels like another world. Slow, deep music fills the space that smells of wood, leather, and expensive cigars. There's a decadence to this place I've never experienced anywhere else. The wallpapered and wood-paneled walls are covered in paintings and vintage decor, dim lamps strategically placed in the space, lighting it in just the right way, hiding some of the faces who are filling the seats. I love that the wooden tables are not all the same. There's a mixture of coffee, dining, and bar height tables, and every chair and sofa is mismatched, adorned in expensive, dark-colored leathers.

But the bar is a work of art and it draws my attention instantly. It's pulled right out of the twenties with its wood, marble, and gold accents. Right behind it, in the center of the wall, there is a gold décor piece made entirely of thin metal strips. Lines that form a starburst, surround the shape of an eye, all inside a circle. It's very stylized, in the nineteen-twenties elegance—apart from the eyeball itself. It looks so incredibly real, you would swear it's watching, following you around the room. It's beauty is slightly unsettling.

Everything in here seems to be left over from the art deco era and it got infused with southern blues vibes.

"I think I'm in love..." I almost whisper, marveling at the beauty of it.

"Thank you."

Carter shows up out of nowhere, giving a courtesy nod, his features as straight as ever, but I swear I can see a trace of a smile on those lips.

"The speakeasy was Carter's idea, same as the decor," Ronan explains.

I can see why. The man looks like he belongs here, with his slicked back hair and undercut, shirt with sleeves rolled up to his elbows, and tailored suit trousers and waistcoat.

"It really is beautiful. It's nice to see you again, Carter." I think I'm lying. I'm not sure, though. It's not like I dislike him, but I'm slightly terrified of him.

We follow him to the back of the locale to a more private area, dodging the curious looks some of the patrons give us—or me. Talking of terrifying, Vincent Sinclair is right there, sitting next to Maddox at a dining table. He's dressed in all black from shoes to shirt, matching his hair and eyes, and a chill runs down my spine at the sight. I have no idea what to make of him. I can't hold his gaze for too long. If Carter's is empty, devoid of humanity, Vincent's is filled with promises of peril. I don't think he trusts me either.

I did steal his money—albeit I did return it, but still.

I take a seat next to Hanna as Maddox pushes toward me a matte black menu with foiled gold accents. The attention to detail in this place tickles all my artistic senses.

We fall into chatter, talking amongst ourselves as the guys seem to have been getting more comfortable having us around, since we returned from the island. I've been more intrigued by Ronan; observing him in this environment has given me a different perspective on him. His shoulders are more pulled back, his head held a little higher, his features more stern. Even now, in what's supposed to be a familiar and comfortable environment for him, he doesn't carry himself the same as he does with me in private, or how he did on the island. I like this side of him. I like both, but seeing him so stern and serious, goddamnit if I don't lo— like him even more.

Christ.

"Excuse me," he says, kissing my forehead before he rises, disappearing behind me.

Maybe five minutes pass, and Hanna interrupts our

conversation, leaning in.

"Jesus, who are those two talking to your man?"

I turn my head to the bar, trying to be as discreet as possible, but failing miserably when my eyes land on two of the most beautiful women I've ever seen. Both of them are tall, gorgeous, and elegant. They're a true vision. Ronan is in a fairly intense discussion with the older one of the two, a stunning redhead with a short bob haircut, while the other has turned her attention to the bartender.

"I don't know," I finally respond to her.

I wish I did though, because there's this burning sensation in my chest, and god dammit if it doesn't feel dangerously close to jealousy. But my insecurities are the ones that are more prevalent right now—I look nothing like her. I'm close to asking myself—and him—what the fuck I'm doing here.

He looks so comfortable and familiar with her. She belongs. In this world, in this space, next to him. I don't.

When she turns her head, her gaze lands directly on me, like she knows my thoughts are of her. Her expression is blank, utterly unreadable, but in such a natural way that it's chilling. It doesn't falter when she sees me watching her, unable to stop. With a woman as beautiful as her, I expect the air of superiority, but it never comes.

She briefly brings her attention back to Ronan, nodding her head once, before they both turn and start walking. In this direction. *My* direction.

I'm slightly nauseous. I can't explain why. Maybe because this could have just been a beautiful dream, and I'm about to find out he has a wife at home who's about to kick my ass out of his life. She has that look about her that tells me she might not be above slitting my throat here, in the middle of this bar.

Finn catches my attention as he slides next to Hanna and says something that seems to go right past my ears.

Ronan and the mystery woman, who looks even more stunning up close, are right in front of us now. They look so comfortable together. Like they've been around each other for years.

"Ekaterina, this is Annika. My girlfriend."

My... what now?!

She extends her hand to me, a prim, elegant smile pulling very gently at the corners of her lips. I push the chair back and rise, capturing her hand and giving it a gentle shake.

"It's a pleasure to meet you, Annika. I've heard quite a bit about you."

The expression in her eyes is warm in such a strange, rigid way. I would have thought she mocks, but no... she looks at Ronan in the same way.

"Oh... it's nice to meet you too."

"Ekaterina is our associate. If you remember our conversation from the car."

It takes me a minute, but eventually, the wheels click into place.

"Associate, yes. Sorry, Ronan didn't mention your name then." Or the fact that their associate who runs the escort service is a woman.

I guess it makes sense. But there's still a tinge of jealousy pulling at my heartstrings. She just smiles, shaking Hanna's hand now as Finn introduces them.

A conversation starts, but I'm not talking. I hear none of it. Ronan doesn't speak either. His head cocked, a questioning gaze aimed right at me. He holds it, yet neither of us speaks. It's intense, growing its own heartbeat I can hear inside of me. Thumping from his blue eyes to mine, grazing my skin with goosebumps from the inside out, my nipples turning to sharp points, my belly fluttering, my core clenching on itself.

A flush heats my cheeks when he leans in, his lips against

my ear, the heat of his breath traveling into my soul.

"I've never found jealousy enticing until it painted your blue-gray eyes in such vivid strokes. It makes my cock twitch to sink so deep into your cunt, I'll fuck all the threads of doubt out of you."

My lips part, eyes widening, as he pulls away and straightens, his composure unbroken, completely nonchalant like he didn't just fill my mind with filth and my pussy with desire.

"Annika, do you want another one?"

I'm startled back into this world when Hanna touches my shoulder.

"Sorry?"

"Another drink?" she asks again.

I turn to find a server smiling at me.

"Actually, just water for me. With a couple of slices of lemon, please."

He nods and walks away. Between the two of us, Hanna is the cocktail drinker. I'll have one once in a while if it's a nice place that does special ones. Other than that I don't bother.

"I hope you all have a good evening. I'm going to go back to my meeting," Ekaterina says, nodding to all of us.

We all sit back down after saying goodbye to her.

"So, do they even know about this bar?" Hanna directs the question at Finn, but lifts a curious eyebrow at me like I'm supposed to know what the hell she's talking about. My mind is still reeling from Ronan's words.

"Who?" I ask.

"Finn and Ronan's parents."

Oh. We haven't actually spoken about them. Only mentioned in passing.

"No. We stay out of their businesses, and they stay out of ours," Finn answers.

I turn to Ronan. "Do they know what you do?"

He takes a sip of the amber drink the server just brought over, and his expression turns serious. More so than I've ever seen before in his features.

"They have some knowledge, but in our business, the less they know, the better for all of us. That way, no one can be accused of anything, be implicated, or held accountable."

"Well, if that's not cryptic, I'm not sure what is," I say, eyebrows furrowing.

"Let's just say our parents have never been your typical involved parents. We grew up with a bunch of nannies, chefs, and drivers while our parents skirted at the edge of the law and every tax paradise out there, adding more and more buildings and businesses to their portfolio."

"It sounds... cold." I can't imagine living like that, being cared for by strangers, without my parents' warmth or love. Yet there isn't even a trace of sadness or longing in his eyes when he talks of these things... it's all he knows.

"It was, in most ways. Their involvement was different. They always made sure we had access to every opportunity. They provided, and took care of us, even disciplined us, but... parenting wasn't quite their thing," Ronan tells us.

"No, we didn't learn many things from them," Finnigan continues. "Except that when it comes to business, turn a blind eye, unless it concerns you. Catherine and Christian Hennessey are quite the pair. To this day, I'm not convinced they actually love us."

"They do. In their own, detached way," Ronan states, unconvinced.

"If you say so. I think that if you died, they would just send me a condolences card." Finnigan says with a laugh, and my curiosity spikes further.

"Where are they?" I ask.

"Not quite sure. They decided to retire early, selling most of their businesses and holding on mainly to the passive ones, like real estate. They've been traveling ever since. Last I talked to them, they were on a yacht somewhere on the North Coast." Ronan shrugs.

"Sounds like a pretty good life."

I'm not sure what else I can say. I never gave kids a serious thought, but birthing two just to have nothing to do with them at all from birth to... well, now, is a bit odd. Cruel even.

He smiles and wraps his hand around my thigh under the table, his fingers running higher and higher, my pulse too.

"I think it sounds like we need to stop talking about our parents and head home," he says with a smile and a quirked eyebrow.

Home.

Only, I'm not so sure it's mine.

CHAPTER 10

I WAKE UP SUBMERGED IN A SHEER darkness, slithers of sunlight breaking through the cracks of the blinds that haven't been rolled down all the way. His scent surrounds every fiber of my being, the same as it has for days now. No. More than that. Has it been more than a week since we've been here? It feels like it.

Actually, it feels more like a lifetime.

The moment he came to the island feels far enough away in my past that a future with him is becoming more vivid. It's not that far at all... a few weeks. But it hasn't stopped him from crawling beneath every fiber of my being, clutching onto each delicate thread that forms me, and making it part of him.

It's fucking terrifying.

He's turning my world upside down, and I have nothing to hold on to. Except for him.

How could I have something to clutch when I've been a nomad for years? I have my family... somewhere on this continent. But my only rock, the only constant in my life, is spinning right along with me. She's currently sleeping on the other side of this penthouse, with the brother of the one currently sliding his hand over my bare belly, pulling me into him.

The softness of his skin against my back sends shivers straight into my skull, ridding all those thoughts that made me doubt, made me question us. Everything about him feels like it belongs with me. Even with the mind of an artist, I'm still seeking the logic in what's happening. Only, I can't find it. It makes no sense.

Maybe I am a witch, like he keeps telling me.

Maybe this is a spell I put on both of us, not just him.

Maybe it's the black magic making us lose ourselves to each other.

Maybe I want to be blind to it, because usually if it's too good to be true... *it's too good.*

"Mmm..." I hum as I press myself against his bare chest.

His hand slides up from my belly, between my breasts, until it reaches the base of my throat, settling there. It puts a pressure on my airways that grows from the inside out, in my lips, my flushed cheeks, and right under my tired eyes as my pulse seems to slow.

"Good morning," I whisper on a raspy breath.

"There's no such thing as a bad one waking up next to you." He says it like he's admitting that to himself, not me.

Holy hell!

His voice in the morning is like raw honey laced with hunger. The vibrations of it run through me like the links of zipper, splitting me apart. He's my undoing.

"If there will ever be, please keep holding me like this, but squeeze my throat harder."

He growls in my ear, and I'm suddenly rolled onto my belly as he straddles me, his cock slapping against my bare ass, sending a shudder straight to my core.

"I promise." His breath tickles my ear as he drops on his forearm next to me.

A warm hand palms my ass cheeks, kneading and spreading them open as it dives down, reaches my folds and parts them with skillful digits that make my hips shoot up. He drives inside of me without warning, his cock twitching against my back, and I get wet so damn fast, I'm convinced the man found an "ON" button inside of me.

"Always so damn ready for me, my fingers, for my cock..."

I'm starting to think he could just snap his fingers and I would be an instant, soaking mess.

All I can seem to do is moan, drawn out, soft... as I sink into the warmth of him, into his slow, deep thrusts. *This* is fucking magic.

He pulls those digits out of me, and I expect his cock to replace them. Instead, he brushes them on my lips, the smell of my pussy oddly arousing. Sliding them into my mouth, he presses on my tongue...

And a very annoying sound pulls us out of this spell. His phone rings on the nightstand, but he ignores it until it stops. Only, it starts again immediately after, and he sighs as he stretches to grab it without getting off me.

"This better be good."

His muscles tense against me, most definitely not in a good way.

There's too much silence. He's listening too intently.

"Where is he?"

He slowly shifts off me, and I roll over to see him. With every second, the frown lines on his forehead deepen. His eyes flash to me, but avert quickly enough that something strange grows in the pit of my stomach.

"How much time do we have?"

I can't put my finger on it, but it reminds me that the man next to me is not just any man—he's part of an underworld I know almost nothing about.

"Ten. Yes. Bye."

He turns completely, throwing his legs off the bed, rising into a sitting position, and sighs heavily as he runs his fingers through his soft blond hair. I want to ask, but I'm not sure where we stand when it comes to his business, talking about it. I don't want to intrude or be nosy. More importantly, do I want to know?

"We have to talk." He turns to me, his gaze not just serious, but it looks somewhere close to being unhinged, cutting off my thoughts.

That answers it—I want to know.

"What happened?"

"Let's get dressed. We need to get Finn and Hanna."

"Ronan, what the hell is going on? Why do we need them?!"

I crawl next to him, sitting on my knees on the bed, not just suspicious, but uneasy down to the bones. This is about me. Hanna as well? He captures my chin between his thumb and index, pulling my lips to his, dropping a quick, but deep kiss.

"Get dressed." He orders me before he rises and disappears in his closet. Moments later, he has sweatpants on, hanging low on his hips, the elastic of his boxers showing just above, then he slides a white t-shirt on.

"Now, Annika. I'm gonna go get them and bring them to the kitchen. Wait there."

I take a deep breath in, and it seems to get lodged in my

lungs until the bedroom door shuts behind him.

"What the hell is happening?"

I make quick work of pulling some leggings and a t-shirt on and all but run to the living area.

Faint voices sound on the other side of the penthouse, the whole place split in two with the living area in the middle, Ronan's side to the right and Finnigan's to the left.

They own the whole building—well, technically, his parents do, but my understanding is that this particular building has been transferred to the brothers. It's a skyscraper reminiscent of the golden age but modernized.

I busy myself with the espresso machine and begin making some coffee, instead of spiraling into my own thoughts.

Before I turn, I already know Ronan came into the kitchen. He's quick, sidling up next to me, one hand around my waist, sorting his own coffee with the other one. He kisses my forehead without a word, giving me a bit of reassurance.

He guides me to the dining table and sits next to me just as Hanna and Finnigan appear, dressed comfortably, but sleepy and confused. At least Hanna is. Finnigan seems to carry the same sort of hard expression as his brother. It looks even more strange on the man who seems to be eternally happy and easygoing.

The morning sun streams through the huge floor-to-ceiling windows, a contrast to the silent, yet heavy atmosphere. Dread has closed in around me, my chest tight as Ronan sets his forearms on the table, clutching his hands together.

"What's happened?" Hanna speaks first.

It's almost like I'm back in our business meetings, craving to blend in with background. It's not an option now, though, with Ronan's eyes fixed on me.

"You said once that you keep tabs on the people who have

bought paintings from you," Finnigan responds, his serious tone making me even more nervous.

"I do... yes."

"Have you heard anything?"

The moment the question lands, Hanna's expression is a mixture of annoyance, dread, and shock. She only manages to shake her head... but we both already know what's coming.

"We're not the only ones who found out about the forged paintings." His words clutch my lungs and rip them straight out of my chest.

I'm frozen, unable to look Hanna in the eyes anymore.

What have I done?

Ronan

"WHAT DO YOU MEAN? HAVE YOU TOLD SOMEONE?" Hanna finally manages to ask, disbelief in her tone.

Finn repeats what Carter told us before we went to the island. That someone powerful is looking for two women who match their descriptions, regarding an art deal struck some time ago.

"That can't be... I would have heard something."

Hanna's eyes become slightly vacant, searching deep into her memories.

"It's my fault. I've done something... I've screwed it up," Annika says, wrapping her arms around herself, her gaze fixed on the dining table, as she gently shakes her head.

An urgent knock on the door interrupts us, and Finn rushes to answer it as we all turn to see who's arrived. Vin, Carter and Madds walk through, keeping the pleasantries brief as they sit around the table. Carter is opening the laptop he brought with him, his fingers sliding fast over the keyboard.

"It's not you." Hanna rubs Annika's back, trying to soothe her shaking as I squeeze her thigh. "I should have heard something. I didn't look hard enough."

I wish I could say their enemy and his team are so good at what they do, that they made sure she wouldn't find out they're looking for them. But the guys and I talked about this... whoever these people are, they're not hiding. Even if they've kept their enquiries within a tight circle, the message is clear—*I'm coming for you.*

"No," Annika continues. "I should have been more careful. I must have..." she trails off, that soft bottom lip trembling slightly, and there's this deep-seated need inside of me to wrap her in my arms, comfort her. But unfortunately... there's more.

"Please stop. We always knew this was a risk. We both understood this right from the start. Even if we weren't fully ready, we knew there was a big chance someone could find out at any point in the transaction or after it." Hanna grabs her friend by the shoulders, forcing her to look at her.

"But that doesn't change—"

"It does, Annika! This is not on you!" Hanna raises her voice, but pain still settles in her friend's features.

"It really isn't on you." Carter's calm tone forces a tense silence in the room, all eyes snapping to him. He stops typing, lacing his fingers together as he settles his forearms on the table and turns to the girls. "There was no mistake in the painting. That's not how he found out it is a fake."

"How then?" Hanna asks.

"The original was found."

"Jesus Christ," Annika mutters under her breath. "Which one?"

"The Punishment of Innocents by—"

"Gravano!" Annika's chair grunts painfully as she

abruptly pushes back, the look in her eyes one of utter terror that I can't fucking bear to witness.

"Little—" I go to touch her, but she's breaking away.

"You're wrong. You're wrong!" She raises her voice in panic. "It's not possible. If it was, the art world would have gone mad over this. It's a Gravano, for fuck's sake! No, you're fucking lying!" She's almost shouting now, pleading with Carter to reveal the lie, the mistake, anything but let this be the truth. The color has drained from her face, building inside of me a rage I never thought I could feel.

"What the fuck did he do to you, Annika?!" I seethe, already plotting the death of a man I don't even know by name.

She ignores me. Hanna turns to her, and I notice now that she doesn't look better at all.

"We'll b—be okay. You'll see. We'll be fine."

What's even more unsettling is the fact that, for the first time since meeting her, I can see that Hanna doesn't believe a single word she speaks, her usual confidence gone. Annika glances at her, almost wide-eyed—she doesn't believe her either.

"Annika," I warn, "fucking tell me. Did he touch you?!"

She finally turns to me and shakes her head.

Fuck. Me. I let out a loud breath and turn to Carter.

"Who?"

"Roberto Bartiste. He works in shipment far from here, right on the East Coast. But from what I gather, he's been expanding his business. He has power, taking over more and more territory."

"Shipment. Drugs?"

"Amongst other things, drugs. But that's not his main business and not the one he appears to be expanding. It's—"

"People," Annika finishes for him. "He is a human

trafficker. Something he is… highly passionate about."

I grip the leg of her chair and attempt to pull it to me, but she plants her feet on the ground, pushing back and standing.

"We have to go. Run," she says with urgency, turning to her friend.

But her words are ringing in my ears. *Run*. Away from me.

"No."

She whips her head to face me as I utter that word, a fear in her expression that I'm not sure I can soothe.

"Sit down, Annika." I grab her wrist, and she stills.

"You don't understand. If this is true, if Bartiste is coming for us, we can't just stay here."

I shake my head as she tries to rip her wrist out of my hold. I pull her until she's standing right next to me, my arm wrapped around her hips, holding her tight.

"Annika…" I both warn and comfort her, meeting the challenge in her steel-blue eyes. The submission prevails, her gaze drops, and she leans into me slightly, before sliding back down on the chair.

"What do you know? Why hasn't the world found out about the real painting being found?" Hanna asks.

"Bartiste is keeping the information under wraps. He's on a mission, and part of that might be to protect his reputation," Vincent answers, speaking for the first time since he walked in.

"Mission?"

"To find you. He wants you to pay, and I don't think it's money he wants."

Annika trembles at his words, and once again I wonder who the hell this man is.

"Your multiple identities probably slowed him down. The Lady in White going out for auction might have been his last lead," Carter continues. "I'm not sure what resources he has to find you, but all I've seen so far suggests he has very deep pockets. He's close. Too close."

"Oh, he has plenty of resources." Hanna sighs, and Annika just retires within herself, her gaze almost vacant.

"Does he know they're here?" Finn asks.

"Put it this way, he's left the East Coast, heading south."

"Fuck... Okay. Can he be bought?"

"We can try, but I guarantee that money's not going to stir this guy. Men like him go to extremes when their ego is played with. Pride and reputation sit above all else," Vincent chimes in.

"We have to run," Annika insists.

"No!" My voice comes out as a growl this time. This idea she keeps pushing irritates me now.

"You don't understand, Ronan, this man... he can't find us," Hanna tries to reason with me, her wide eyes pleading.

"How exactly did you get into business with him? I thought you vetted everyone beforehand," I ask her, yet my eyes stay on Annika, who looks paler by the second.

"Our contact was an art dealer. Not uncommon. Trying to figure out who the buyer was turned no results, but their client list looked fairly safe. We agreed to keep working with them, and everything went smoothly, as it usually did, until the day we closed. Buyers always left these things to their dealers... but *he* came. It was too late for us to back out once we realized who he was." She pauses, taking a deep breath and rubbing her eyes. "He took a liking to us. Annika, in particular. This man... he speaks in constant threats, and the one he gave Annika, concerning the authenticity of the painting, was bad. Sexual trafficking bad."

Before Hanna speaks the last word, Annika pushes her chair back violently, ripping away from me, her hand on her mouth as she sprints away into the corridor. I'm already on my feet, but Hanna stops me and follows her.

"We have to help them," Finn says, palpable fear shining in his eyes as he looks at me.

"How deep are you both invested in... them?" Vincent asks, leaning back in his chair, arms crossed over his chest.

I don't miss how Carter cocks an eyebrow at the question, like it's a stupid thing to ask since the obvious is staring us straight in the face.

A part of me is in disbelief at how fast this woman crawled under my skin. It's almost hard to admit it to myself, like it's some sort of weakness. It's been a few weeks, but somehow it feels like eons.

"Deep," I answer in unison with my brother.

"It's a big risk. This could make or break us."

"It better fucking make us. If anything's going to be our mark on the underworld of this city, breaking a man like him will be it. I don't give a shit about a lot of things. I'll deal, blackmail, steal, con, and kill, but human trafficking?! If there is anything our organization has to take a stance against on our goddamn turf, and hopefully beyond, this is it."

"Agreed." Maddox finally speaks, nodding as he looks to Vincent.

"We're moving in different circles right now. Lower risk. We have power, but this will change our reputation," I continue.

"We have to be careful, brother. We are doing this for them, not for our syndicate's benefit. Hanna and Annika are the priority."

Finn looks more concerned than I've ever seen him.

"*We*"—I point between the two of us—"are doing this for them. Our brothers might need more motivation."

"We should be motivation enough," he says with a chilling glare, yet it turns pleading when he turns to them.

I get it, but I think somewhere in my brain, there's a bit of a disconnect between keeping Annika safe and not getting my *brothers* killed for my own selfish reasons.

"We would never leave you in a situation like this." Maddox's expression darkens.

"I'm going to keep Brendan, Tina, and Jian on his tail. We can use CCTV and traffic cams to track him and at least know when he's in town." Carter turns his laptop screen toward us to show what he has so far.

"We'll have men tail him the moment he gets in. I'll keep an eye out and get my hands on one of his guys. That will help us to find out their plan," Vin continues.

"You might not need to. If you can get me one of their phones, I can try to sneak my way through their network. I might find out more that way," Carter adds.

"Can't we do both?" I ask.

There's a pause, and I can almost hear the wheels spinning in their brains.

"Yes, we can." Carter confirms with a nod. "But what about the girls? Is it wise for them to be here while all this goes down?"

I look at my brother, the question lingering between us. I know what I want to do, but I also know what's safer.

"They should stay with us." He speaks first, saying exactly the thing I want, but hearing it confirms my fears.

"I don't think that's the best idea." I counter. If only there was more confidence in my tone of voice.

"But it is."

We all turn at the sound of Hanna's voice, as she and Annika walk back in. They've gained a bit of color back in their complexion, but not near enough for me to stop worrying about my little witch.

"We have to go. This is on us. Our mistake. Our problem.

We're not bringing this on you."

"What the fuck, Hanna?" Finn rasps. "Just like that, you want to fucking leave me?"

She shakes her head and smiles, but it doesn't quite reach her eyes. I extend my arm, willing Annika to come to me, and like in a trance, she complies in a heartbeat, sitting back down.

"Of course I don't want to leave you," Hanna replies to my brother. "But I also don't want you to take the fall for us. I can't have any of you hurt."

I pull Annika's chair as close as I can, and she settles into my side, her small hand on my thigh, and I can't help but cover it with mine. Just as I want to cover her, wrap myself around her, and keep her safe forever.

"We can't force you into this, into our mistake." She sighs. "We know Bartiste. It could turn so, so ugly. We cannot be the reason why something happens to you."

"While I appreciate the sentiment, little witch, I'm helping you. Whether you like it or not."

"*We* are helping them," Finn rasps.

"He's right," Maddox says. "We are helping you."

Silence descends upon the room. Annika looks around to all of us with red, tired eyes, worry painted far too vividly within them.

"Thank you. Really, thank you."

"We're still leaving, though," Hanna says. "Anni and I talked about this already. I think we should go back to Bovely Island."

It's not the worst idea. Vin nods, Madds cocks his head, pondering, and Carter's stance is unchanged.

"We'll send as many men as we can spare with them for protection. Bartiste obviously caught a trail to them into Queenscove, but there's a smaller chance for him to be aware of that island. We'll go to old man Bovely, explain to him how important it is to keep his mouth shut, and maybe even take him into hiding to be safe."

"This is absurd!" Finn rages. "How the fuck will they be safe if we're not there to protect them?! It's madness!"

"We have to go…" Annika says to me and me alone. Like she knows that I understand somehow.

"I don't want you to."

"We won't be that far, only Bovely. We can't be in your way. I'll never forgive myself if something happens just because I dragged you into this."

"Annika, baby, you may be a witch, but even you don't have that sort of power over me, the ability to drag me into something I don't feel like doing."

"You gotta be kidding, Ronan!" Finn turns to me now. "Fuck!"

"I'm considering it because there is a big chance Bartiste is unaware of the island. No matter what, we'll go head-to-head with this guy, and we don't know what to expect from him. Not now anyway."

"What if he finds them and we're nowhere near there?!"

"How is it different with him sending his men here while we're out there fighting?"

He's stunned into silence finally, pondering my words. I know why he's arguing, I want to argue with myself on this too, but… fuck, I don't know.

"Finn, listen, I'm not saying that this is the best solution. I want them close too, but what if Bartiste comes with more firepower than we can handle? Or more men? We don't know this guy. The only advantage we have over him is the fact that we know our territory and he doesn't. At least… as far as we're aware."

My brother is stretching this silence for an uncomfortable amount of time. Enough for Madds to get restless, the tapping of his foot making a hollow noise on the wooden floor, while doubt starts to creep in the quiet threads of my mind.

"What if—what if he finds them, and we're not there to save them? I just can't stop thinking about that possibility. Fuck, Ronan!" He gets up and starts pacing around the table.

Annika still looks a little pale, further making me question my point of view on the matter. I need to be with her. How can I abandon her when this whole thing just makes her sick?

I pull her harder into my side, pressing my lips to the top of her head.

"I'm okay. Just a bit queasy," she whispers my unspoken concern.

"Your brother's right, Finn," Hanna answers instead. "If we're here, you'll worry about us more than the task at hand. Your mind won't be in the right place. Obviously, neither of these two situations are ideal, but considering that we got ourselves in this mess, I would rather stay out of your way. We'll be okay." She cups his jaw, soothing him just as he's about to argue some more.

"Baby..."

"It's gonna be okay," she insists, and he slowly seems to accept our fate.

We exchange looks, then we all turn to Vin, Carter, and Madds for their confirmation as well.

"We've already started the work," Carter says with nonchalance. Like it was the most obvious and logical thing in the world to do.

"I have men on standby. As soon as Carter gives me a name and a person, we'll bring them in and find out as much as we can. He's convinced there's a scout in the city already."

Did these three come here out of damn courtesy? Because they seem to have anticipated the outcome.

"If there is, shouldn't we find him before Bartiste arrives?"

Finn asks.

"Yes, but we don't know who to look for. We're keeping an ear out for people asking questions, but I'm not putting my hopes on finding this person," Vin answers.

"We must lay low. You'll make a list." I turn to Annika. "Everything you need for the island. We'll send someone to buy it all, then you'll go. You might even have to split, just in case there is a scout here for you. Maybe even disguise yourselves." This sounds surreal.

I harshly swipe my hand over my face, wishing I could fucking wipe away this whole goddamn day. This whole problem. I have this gut feeling that it will turn ugly and it's eating me inside. But I have to get over it, all that matters is keeping Annika safe.

"Sounds like a plan. Thank you," she says, smiling at me, and I swear I already feel a bit better. "To all of you, thank you."

Carter nods, then stands, the other two frowning.

"This needs to happen fast. I'll be back tonight to finalize the plan."

He shuts his laptop, and walks away, toward the front door. Vin and Madds get the message and follow him.

I'm not sure how much time we have, but I plan to spend all of it with her. I don't linger. I need to get the fuck out of here, away from my brother's scrutinizing gaze. Grabbing Annika, I head straight to my side of the penthouse and into our bedroom.

"Are you okay?" I ask, shutting the door behind me.

"I'm fine. I just got nauseous. The thought of that man... he gives me the creeps in the worst way possible. I think I just got overwhelmed for a moment. This is not how I expected this day to go."

I narrow my eyes, watching how she drops her gaze to the

side, rubbing her arm.

"Are you sure you're okay?" I ask, since that doesn't sound like it's the entire truth. But then again, even Hanna looked a bit sickly at the sound of his name.

She nods, meeting my gaze as she sits at the edge of the bed.

"I think my *profession* has given me this badass image. You know by now that it's not me. Blending into the background is my thing, observing and staying out of trouble. I wasn't naive; I prepared myself for some form of danger. I weighed the risks, and of course, some situations were unavoidable over the years."

The thought of her being in danger riles up a feral instinct inside of me that begs to find every single fucking soul on this Earth who wronged her, whoever put my little witch in harm's way, and rip them to pieces.

"But this—Bartiste—is different. When he looked at me, there was no humanity in his eyes. It's like he saw potential, a price tag on a precious stone that he could cut and shape into the exact gem he needs to fulfill his fucked-up purpose. Use it, chip it away bit by bit, until there's nothing but dust left behind, and the world forgets there was anything precious occupying that space to begin with."

A pressure grows in my head, my bottom lip pierced from biting it too hard, and my jaw hurts from the constant flexing.

"Hanna said he threatened you. What did he say?"

This is going to get me even angrier, but... I have to know.

"It's been over a year; I don't fully remember. He didn't threaten me with death, but one of the things I do remember him saying was that if he ever found out that there was something wrong with the painting, he'll hunt me down, and make me pay in flesh and blood, before he'll sell me to people who will do much more to me than get their dicks wet with my cunt."

My blood is no longer boiling—it turns cold. I have a feeling that the type of human trafficking this man enables is not the virgin auction type of affair.

"Listen to me." I close the space between us, dropping to my knees in front of her, cupping her jaw in my hands. "You don't have to worry about him. He won't get his hands on you. He won't even get to lay his eyes on you. Do you understand me?"

"You can't promise me that. No one can..."

She looks at me with doe eyes, innocent and scared, and it fucking kills me not being able to turn my words into a promise. I want to give her the world, the whole goddamn thing. Just wrap it up in a pretty bow and place it at her feet for her to do whatever she pleases with it.

But I'm terrified this enemy will be too much.

"I'll do everything I can to keep you safe. You know that."

She nods, but she still seems reserved.

"I know you will, but I'm scared."

"You'll be—"

"No, you don't understand," she interrupts. "Not for myself. For you. All of this, the danger you're putting yourself in, your brother... the rest of your friends, it's because of me and Hanna. If anything happens to any of you, it will be all my fault. I cannot bear the idea that you are putting yourself on the line for me."

"We're big boys, darling Annika. The only choices we make are the ones we deem right," I say, gripping her jaw and holding her attention to me.

She tries to shake her head, but my hold tightens.

"I'm just a random woman..."

"That's where you're wrong, little witch. You're the right woman."

Her lips part on a muted gasp, her eyes widening, fixing on me, and I think she's stopped breathing. I'm trying hard not to close the distance between us; I don't want to be an asshole after the fucking news we just threw at her. But she has this pleading look in her eyes that I ache to soothe.

I pull her to me, pressing my lips to her delicate ones, but a switch flips, and she pushes against me until my ass is on my heels and she's straddling me. Her nails dig into my sides, almost clawing at my t-shirt, trying to force it off my body.

"Annika…"

"I just want to forget… just for a moment. Please, Ronan, make me forget."

I can't deny her. I let go, raising my arms and giving her access, and before I can do the same to her, she's already stripping her top, exposing those luscious tits. I sink between them, kissing my way to her perky nipples, her back arching, head falling back as a shudder shakes her flesh, her skin bursting in goosebumps.

"Fuck me, Ronan…" The breathy whisper is a command I'm following before my brain acknowledges the movement.

Her back hits the bed at the same time my sweatpants drop to the floor. I pull her leggings off, happy to see she didn't even bother with underwear today.

The witch reaches for me, spreading her legs in a spellbinding invite, exposing that pretty pussy as I stroke my shaft. I could come on the spot when she reaches down, splitting her lips apart with two fingers. But a devious grin pulls at my lips, and I reach over, flipping her onto her front before I grab her hips and jerk her up, that soft ass in the air as she yelps. She's glistening already, her slit so goddamn inviting, it takes too much effort not to sink my cock inside her.

But I want a taste first.

I drop onto an elbow, splitting her slowly with my tongue, from her clit, up to that tight asshole, enjoying how every muscle in her body seems to quiver all at once. I do that enough times that she begins begging me in hushed tones, her face buried in the pillow that she fists in her small hands. I sink my tongue into her sweet pussy, lapping her in the same rhythm as her increasing moans, and when I press two fingers against her clit, she screams into the pillow.

"Fuck! So close... so close. Don't stop! Please!"

A few more seconds of this assault, and when I pull away completely, she turns feral, her head whipping back, reaching over to force me back between her legs.

"If only you were the one making the rules here," I say with a grin.

"Ronan, what the fuck!"

I laugh as I flip her on her back once more. Wrapping my hand around her frail neck, I sink two fingers into that tight cunt, smirking as she gasps and grabs my forearm with both hands. I finger-fuck her slow and hard, with every other thrust rubbing that bundle of nerves with teasing movements, as her heels dig into the bed, her whole lower body rolling on a frantic rhythm.

I feel the spasms in the walls of her pussy before her legs begin to shake. She squeezes her eyes shut, but I tighten my grip on her throat.

"Eyes on me, little witch."

When they flash open, she goddamn glows. Pleasure ripples through her and my hand on her throat is the only thing keeping her from screaming this house down. She's fucking mesmerizing and I can't wait anymore.

I line up my cock with her twitching pussy, and push through those spasms, through her nails clawing at my back, through her breathy curses, until I reach the end of her and almost come on contact.

But before the last ripple of her orgasm ends, I pull out until she grips only the head, and slam back in on a thrust that makes her slide up the bed. A pleasure-filled grin paints her lips as she props her hands against the headboard, and it's my cue. I do it again, pulling almost all the way out before I slam back in. Over and over, as she cries out with each thrust, that smirk fueling me to keep it there, to see her come while smiling at me, because it might just be the most stunning thing in this cruel world.

I'm falling over the edge, the euphoria taking over all the nerve endings in my body, so I reach between us, finding her clit, because I refuse to come before her. Two fingers against that nub of flesh, rubbing in small circles, just how she showed me she likes it, and it's all it takes. Stars explode behind my eyes when her walls clamp down on me. Spasming, she drives me mad, her moans turning to music to my ears, and I spill inside of her on a low grunt. It goes on and on, and I can't fucking stop it.

All because of her... everything about this woman makes me come in my pants like a damn teenager.

I crash on top of her, trying to prop myself on my elbows so I don't crush her, but the woman pulls me tight.

"I like..." she pauses, panting like she ran a marathon as she comes down from that high. "I like your weight on me. It's satisfying."

I give her a little bit of it, pressing her into the mattress until I can tell it's too much, and I hold back, brushing the loose strands of hair from her face.

"I need to know that this is real."

I have no idea where that came from. The blood hasn't returned to my fucking brain.

"Your cock is still buried inside of me, Ronan."

She has an amused look on her face, and it calms me a bit. I shrug because I have no fucking clue what else to say. I would slap myself if I wasn't lying on top of her.

"I didn't know it could be... I thought you would just be an adventure, something I never had and desperately needed. I guess I was more right than I planned. You are exactly what I need... This is real, Ronan. As real as you want it to be."

I think I want it forever...

CHAPTER 11
Annika

I HELD IN A NAGGING NAUSEA ALL DAY. I held it in while I got dressed and packed my small bag. I held it while the guys were running over the next steps. I even held it in when Carter told us Bartiste was in the neighboring city.

They had the suspicion that he knew we were in the area, but not Queenscove specifically. This was our opportunity to go.

I swallowed through that bile as Ronan held me like he really didn't want to let me go. Like in this short amount of time he's actually attached himself to me. Has he really? I've been telling myself that this was nothing more than a summer adventure, but with the way my soul has been feeling... like it would get ripped out of my body if he wasn't part of my life, I'm pretty sure I'm fooling myself. He held my head in his big hands, whispering promises of safety and happiness, before kissing me like he was going to war. I suppose in a way, he is...

Then we were picked up by one of his men in an inconspicuous car, and we got on a boat.

There, I couldn't hold the nausea in anymore. I was sick until my throat was burning and my stomach screamed in pain. I've never had motion sickness, but if it was going to happen, it makes sense it was today.

Now, as I sit back at the round table overlooking the sea through the bay window of Bovely Island's villa, I wonder if it was all a dream. Ronan and I here was like living in a bubble of discovery, laughter, and lust. I thought it felt like a dream, but I was wrong. Queenscove was the real dream, because it's there I got a taste of what life would be like by his side. Actual life, in the real world, not isolated here.

It all happened so fast. Yesterday, I woke up in a dream. Today, it marked the beginning of a nightmare. Now... it feels like I'm trapped in an omen.

"They'll be okay," Hanna assures me as she places a steaming cup of chamomile tea in front of me.

I try to smile at her, but I'm not entirely sure if my lips moved. Her expression is so gentle, though, and I appreciate how she's trying to be comforting. Even as I see the worry in her own eyes. She's my voice of reason, my rock, why I'm not a total recluse, the one who has fed my happiness in these last few years. She always buries her own worries to settle mine.

"Are *you* okay?" I take her hand and squeeze it.

She opens her mouth, but pauses, before letting out a heavy breath.

"Yeah. I'm fine."

"It's okay not to be okay. You can let go for once..."

Tears slowly pool in her eyes, yet she doesn't say a word.

Her eyes redden, her jaw gently trembles, and she shakes her head, letting those tears fall down her cheeks.

"It's all my fault," she finally whispers.

"Don't be ridiculous." My sadness is forgotten when I see the guilt splashed all over her face.

"I should have known; I should have kept better tabs on Bartiste. That way, we could have had an escape plan formed and we would have been long gone. Safe." More tears fall, her voice cracking.

Technically, that's true. She takes it upon herself to keep tabs on everyone, and find out if they discover that the paintings we sold to them are fakes, but...

"We both know that if a man like Bartiste wants to find us, it happens sooner or later. Him discovering the real painting was a chance in a damn million. But whether you would have found this out or not doesn't change the fact that the asshole would have still hunted us down."

"We would have been better prepared..." she tries to argue.

"To run. From one hiding place to another, constantly looking over our shoulders. Now we have an entire mafia helping us."

She takes a deep breath in, wiping her eyes as she exhales and gathers herself. Slowly, the normal Hanna falls back into place.

"You're right," she says, nodding. "But I still fear that nothing can protect us from Bartiste."

I fear she may be right.

Ronan

I'M NOT ENTIRELY SURE WHAT I EXPECTED WHEN I looked at the footage our hacker team recorded of Bartiste. This wasn't quite it, though.

Maybe I envisioned a suited businessman who made you stumble on your own feet whenever he showed up in your path, dripping with power and respect.

What I saw on that screen was nothing like that. He's the definition of average—medium-short haircut with a receding hairline, oval head, not much of a defined jaw on him, crooked nose. His choice of clothes made him look like he was going to his job as a mid-level manager at some finance company, not on a manhunt for two women who cheated him out of millions.

The motherfucker would blend in anywhere.

And he's currently blending here, in Queenscove. He arrived the evening after Annika and Hanna left for the island, and we couldn't waste any time. We're still trying to figure out how the fuck he knew to come here. But Carter's been bumping into some invisible walls, more proof that Bartiste has some smart people on his team.

We're trained to expect the worst, but we've been thriving on owning and juggling information, and this particular one has eluded us.

Carter's little birds have been doing a good job of keeping track of him and his men throughout the city. We know where he's staying, who he's met so far, and most importantly, where he is right at this moment—Rosenberg. In the same goddamn private room we met Annika and Hanna in when we bought the painting.

Two cars with our men pull in behind us as we park at the back, where the private entrance to Rosenberg is. Eight men exit the cars, the drivers staying put, and two others stay outside in case anyone plans to sneak up on us.

"I think they're announcing our arrival." Finn jerks his head in the direction of one of the two men posted by the entrance. He's looking right at us, tilting his head as he speaks, far too obvious that he's talking in an earpiece.

"Good," Vin says with a deep rumble.

The man thrives on pulling metaphorical teeth, harnessing secrets and confessions from his victims, sometimes without lifting a finger. But other times, you see it in the dark slits of his narrowing eyes, he wants to lift more than just a finger. He craves the violence that our life choices can deliver. A man like Bartiste can awaken a monster in everyone who has basic morals. But it's even worse when the morals are ingrained in a world of possibilities, where death is never out of the question.

"This entrance is closed." One of the men standing by the door raises his hand to stop us, while the other looks us up and down.

"Take a picture, sweetheart. It will last longer." Madds steps up, looking down at him, dead in the eyes, with a challenge.

"This entrance is never closed for us. Step away. *Please*." I feign politeness.

"It is today."

"Move."

My ears vibrate when Finn speaks, his voice rough with anger, fear, and anxiousness that seem to be rising every day he's without Hanna. I, on the other hand, have spent every second of waiting time in the fighting ring under the speakeasy with Madds, my dark blue suit covering bruises that calm my unease toward this situation every time I touch them.

"I don't have time for this." Vin steps forward, getting right in the man's face. "Your friend over there is going to open the door for us and bow as we walk past."

"Step—"

But Vin interrupts him and tilts his head with a devious grin on his lips. The unmistakable sound of a gun cocking pulls the man's attention down to his crotch.

"Door, please." Vin jerks the gun, and the man sucks in a breath. He attempts to protest, but something in the way Vin tilts his head and looks at him makes him pause.

"O-open it," he tells the other one.

His *friend* follows the order, holding the door open for us.

"If any of you dare to even look at us the wrong way, I'll pry your eyes out with my fingers and feed them to each other."

On that disturbing image Vin leaves us with, we all pass through the door, walking straight to the room where we know their boss is. Two other men stand by the door.

"Gentlemen. A word with your boss, if we may." Finn

approaches, but one of the gorillas standing there scoffs without even looking at him.

We surround the men, staring them down until one of them rolls his eyes and enters the room, leaving us there to wait. When the door opens again, he moves out of the way to let us pass. I nod to two of our men and they remain outside. The door closes behind us, and we're met with a twelve-seater table, but only two of the chairs are empty.

"Let me guess, you're here to piss on the walls and let me know it's your turf."

I raise my eyebrows and turn toward the owner of that voice—Roberto Bartiste himself. I get it now. As average looking as he is, there is nothing average about that filthy look in his eyes, the weirdly curved shape of his lips, and those inward tilted teeth exposed to us as he blows out the smoke of his harsh cigar.

"We have toilets in this part of the country, and the only thing that wets our walls is the blood of the people who think they can piss on them." I take a step forward, looking at the man who sits at the end of the table. "What's your business here?"

He glares at me, like I disrespected him in his house. But this is *my* goddamn house.

"I don't see how that's any of your business, boy."

Boy... I force myself not to grit my teeth or pull my gun out and sink a bullet between his eyes right here. The only thing stopping me is how outnumbered we are in this small room. We have to play our cards right.

"You're on our territory, old man," I bite out at his reference of me, enjoying the twitch of his mouth, "and nothing moves around here without us. Now, I will ask one last time, what's your goddamn business here?"

He leans back in his chair, taking another puff of his cigar.

"No business. Just pleasure," he says, a sleazy grin pulling at his lips.

His attention is suddenly shifted next to me, his expression faltering for a mere second, enough for me to know there's something in Vin's eyes that makes him uncomfortable. I let it sink in for a moment longer.

"There's no pleasure for you in Queenscove, Bartiste," I all but growl. "We know what you do, what you deal in. There's no place for you here at all."

His whole expression mutates. If I thought the man's aura was doused in filth, it's goddamn dripping off him now.

"You have the pleasure of knowing my name, but I don't know yours."

He takes another puff of that cigar, filling the room with its sickly scent.

"You can pretend all you want that you don't know who we are. Just like we're pretending we don't know why you're actually in Queenscove." Finn speaks, and for a moment, I want to punch him.

We needed to hold on to some advantage. But I'm itching as well to lay all the cards on the table and get this over and done with.

"Name your price," he continues.

Surprise flashes in Bartiste's features, quickly morphing into a widening grin.

"They got you boys too, didn't they? Little whores. It was only a matter of time until some suckers fell for their charms and did their dirty work."

Finn seethes, ready to pounce at the man, and I take a deep, painful breath.

"Watch your fucking mouth," I warn. This asshole thrives on weakness, and I'll fucking die before I show him any.

"The only way I'm leaving this place is with those bitches

gagged and bound in the back of my car."

I shake my head once, pushing back at the rage filling my veins with every second that passes and every word Bartiste spits our way.

"That's not an option."

"You know the rules of the game—stay in our way and you die."

I cackle at Bartiste's threat because I can't quite believe the disrespect and audacity.

"There's no game here, old man. This is a goddamn jungle, and the rules are clear. You don't eat on our territory, you don't touch what's ours, and if you don't leave empty-handed, you don't leave at all." This time around, no self-restraint in the world would have kept me from growling at the man, watching as the veins in his temples swell by the second.

"I think—"

"The money you lost on the deal will be returned to you," I interrupt. "We'll add ten percent on top for the trouble. But only if you leave in the next twenty-four hours."

"I'm not open for negotiations," he seethes and as the look in his eyes darkens, I wonder if we're actually going to leave this room alive.

"We are. You get what you're owed, and everyone's happy," Finn says.

"That's not how it works in my world." Bartiste rises, stubbing out his cigar on the plate in front of him. All his men tense at the same time.

"You're in our world now." Vin speaks with a voice so cold the temperature in the room seems to drop.

"We're not negotiating for women, Bartiste. We're negotiating for the terms of your departure," I continue.

"Expect a call tomorrow," Finn finishes.

"Fine. But only if *you*"—he points his stubby finger at me—"are the one to make it."

And with that, we turn around and leave the room, our men ensuring our backs are covered all the way through the corridor and out of the back door.

Maybe there's a chance he'll take the deal.

When we reach the car, we all seem to breathe a little easier.

"We have to go and protect the girls. This deal isn't going to work." Finn breaks the tense silence.

I shake my head and rub a hand over my face, scraping the five o'clock shadow I didn't have time to shave.

"It's not a good idea," Carter replies before I get to shoot down that idea.

It fucking breaks me. I want to see her, hold her, kiss her. Worship the fucking ground she walks on. Choosing the right thing is getting harder and harder, because every step of the damn way, I'm questioning my decisions. The analytical side of my brain is slowly being drowned by fear.

"They need more protection!" Finn argues. "You've seen that motherfucker! He made even my skin crawl, for fuck's sake!"

"He knows who we are, what we look like. We have to assume he knows more about us than we think. We cannot be the ones to go, we can't risk it. We'll be followed."

"But you agree they need more protection?"

Finn lays back in the backseat.

"Definitely," I say with a nod, looking out at the moonlit streets of Queenscove as we pull out into the calm traffic.

"I'll send another team."

Even though we can barely spare a few. We're not deep enough in this business to have armies... and we're going to need all the men we can get for whatever Bartiste could have in store for us.

"Not on our boat, though," I continue. "Carter, talk to Jonathan and ask him if he can lend us one. Finn, choose the men you want to send over, but make sure you give them specific instructions and explain how detrimental it is to take precautions. They cannot be seen or followed. And tomorrow... we find out what kind of man Bartiste really is."

But Carter ends the exchange on a chilling, ominous note. "I think we're going to war."

Annika

HE'S SO GODDAMN BEAUTIFUL. MY HEART HURTS as I stare at Ronan in this video call. I don't know how I got here from lusting over a guy I saw in a photo, to begging him to come to me and not risk his life trying to get me out of the shit I caused. I miss his touch, crave his rumbling whispers in my ear, his possessive grip on me when he sleeps.

"I can't bear the risk you're taking for me. Please send someone else. Or just... run. Come to me."

I can see the fall of his chest as he exhales, the expression on his face holding a hint of pity.

"It's too late, my little witch. He wants me there, and if there's any chance he'll be willing to make a deal with us, I can't risk pissing him off by not being there."

"What if he says no?"

I dread the answer or the prospect that question poses.

"We'll kill him."

Such a short, matter-of-fact answer. I was always running

around dangerous circles, but never have I been posed face to face with the prospect of a man being killed for me without a second thought or a shift in expression. This man right here would do it without even flinching. He would kill for me. I should tell him it's wrong. Murder is wrong. But I can't even convince myself that it is.

"Just like that," I reply.

"I wanted to do it the moment I entered that room. I understood the fear in your voice as soon as I laid eyes on him. But we were outnumbered... it was risky."

"Not to mention, you were in a busy restaurant?!" I point out the obvious.

"Yeah, not gonna lie, if we weren't outnumbered, I would have done it anyway. Public place or not. The room was private enough."

"You would have gone to jail." I shake my head.

"But you would have been safe."

I swallow the knot that's suddenly formed in my throat as I take in those words. They're heavy. The implication is so much more than I expected.

"I would have waited for you," I all but whisper.

"You would have had no choice."

A cheeky grin pulls at his lips and suddenly that heaviness migrates somewhere deep in my belly, and I miss him for a whole other reason now.

"Being away from me might do you some good," I say, matching his expression.

"I doubt it. I'll come in ten seconds flat when I finally get my hands on you."

"It's only been a few days, Ronan." I playfully roll my eyes.

"Like your panties aren't wet right now, and you haven't even started properly imagining how hard I'll fuck you when I see you again."

I bite my lip as an image begins forming in my head, and I'm just about to respond, when a door opens behind him, and someone stands in the frame.

"For fuck's sake," he mutters as he turns around, rolling his eyes.

"*Something's happening.*" I hear someone speak.

"I'll be right there."

When he turns back to me, the look in his eyes tears that muscle that sits in my chest.

"I think I have to tell you something." My voice cracks.

"No, baby girl. Tell me when you see me."

He shakes his head and bites his lip, his nervousness reinforcing my uneasiness.

"I just—".

"Annika," he warns. "Don't look at me with those pretty eyes of yours like it's the last time. I'll get you out of this. I promise."

I'm struggling to hold back my tears. I want to be strong. I want to be like Hanna, ready to fucking take on anything and everything, doused in main character energy. But I have no superpowers, no hidden talents to magically make everything better.

"Are the guys we sent, okay?" He quickly changes the subject.

"They are. A few of them are patrolling the island, and six, I think, are in the house."

"Good. Stay with them at all times."

"I will." I sigh. I would rather him be with me than risking his life out there. Nothing about me is worth all this trouble.

"I'll see you soon, little witch."

He smiles as I say my goodbye, and when the screen goes black, I feel like my whole world goes right along with it.

CHAPTER 12
Ronan

THE PRIVATE CLIFF-SIDE TERRACE OF Coveview Estate has enviable views of Queenscove shores, the marina, and on a really clear day, some of the islands off the coast. However, I'm not entirely sure why Bartiste chose this place to meet us this morning.

I step onto the flagstone floor, joined by my brother, Maddox, Vincent, and eight of our men. We're stretched thin. I wish we were more established than this so that we could afford an entire fucking army. But good help is hard to find. At least we have enough men to watch the girls and some to lurk around in the shadows of the estate. Carter is with the hacker team, just in case.

"I take it you have my answer," I say, nodding to the man as he turns away from the view.

"You're quite the morning person, aren't you?" he

deflects. "Seven in the morning is definitely not the time I was expecting you to call at."

"You're an experienced businessman. I presumed you made your decision long before that. Was I wrong?"

He's brought just as many people as us. I don't feel outnumbered anymore if this deal goes south. But I would lie if I said at least two of these motherfuckers didn't scare me. More scarred than Maddox, and just as tall and broad.

"I have. But that doesn't mean that I appreciate being rushed."

That sleazy grin makes another appearance on Bartiste's face, and goddamnit if I don't want to wipe it off with a bullet. But I don't know the man, what contingencies he has in place. As much as I want to kill him right now, I can't until I make sure there's no ace up his sleeve.

"I see no point in wasting each other's time. We both know what we want, so we might as well get it over with," I say.

He takes a few aimless steps, hands clutched behind his back, as his gaze moves between us.

"You're still quite young. There's so much more to learn about this work of ours. How to handle business. What things to let go. What matters and what doesn't."

I sigh as I urge my patience to hold on, because all I want is a goddamn answer. The pulse begins to hammer in my temples.

"Some very important rules are," he continues, like he's checking off a list, "to always take back what you're owed, never give anyone a second chance, and keep your word. You see, I may not have many morals, if any, but I will always make good by my promises. No matter what they are, or who I made them to. Why is it important to be strict about these rules, you may ask?"

No one did. But I'm starting to hear the pulse in my ears now. He makes me more nervous by the second.

"Because there is one thing the underworld values over everything else—reputation. You should know this. And you should also know that money is only a printed piece of paper that anyone can make. I don't give two shits about theirs or yours."

My fists are itching to flex, fingers needing to feel the trigger of my gun, because I don't like this one bit. It's creeping up my spine—a sense of terror that's settling deep in my chest. Suddenly, regret replaces it.

I should be with Annika.

This was a fucking mistake.

"Money means nothing when reputation is at stake," Bartiste continues, and I'm so tense, I could snap in half. "I'm keeping my promise to those whores of yours. I'm going to take them, put them to some hard, grueling tests to see what they're made of. I'll do that shy bitch myself, just like I promised. And then we'll use them the best way we know how. Hard—until their cunts wither and nothing will be left of them. But that shy one might go up for auction. She has what it takes, that innocent look about her. Well... we'll see once I'm done with her."

Darkness descends upon me. Visions of this slimy creature putting his hands on *my* woman. His guts on the floor in front of me. His head mounted as a trophy in my office. He will never. Ever. Get to even look in her goddamn direction!

I suddenly realize that my gun is aimed straight at Bartiste.

"Cheeky. You sneaked that piece in. You better put it down, boy," he warns.

There was a *no gun* rule. We all checked each other before we entered, but I know how to hide mine.

"That's not how it works, old man. You can't come on

our turf, threaten our women, and make the rules. No matter what happened in the past, we approached you, gentlemen to gentlemen. Proposed a fucking. Generous. Solution." Each word I speak comes out more seething than the last, my throat straining as I struggle not to rage at him. "So, considering the circumstances, if I were you, I'd count myself lucky I'm not chewing on a bullet right now. This gun stays up until you agree to the offer, then fuck off from the South Coast. If you do not agree, none of you motherfuckers leave."

The tension in the air isn't cleared up by the contrasting gentle sea breeze sweeping the terrace. The complete opposite happens. I don't even dare to turn and look at my brothers, at our men. I know they're ready to fight, even if some of them might think I'm fucking stupid right now for being so goddamn emotional and reckless.

But was there another choice? No fucking way. Not when this pitiful excuse of a man speaks that way about them. About *her*. Annika.

My fucking Annika!

Goosebumps snake around my neck, along with the need to crack it, just as the expression in Bartiste's eyes shifts. They look exactly the same, it makes no sense, but something in them is almost unnoticeably different and my gut tells me to press the trigger. He knows something we don't.

This is bad. This is really bad.

It lasts a moment more before the unnoticeable becomes very much noticeable, cracking into a grin just as he turns his head slowly toward the sea. He doesn't seem to give two shits about the gun aimed perfectly at his chest.

I don't have time to wonder why he turned his attention. A blast splits the eerie silence, breaking my attention from the man. First instinct is to check if I have to take cover. But it sounded like it came from afar. Second instinct is to look in the same direction as Bartiste. But I only dare to peek for a split second—*the marina.* I keep my eyes on him with a sinking feeling in my gut, but I swallow the bile and stay silent. My phone vibrates in my pocket, and I hear the same distinctive noise from the guys around me.

"You should check that," Bartiste says as he turns his attention back to me and nods with that slimy grin.

I quickly pull out the phone and a message from Carter lights up the screen.

Our boat was blown up in the marina. Something's not right.

"All it took is one of your men. The right one. He broke so easily. Turns out, there's some pretty islands around here."

Fuck this shit!

I shoot my gun at Bartiste, but some asshole jumps and takes the bullet for him as he hurries away. Then it happens all at once. His men crowd us. Knives out. A cacophony of grunts and roars sounds as we jump straight into action. More men show up out of nowhere to pull him away. I hear Maddox's distinctive raging growls somewhere around me. Something hard and sharp slams against my right cheek as I'm distracted trying to aim for that slimy motherfucker again. I manage to shoot three more rounds in between punches. Screams sound, but I don't know where they're coming from. Did I hit him?

There're two on me now and no sign of their boss. Instinct kicks in and I pistol-whip one straight in the cheek, the distinct crack of bones fueling me. But I get tackled and, in this madness, I can't even tell how many are on me. I struggle against them, punching and shoving into them, yet I can't seem to get unstuck. Annika's beautiful face flashes for a moment before my eyes. A deep roar shakes everything around us, and I manage to break free and get back on my feet. *Was that me?* The predicament sinks into the depths of my goddamn soul and when another man tries to come at me, I fall into a frenzy, punching him in the ribs in rapid succession, backing him up until he's bent over backwards against the stonewall of the terrace, choking on his own goddamn blood.

Another man grabs me from behind, and I shift against him, but not quick enough to avoid the blade that sinks in my back all the way in. Before I can even think to move away, another guy approaches from my left and something slams hard against my cheek turning my world upside down. The impact echoes inside my skull, creating a strange sort of hollowness.

I don't hear a crack, though. And the knife's still in.

Good. At least I'm not bleeding out.

Yet I wish it would hurt. I wish adrenaline wouldn't fuel me because I fucking deserve the pain.

Annika's sweet voice echoes in my mind. Begging me to come to her and not do this. Run away, hide from the man who is now so much closer to her.

Because of me.

I failed.

I snap my head back, feeling the crunch of bones as it connects with the asshole's nose, then I elbow him hard enough that he releases me. I dodge the next punch from the guy to my left, charging into him until we crash into a hard wall.

Only it's not a wall at all—it's Madds.

He stands behind the motherfucker, bloody and bruised, like a berserker in battle. Looking down in disgust at the man trapped between us, one second his hands are on the sides of his head, the next one his head is facing the opposite direction on a chilling crack that creeps up my spine. The guy crumples to the ground just as I realize the commotion has subsided.

Looking around, the last of Bartiste's men go down at the hands of ours. It's a goddamn bloodbath.

"The girls," Finn heaves, as blood rushes from the split skin on his lip and brow arch.

"Call the clean-up crew now!" Madds orders our men.

Finn comes to me and checks the knife stuck in my back. It's in my right side, close to my waist. I think it missed everything vital. With a nod, he plants a hand on my shoulder, and fire splits my flesh as he pulls the blade out. I don't dwell. There's no time. Quickly ripping my suit jacket off, I tie it around my waist, putting as much pressure there as I can. The blade is thin, so I don't think it did much damage.

"I'm going to go sort out this situation with management. Make sure it's under wraps. You guys go!" Vincent orders us.

I don't need to hear more. I run down the terrace steps, thankful I don't have to go through the main grounds or the reception area of the estate, and head straight to the back parking lot. I really hope our damn car is okay; otherwise, we're fucked. I hear others running behind me, but I don't care who came. I just know I need to get there.

When the car comes into view, I turn on the keyless ignition, sighing with relief when there's no bang. Madds drops to the ground and looks for any surprises underneath it. Ben, one of our guys, pops the hood and does the same.

All clear.

By the time I'm in the passenger seat, my phone is in my hand, finger just about to swipe on Annika's number, but her name lights up on the screen before I get the chance.

"Are you okay?!" I almost shout.

"Someone's here, Ronan! Two boats came." Her voice is shaky, quiet.

"When?"

"They docked some time ago, maybe ten minutes. We were outside, we thought it was you guys..." She's heaving like she's been running a marathon, and I don't know if it's from fear, anxiety, or if she's actually been running. "We wanted to go meet you…"

"Baby, where are you?!"

"Then we heard shots fired. We ran back…"

"Where are our men? Is there someone with you?" I rasp.

"Louis and Dan were out with us. Another one remained at the house. But… Ronan, I can't hear anymore gunfire."

Shit.

Either our men eliminated the threat, or… the chilling alternative I can't bear to think of.

"We're coming, baby, we're on our way."

"You're on a boat? I don't hear a boat. Where—" Her voice breaks with hope. "Where are you?"

"Tell me you're hiding right now."

"Ronan!" she warns, but it comes out more as begging.

"We're not on a boat, but we're on the way."

All the rage I felt earlier has now seeped into a fear so deep, the knife wound in my side is a tickle compared to the pain this terror brings.

"Please hurry." She sounds so goddamn pure, so soft and breakable.

And I'm failing her.

"We're in that hidden room that leads from the library to the dining room. Louis and Dan are with us. I think there're two more in the house. Maybe. I'm not sure."

She's not alone. Good.

"Hide anyway, even if it's under a goddamn desk, just hide, okay? I'll be there before you know it, baby." But I'm struggling to believe my own words.

Our tires screech on the asphalt as Ben speeds down the serpentines of the hill. I can't believe Bartiste pulled a stunt like this in the middle of the goddamn day.

"What if… what if you won't?" she whispers.

"Goddamnit, hurry the fuck up, Ben!" I yell so loud, my throat hurts and the man flinches.

I can't. I can't answer her. I can't allow myself to think this could happen.

I have no idea how it came to this. How my life turned upside down on its axis in such a way that it only makes sense with her in it. I rolled my eyes at people claiming love at first sight, or merely a few dates before they claimed mad love. It made no sense at all. Until it did.

"Baby, I..."

"Ronan..." she interrupts on a shaky whisper. "I'm late. I think I'm pregnant."

CHAPTER 13

Ronan

I THINK I'M PREGNANT... I THINK... I'M *pregnant.*
The echo of each word falls with each thump of my heart. My mind is devoid of anything else, and the haunting sounds trap me inside of it. I can't escape. It goes on, and on... and on.

Ronan....?

"Ronan?" Her sheepish voice manages to catch my attention. Barely.

Then the car swerves as Ben takes the last sharp turn down the hill and onto one of Queenscove's main streets, pulling me fully back into the now.

"I'm sorry, I didn't mean to... uhm... I just thought you should know."

Oh hell, there's a whole fucking criminal organization knocking at her door, and she thinks I might have a problem with what she told me? God, I'm a fucking idiot.

"My little witch, we'll have all the time in the world to talk about anything and everything. For now, I want you to stay safe and hidden until I get there." My words come out with such conviction, I think I manage to fool even myself.

"I don't know if I can do that," she says in a shaky voice.

"Do they know where you are?"

"I don't think so. No one's attempted to get in yet."

"That's good. Stay low to the ground. Away from any window and have as much furniture as possible around you. Okay?"

"Okay."

I can tell how hard she's trying to show that she's strong, even in a whisper.

"You're going to be okay, baby." I wish I could turn this into a promise. "I know I fucked up. I should have been there, and I'll spend the rest of my goddamn life making it up to you."

"All of it?"

"I would spend more if I could."

A low chuckle coming from her breaks my fucking heart. What if... What if this is the last time I hear that sound from her? The last time I hear her voice. The last time I make her smile.

Suddenly, I hear a commotion in the background and a yelp from her, but she quickly muffles it.

"They're here..." she whispers, and I think I stop breathing.

"Stay quiet, baby girl, stay quiet. They might not know you're there yet."

"Ronan, I'm scared."

"Just focus on me. On us. On the whole life that we have left to live together now that we found each other. We can do anything we want."

"Like what?" I can barely hear her, she's whispering so low.

"First, I'll take you to Venator Castle, walk into the footsteps of your great-grandfather, since I hold the man responsible for meeting you. Without him and this painting... who knows how long I would have been wandering this continent looking for you."

The commotion sounds even louder now, strong bangs frightening her, her breathing staggered, jumpy with every hit.

"A—And then?"

"Then we can go up north, beyond the hills of Venator, up in the mountains. Rent a cabin in the middle of the forest... chase you amongst the pine trees while you let out that songbird of a laugh of yours, before I eventually catch you and..."

I twitch, almost jumping in my seat when I hear a heavy bang and Annika's muffled cry. They know they're in there. They're gonna get in. I can barely fucking breathe.

"Then we can go to the West Coast," I continue, attempting to distract her, keep her calm. "Travel the length of it and hit every remote beach we can find, every hidden lagoon, and waterfall. We can spend every minute of every day swimming and floating around, as the sunshine, then the moonlight hits our skin."

"You would do all of this, with me?"

"Not would, but will. The first time I laid eyes on you, I was sure you were the end of everything I've known up to that point. You're my wicked beginning, the start of a life I never knew I needed. If I can figure out a way to find you even after we perish of old age, I will."

She's about to speak, but gunfire and a sharp scream interrupt her.

"Hanna!!!" Finn shouts from the backseat. He's on the phone too.

"They're shooting through the wall," Annika sobs.

"Ben, for the love of all the fucking gods, drive faster!" I turn to the man, seething through gritted teeth. If he can find a goddamn way to fly, I need him to do it right now!

"They stopped. I heard shouting behind the wall."

But heavy, loud bangs replace them. I can hear them disturbingly clear even through the phone.

"Bartiste doesn't want to kill you. They wouldn't want to risk shooting you and Hanna by accident."

"You saw him..."

"Don't think about him right now."

"Where are you, Ronan?" Her voice breaks in such a tragic way

"On my way, I promise, I'll be there in a bit."

"You're lying to me..."

I am...

"I wasn't lying about everything I want to do with you. I want to see this continent with you, discover its hidden gems, discover all of yours too."

"I haven't had enough time with you. I need more."

"You'll have more."

"I'm falling for you, Ronan."

"I fell the moment I came for you and all I found was the painting of yourself you left for me."

"Nooo!!!" Her scream is followed by a thundering crash and someone else's cries in the background.

"*Get away, you asshole!*" I hear Hanna.

Finn yells behind me, begging her to hide.

The distinctive sound of breaking wood makes Annika yelp. Thuds and violent noises make me dizzy, the pulse in my temples sending me into a silent frenzy.

I'm not there, goddamnit! I'm not there... She's alone because of me! In danger because of me!

"Annika, baby, please just hide. Stay low. Please..."

"They're inside, Ronan! Ben and Louis are trying to—"

"I want you to listen to me. No matter what happens, I'm coming for you. No matter where you are or where you will be, I'm coming for you."

Her staggered voice turns to whimpers, and through tears, the rage comes through. That unmistakable fury that only comes out when you're backed up into a corner and there is no escape in sight. And she lets it all out on an ear-piercing howl.

"Annika!"

"Ronan, please..."

Gunfire interrupts her and more screams fill my ears, seeping fear into my gut.

"They're dead... Nooo! Let her go! Goddamnit, let her gooo!"

With a loud crash, the line goes dead. Finn hollers in the back of the car, but a sort of shocked numbness fills my veins. Disbelief... utter and total disbelief.

This—no, this didn't happen. What have I done?

A thundering roar rattles the windows of the car, blind rage replaces the numbness, and I don't realize I've been banging my fist on the dashboard until pain slices through my hand, a deep dent left in its wake.

What the fuck have I done?!

* * *

Jonathan, *The Ghost*, lent us his boat and even at full

speed, we knew there was no chance. It was too late. When my feet touched the sands of Bovely Island's shore, I ran inland through the trees of the small woodland, plagued with memories of the last time I did that... *chasing Annika*.

I was holding on for dear life to my self-control as we were spotting our men, lying lifeless under the shadows of the trees. As much as I was running after Annika, I couldn't help being pained by the heaviness of having to break the news of their death to whatever families they had left.

The torment grew every time I had to get close enough to make sure none of them was... her.

Then we got to the house, heart in my throat as I walked through, witnessing the destruction. Pain splattered in shades of crimson on the walls, through the shards of broken furniture, the bullet holes. I knew in my gut that what I was looking for wasn't there... I knew she wouldn't have magically fought the beasts that came for her. It was then that I acknowledged hope for what it truly is—the cruelest form of torture.

As I walked through the broken wall of the hidden room, the absence of her body was the only saving grace.

"I know who we need to go after." Carter rushes through the door, in the empty main room of Midnight, pulling me out of the painful flashback.

He's been in the office, checking in with his team, while the rest of us have been devising a plan out here. Far too many hours have passed since we returned, since they were taken. Finn gets off his chair, anxiously waiting for Carter to approach and continue. I down my drink and lean forward, bracing my forearms on my knees, nervously rubbing my thumb over the palm of my hand.

"There." He pops the laptop he was carrying on the table and points to a spot on a map.

"That's fucking hours away. Is that where they're keeping them?" Finn asks.

"No. That's where Nathan Hayes is. I've been trying long before we even met Bartiste to find this man."

"And we fucking care, why?" I ask with an unintended bite.

"As much as he is the boss, he would be nothing without Nathan. He's the little mole working in the background, orchestrating the whole operation, and I finally fucking found him!"

There's a sparkle in Carter's eyes. This is a vengeful victory for him. He pops a grainy photo of the man on the screen.

"He wasn't with Bartiste either time we met him," Vincent points out.

"No. He's highly important to Bartiste. He would crash and burn without him. So he keeps him out of harm's way, hidden."

"Then, we go get him."

"No."

We all stop and look at Carter, pulling our brows together almost in unison. He straightens, sliding his hands in his pockets.

"It's almost six hours away, too much can happen by the time we get there."

"Okay, what now?" I ask him.

"Don't you see where he is? Venator, specifically Alnit Hill territory..."

"Oh."

"I think it's time to reconnect with your cousin."

"I think you're right." I nod.

"You're talking about Buchanan?" Finn steps forward, frowning at me.

"He runs Alnit. We would be stupid not to ask for his

assistance."

"Make the call," Carter growls, his gaze darkening with bloodthirst vividly painted in his blueish-hazel eyes.

"We barely know the man, brother. Why would he help us?" Finn asks.

"Because this is not about us, this is about our women. Sloan would never say no to that."

Annika

I THOUGHT I KNEW WHAT FEAR WAS. HOW IT shattered your will and stinted any self-preservation instincts.

I thought I felt it when those men quite literally burst through the door and killed the ones who were protecting us.

That wasn't it.

I thought I finally felt the worst of it when we struggled and tried to fight our way out of the boat that was ripping us away from our life. Then that first punch hit my ribs, before it landed in my temple and knocked me out.

I thought it couldn't get any worse than the moment I woke up in pitch-black darkness, willing my eyes to adjust, but to no avail. My head was pounding, every bit of my body shivered, but I managed to find Hanna as she was waking up, probably with the same concussion I had.

But that wasn't it either.

Real fear is staring into the eyes of death and knowing that it's not coming just yet. It's the constant expectation.

The road leading to it. Torturous, grueling, painful. It's not knowing when it will all finally end, and you will be taken away.

The anticipation of death—this is real fear.

"I wonder what I can fit in this tight cunt of yours?" Bartiste grips me harshly in his hand, squeezing the part of me that was only meant for one man.

But I can't seem to react. Numbness fills every vein. There's nothing I can do to stop him. Not when I'm hung by my tied wrists on a meat hook fixed in the ceiling, painfully naked.

"I still haven't decided how I'm gonna take my payment. Which bodes well for you, since I haven't ripped you to pieces. *Yet.* Lucky bitch."

He's annoyed with his own decision, and lashes out at me, pulling his fist back. I start crying out before it even connects with my middle. Through the pain that brings violent nausea, I breathe a sigh of relief because he hit me in the stomach, not the belly. There's little to no chance that we will escape this, but if we do, and if I'm really pregnant... I can't let him take it away from me.

"Too bad you don't care as much about her friend," a pitiful excuse of a man says with a sleazy chuckle from his spot in the corner of the room. He pushes his heavy boot on the back of Hanna's limp body, welts and cuts marring her once perfect skin.

A shudder rips through me, and I want to cry when Bartiste grips my core tighter with a sordid grin on his face before he slaps me harshly.

I would beg for my life, for Hanna's life, I would beg him to stop hurting us, to stop touching us, to kill us, to take our money, to do anything other than what he's been doing for however long he's had us. But we've already done all that. All that and more. He doesn't care about anything else but our slow punishment.

Grueling, never-ending punishment. All I can do is cry, hiss, and yell. Nothing more, nothing less... and even that's getting old.

"Maybe I should start treating you the same. Shove my hard dick in that little slit of yours, and pull you apart as you bleed for me. But your greedy cunt might like it and we don't want that. Do we?"

Bile rises in my throat, and I swallow when it threatens to reach the surface. His hand slides farther back and that vile grin spreads. "But this tight asshole is guaranteed to rip and bleed."

An unfamiliar chill rushes through my body as his finger pushes against that ring of muscle and suddenly my knee connects with a soft part of him. The movement happens before my brain registers it, or the potential consequences. But somehow, I found that power in some newfound anger-fueled adrenaline.

"You bitch!" He grabs onto his middle, right above his dick I'm sorry I missed, and his other hand connects with my face so hard, I'm swinging as I dangle from the ceiling.

When he comes back into view, he hits me a second time, the whiplash so harsh I'm amazed my neck didn't snap.

The third time, the world goes black.

* * *

No matter what happens, I'm coming for you... I'm coming for you... I'm coming...

That eerie voice echoes, and I wake up with a start. For a

moment, for one excruciating moment, I thought it was real. But once more, only darkness fills my vision, no Ronan, no light, no hope.

Only a dream... a cruel memory.

"Are you okay?" Hanna's strained voice sounds in the darkness.

She's lying next to me. Shivering. But it's not cold here.

"Yeah..." I lie.

I rise into a sitting position, resting my back against the concrete wall, then I grab onto her and pull her to me until her head rests on my lap. We're both naked, but it stopped mattering a while ago. She wraps an arm around me and pulls the rest of her body until she's nestled against mine, her shivering subsiding.

"They're coming for us," I tell her as I stroke her hair.

I don't fully believe they'll actually find us, but I want to give her something. She needs hope. These people have ripped the fight out of her after the second time they took her away and brought her back beaten, bleeding, and... broken. There was nothing we could do to stop the bleeding. It flowed freely between her legs until it eventually ended.

The guilt riddling me is indescribable. It should be me. I begged them not to take her. It earned me a brutal slap that sent me straight onto the floor. Still, they haven't done that to me, haven't raped me. Only her. Making me watch my best friend go through this, planting this seed in my mind and soul, is a whole other form of torture.

It's a while until she talks again.

"If they don't come in time..."

"They'll be here soon," I interrupt.

"You never were a good liar."

For the first time since I've been here, I almost smile. She's right.

"I'm sorry."

"For what? Your lie? I get it. There's no light at the end of this tunnel, so we might as well make ourselves feel better." She speaks those words so slowly, no energy left in her.

"No. For what they did to you, Hanna. You… and not me."

She stiffens against me, but soon begins to soften. Relaxed or defeated?

"I'm not sorry. I love you, Anni. Don't think for a second that I have some fucked-up feeling of anger that they haven't touched you too—in that way." She adds that at the end, knowing that they've touched me plenty.

But her words don't soothe the guilt; they give me a sense of relief for a whole other reason. One I haven't shared with her yet.

"I love you too."

If we really aren't getting out of here, I might never get the opportunity to share this. "I have to tell you something."

"What is it?" she asks when the silence stretches too long.

"I think I may be pregnant."

"What?!" Old Hanna rises to the surface for a few moments, her voice close to the normal pitch it had before we were brought to this place.

She gets up to sit next to me, which is pointless since it's pitch-black in here and we can't see each other.

"I'm not a hundred percent sure, since I obviously didn't have a test handy, but I missed my period."

"And you've been nauseous and sick recently. I thought it was this whole situation."

"It's probably part of it. But I'm sore, my breasts feel different, and they ache, my nipples extra sensitive. I don't know. Maybe I'm imagining it."

"But if you're not…"

"Yeah."

"Fuck."

"Yeah..."

"This is not a great advertisement for the brand that made your IUD. How do you feel about it?"

"I don't know. I didn't exactly have time to adjust to the idea. With everything that's been happening, I lost track of time. But it's been in the back of my mind for a few days, when I realized that I should have had my period by now."

"Wow... I wonder what Ronan would think about this. And Finn..." Her voice trails of with longing as she talks about the man she's been falling for. "He would be an uncle. And I'm Auntie Hanna. Huh. I love the sound of that."

For a moment, it seems that she's drifting into a dream... an illusion of what our lives could be. And probably never will.

"I told him. Before the assholes broke in when I was on the phone with him. I couldn't... I couldn't disappear without telling him. It felt wrong for him to never know it if I die. Maybe it was selfish of me too. Maybe out of desperation, I thought that the revelation might make him search harder..." God, this is terrible to admit.

"You thought you weren't enough?!"

"I don't know."

"You're blind if you haven't seen how that man looks at you, Anni."

"Like Finnigan looks at you?"

I smile, even if she can't see it in this darkness. She sighs, and I wish I could soothe her. But here... nothing can.

"I miss him," she continues. "He crawled under my skin so deep... He's younger than me too. I have no idea how I've allowed this."

"Allow? Nothing allows Finnigan Hennessey anything. The moment he laid eyes on you, you had no way out."

"I really didn't. He's honest. Wears his heart on his sleeve.

So open to show it all to me, his heart, his soul, his dirty as fuck mind. It's refreshing meeting a man like that."

Those beautiful thoughts end in a muffled cry. I know what she's thinking—she'll never see him again. I know because that's exactly what I'm thinking about Ronan. My parents too... they'll never know what happened to me if I die.

I don't doubt that Ronan's searching tirelessly for us. I truly do not doubt it. They put their asses on the line for us. But that doesn't mean they'll find us.

Roberto Bartiste is a resourceful man. Cunning. And vengeful.

He's doing everything in his power to keep us.

Keep me.

CHAPTER 14
Ronan

"YOU'RE SURE HE'S COMING?"

Finn is getting on my nerves, asking this exact goddamn question for the third time now. Second time since we arrived at our meeting location, midway between our cities—about three hours away from Queenscove.

I'm struggling to keep it together. I haven't slept in two days, since Annika was taken away from me. Yet somehow it feels like it's been longer. Much, much longer.

I never knew love could be like this. So ruthless and all-consuming. Giving you the very essence of your existence, only to feel like your soul is ripped away from your very being when they're not around.

"How do you know we can trust him?"

"I swear to God, Finn, ask me one more time and I'm

gonna put you into a grave myself." I turn to him, my lips in a tight line, glaring as I flex my fists.

"Well, fuck you too! Like this whole thing is easy! What kind of cold bastard are you?! I can't fucking breathe, Ronan! I can't breathe knowing she's out there. That these motherfuckers put their hands on her! Knowing I can't get to her fast enough! I can't risk it, not on some guy who's supposed to be family, who I've only met a handful of times and don't know if I can trust!"

I wipe a hand over my face, tightening it around my jaw like I can physically rub away the weight of it all. The weight of my brother's pain... my own.

"So ex-fucking-cuse me for asking a million times! We can't all be cool and collected like golden boy Ronan!"

"You're crossing a line, Finnigan," I seethe.

"Guys, this is not the time," Madds tries to interrupt.

"Stay the fuck out of this!" I turn and shoot him a look that makes him raise his palms at me in defense, before backing away and joining the others by the car.

Then I spin back to my brother. "You think I'm cool and collected? You think I'm not in pain?" My tone lowers the angrier I get. "That I can close my eyes and suppress her helpless cries, ignore how they get louder with each echo inside my head? You think I can allow myself to breathe, knowing I'm the only thing that can get her and our baby out?!"

"W—what?"

Finn's eyes bulge, and I'm confused for a second, before I realize what I said.

"Is Annika..."

"Fuck!" I grab onto the sides of my hair, pulling hard enough that the pain reminds me I need to chill the fuck out and stay rational.

Anger will fuel me, but I can't allow it to turn reckless. I let out a long, strained breath before I turn back to him.

"Yeah, I think, I don't know. Before it all went south on the phone, she said she thinks she's pregnant. She obviously didn't have tests to take on the island... It doesn't matter. Even if there's the smallest chance, I can't ignore it."

"Why didn't you tell me?"

I don't know... denial?

"I needed to stay focused. If it's true, more than two lives depend on me. I can't fuck this up. Thinking about it too much distracts me."

Finn's finally speechless. There's something in his eyes that resembles pity, and I would erase that expression off his face with a punch if I didn't see headlights approaching from the distance. Blood pressure rises in my veins at the prospect of what's to come.

Three SUVs stop before us. Passenger doors open and a bunch of men with fierce, hard features, climb out. But it's the one with the thick, short beard, disheveled black hair, and vivid green eyes who we're interested in. Sloan Buchanan steps out and wastes no time as he walks straight to us.

He's different from the last time I saw him. It's been less than a year, yet he seems older, tougher, wiser somehow. Being both a young single father of a teenager and the head of a crime syndicate has taken a toll on him. Yet the man looks fitter than ever. Sharp. His strong shoulders pulled back, head held high, chest pumped, he walks like each step shakes the earth around him. But there's a softness flickering in his eyes at the sight of us.

"Sloan," I say with a nod and extend my hand, but the man takes it in his and pulls me into a quick hug with a strong pat on my back.

He does the same to Finn, who looks more uncomfortable with it, but doesn't pull away.

"Ronan, Finnigan, I must say, I'm not happy to see you under these circumstances."

He doesn't beat around the bush, snapping his fingers twice, and two men open the back door of the car Sloan drove in. They pull a bound man out of it, dragging him right to our feet. A gift wrapped so nicely for us.

"You rode with him," Finn states, narrowing his eyes on our cousin.

"I wasn't going to let him out of my sight." He says it like the alternative is absolutely ridiculous.

My brother is more than satisfied with that answer. I catch a glimpse of Carter who came up beside me, and even through his cold demeanor, I can still catch a glimpse of respect for Sloan. Respect for understanding the importance of this and making it his personal mission.

"Thank you. Did he by any chance spare us the time and say anything to you?"

Sloan looks down at the sack of meat that stares at us with hate and masked fear.

"We tried. But our mission was to get to you as fast as we could. We didn't want to waste any time."

"I appreciate that."

"We put feelers out, talked to some people to keep an ear out in case his boss is hiding in Venator. It's not easy, with Onasis and Santo so overprotective of their territory."

Venator is an old city built on three perfectly aligned hills, but they all almost work as individual territories, and these three crime families run each of them.

"But at least the youngest of the former can understand reason. To an extent," Sloan continues.

"Pandora?"

I turn to Carter, confused by his question.

"You know her?" our cousin asks.

"University. She was quiet."

That's all he offers. Quiet, in Carter's book, is a good thing. He likes quiet.

Sloan nods in understanding. "Do you need more men for the rescue? My team and I are more than willing to stay. I can call over more."

I turn to Vin and Madds, who are both a few steps behind, watching us. Vin approaches first.

"It would be much appreciated, thank you. We lost too many of our men."

"This is Vincent Sinclair, and Maddox Severin."

Sloan nods and shakes their hands firmly, but pauses on the former, cocking his head.

"The Serpent," Sloan acknowledges in a low tone.

I nod, trying to ignore how far his reputation has traveled, then turn to the last of us. "And this is Carter Pierce."

My cousin acknowledges him, but neither of them says anything.

"What about the other one, boss?" one of his men asks.

I lift an eyebrow at our cousin.

"Hayes wasn't alone, and we didn't want to separate the couple." He pushes the man with his foot, rolling him a little closer our way, just as the other guy is dragged out of the car.

"Couple?" Finn asks.

"That one's cock was buried deep into Hayes's ass when we busted in. Not sure if he's important to him, but thought we would bring him anyway."

"He's important."

Carter steps a foot closer, cocking his head as he observes. He has this look in his eyes—annoyance. "He covers their tracks. Blocking my search almost every step of the way. He works hand in hand with Hayes."

"Well, well. How lucky for us."

The expression on the man's face as he stands, all bound gagged, is smug, but none of us could miss the fear in his eyes. As much as he wants to hide it.

Sloan turns slightly toward his car. "Now, should we get to it?"

* * *

Carter found us a cozy little place in this area. In the middle of nowhere. Abandoned. Perfect for the job. And *my oh my* what a job this is.

We're usually patient men when it comes to extracting information.

Normally, it would be Vincent doing the delicate work. His form of torture is almost free of violence. Sometimes he simply stares at a person for long enough and they spill their deepest, darkest secrets. But most times, he uses carefully curated information he has on them to torture them with visions of the future, with endless possibilities of their life burning to the ground, while all they can do is watch and suffer. Information is power and Vincent *The Serpent* Sinclair knows how to wield it.

But this situation calls for physical torture. Plus, Nathan Hayes is mine. As much as my brother wanted to sink his claws into him, he's fucking *mine*.

Finn got his friend, the one currently kneeling between us, who I'm holding by the hair so he can focus on my brother. We've been hoping that smashing this one's face in will make Hayes talk, but maybe they're not as close as we thought, since he hasn't spoken a damn word. Maybe only a fuckbuddy, then.

"Fucking talk, you goddamn piece of shit!" Finn rages, thick veins marring his temples, eyes red as he lands another punch on the side of his head.

He didn't even wait for the answer. He knows it's not coming. We all do now. Finn lands one more hit on his cheek, brutal enough that when his head snaps to the side, blood splatters even on me, and I'm left with a chunk of hair in my hand. I'm certain there's skin attached to it too.

Not that it matters much. The guy's not going to care either. We all heard the crack of his bones—once when Finn's punch landed, and the second when his head hit the concrete floor.

If he's not dead now, he will be in a minute.

I didn't beat the guy, yet I still seem to be panting heavily. I can taste the blood in the air.

But I don't linger. I grab the metal chair we found in this abandoned place, a shriek of metal on concrete echoing in this desolate space as I drag it in front of Hayes. He's tied to another one of these chairs, not gagged, though. Yet he has not spilled a word. He flinched. Whimpered once. But he stood his ground. Metaphorically, of course.

That ends now, along with my patience.

"Not sure which one was more heartless, you or us? You're just as guilty for what happened," I say, pointing to the man currently bleeding on the floor. "You could have stopped it, Nathan."

For a moment, I search his eyes for remorse, an inkling that he's ready to talk. He's looking everywhere except at me or his friend, his mouth sealed shut. Finn breathes heavily behind me, ready to split this guy's skull open so he can get the information out of there himself.

"Where the fuck are they?" I seethe.

"Who?" He speaks for the first time, and the goddamn

audacity makes my ears ring. My restraint is officially gone.

I slam a blade right above his knee, the vibration of the crunch to the bone tickling my palm. But his pain filled cries are annoying me with their delay.

"Focus." I slap him against the jaw. "Right here, goddamnit. Or I'll slice through your kneecap and rip it right out. Where the fuck are *our* women?"

He yells as spit falls from his lips, pain clouding his mind.

"I said focus!" Rage spills from my lips as I twist the knife, the grind of it against the bone jittery in my hand.

"Stop! Stop! Stop!!!" he finally cries.

I do it, giving him a chance to speak. He takes a deep, shaky breath as he fights through the pain.

"Burfield, in the industrial area at the..." He lets out another cry, and it earns him another smack across the face to keep him focused. "...the old pipe factory. He takes them to warehouses and..."

He trails off, and Finn loses his patience, stepping right behind the man, and bending his head back until his breaths are strained. He points a knife right at his eye, bare millimeters away from his pupil, and the madness I see in him is as disturbing as it's excruciating.

"And what?!" I shout, tilting the knife under his bone.

The man is almost choking on his own saliva as he hollers in pain, his throat stretched so far back that his Adam's apple looks like it's about to pierce through his skin.

"He gets them assessed, prepared..."

Finn doesn't even flinch as he slowly sinks that knife down. It slides into his eye like butter. Even through the excruciating screams, he pushes the thin blade until all I can see is the hilt. Screams turn to whimpers. The shaking dies down. Then the man dies too.

Good. I didn't want to hear anymore, didn't need the

mental image of his implication.

"Burfield…" I whisper on an exhausted exhale.

I'm tired, so goddamn tired. It's not because of the sleepless nights, the fights, or the stress—it's the fucking fear. So far, it's both fueled and drained me, but more recently, it seems to be draining me more.

I pull the knife out of the man's leg, but Finn leaves his stuck in his skull. When I turn around, Carter's looking right at me, an unbothered calmness in his eyes. I used to wait, expecting some sort of change in his demeanor, but I no longer expect any of this to affect him. He's like a statue as he stands by the wall.

I wonder if one day I'll find out what shakes this motherfucker.

Maddox is untroubled too, but not in the same lack of soul or empathy kind of way. He's seen and inflicted enough pain in and outside of the fighting ring that he's grown accustomed to the violence. But at least he flinches from time to time. He reacts.

Not Carter, though. The most he'll do is cock his head, and I'm convinced he does it so he can examine the destruction from a different angle.

Suddenly, he moves, walking to the guy lying on the floor. He stops a few feet away, observes him for a moment, and I don't know if it's the exhaustion in me or if the guy moved, but in one fluid motion, Carter pulls his gun, aims, and shoots. Brain matter paints the floor, yet he fires one more time. Then he spins around and heads toward the exit, calling for us.

"Time to go."

* * *

I think I'm pregnant... pregnant...
I'm falling for you...
Ronan...

I jump in the seat, turning to the space to my right. *Shit, I fell asleep.*

"You okay?" Carter asks, narrowing his eyes from his spot in the backseat next to me.

I nod and turn my attention out the window. Her words still echo in my head like it wasn't a dream. A goddamn nightmare! I shouldn't have fallen asleep, for fuck's sake.

"Was I out for long?" I ask Carter, who's still watching me.

"Not long enough. Are you up for this?"

"Are you doubting my abilities?!"

"You're capable and motivated. I don't doubt that. But you're running on no sleep."

"Aren't we all?"

"Not like you. Or Finn. We're forty-five minutes away. You can still sleep for half an hour more."

"I'm fine. I need to be alert, not groggy."

I'm lying, I could sleep for a year. My body is already shaky, struggling to regulate its temperature. It needs rest. But I can't bear hearing her voice in my dreams anymore... that haunting echo. It's tearing whatever's left of my heart and destroying my focus.

Carter nods, but the bastard knows me all too well. Out of all the guys, with my brother's exception, I'm closest to him. Finn and he are the same age, both twenty-one, but you couldn't guess it from looking at him. He gives off the most confusing aura; it's like that *old soul* expression bled out of him and shows on the surface.

He's *different*. Lacking empathy, but not emotions. I've seen him experience annoyance, slight rage, even joy, in small amounts. Yet, everything else that makes us human, Carter learned. He copied. He adapted. Highly intelligent, logical, most likely a genius by normal standards. Which is why his age, or most of anything about him, is hard to pinpoint. I'd say he's a chameleon, but in reality... I think he's wearing a mask. Showing people exactly what they should see.

Sometimes I wonder if he's doing it with us too.

I trust him with my life and, logically, I know that he would never fuck us over. But he's the kind of man who's only guided by practicality and reason. If he stops seeing it in us, will he leave us too?

His eyes narrow on me for a split moment. At times, I wonder if he can read minds too. I swear he knows I'm thinking of him now.

I turn my attention back out the window. It's a new moon tonight, and we're in the middle of nowhere. There're no streetlights, and too late for traffic, so we're immersed in darkness.

"I know you're staring at me, asshole," I spit at him without turning. "Do you have something to say?"

"Do you?" He doesn't waste a breath and takes me by surprise with the question.

"No."

My lungs begin to burn, and when I feel free of his gaze, I finally breathe again.

After too many moments of silence, we start running through the plan we fleshed out before we set off. We've done all the remote research we could have possibly done in the limited time we had. Our strategy is challenging, and once we get there, we might have to adapt. I pray the location won't raise too many unanticipated issues.

I wish we could fucking fly there. It's only fifteen minutes away now, but I swear the closer I get to her, the

farther it becomes.
What if this doesn't work?
Will I fail again?

CHAPTER 15
Annika

"PLEASE... PLEASE, DON'T DO THIS..."

I have no soul left in my voice. The hoarseness taking over from too much crying and pleading Bartiste to stop.

"You're truly boring me now. I would say I'm losing interest, but in truth... you haven't begged for your *own* life yet."

How could I? It's Hanna lying on the floor, on her belly, being ripped apart by the brute thrusting into her. Her eyes are closed now; I'm not even sure if she's still conscious.

I'm praying she isn't.

It's a different type of torture, letting me witness all the horrible things he's been doing to her.

This is what I want to do to you, sweet Annika. He told me that as he swiped the tip of his knife down from the base of her throat, long past her belly button, leaving a thin trail of blood behind. He said it again as he ordered one of his men to spin her around to face me, bent her over in front of me, and ripped into her from behind. Even after she closed her eyes, he threatened to slice her throat in front of me if I closed mine, if I stopped watching. One of his men has a rough rope around my throat, holding me tight in this chair, even though I'm not tied to anything.

He's been using Hanna like a voodoo doll. Hurting her where he wants to hurt me. And goddamnit, I can almost feel it all...

Only, this torture is different. The guilt is ripping me apart, and I've begged and begged to take me instead, to let her go. To no avail. Even Hanna has screamed at them not to touch me.

I have no one to pray to anymore, no one to sacrifice my soul to so I can save her...

"You've begged repeatedly to stop. You've been annoyingly selfless and attempted to sacrifice yourself for your best friend's life. But... it's not quite enough," he continues, as he moves a bit sluggishly.

He's been limping since he brought us here. I don't know why. I tried kicking him in the leg to use it against him, but I didn't manage.

"Just... let her go. Give her, safe and sound, back to Hennessey, and then you'll just have me. I'll have myself to beg for."

He's slowly swiping his thumb over the blade he holds, the madman actually cutting himself, cocking his head as his blood mixes with Hanna's on the metal. For a few moments I start to believe he's pondering the option. There's no time to acknowledge the shift in him.

"How about we do something else instead."

Fire slices through my thigh, jostling me up in the chair I'm forced to sit in, the rope tightening suddenly around my throat. Bartiste's blade sticks out from my leg and tears fall from my eyes. No whimpers, though, no sound leaves my gaping mouth. I'm too stunned by the agony.

"I should have shot you there, just like your fucking piece of shit of a boyfriend did to me."

That's why he's limping.

"If I leave this in, you'll live. But if I pull it out, my men will be annoyed at the mess they'll have to clean up after you bleed out on our floor." He huffs, but even in this state, I can't miss the sparkle in his eyes as he orders. "Beg me."

Somehow, I manage to take a breath, not a full one, but enough.

"Beg for what? You'll kill me anyway. I told you…" I take a deep breath to push through the pain. "Let her go. Alive. Then it will only be me to inflict your pain on."

"I'm already inflicting pain on you. And you know I'm not referring to the knife fit so snug in your meat."

Meat. This is what we are to him—meat.

"There's no point to this…"

"Oh, but there is—my pleasure. After the humiliation of cheating me, I'm taking my revenge."

"Haven't you taken enough?"

"You haven't begged yet." He's getting angrier.

"I've begged plenty, goddamnit!"

"Not for your own motherfucking life!"

The burning brightens, as in two swift movements, he pulls the blade out and slams it into my other thigh with such force the hilt bruises me. This time, the adrenaline escapes me, tears fill my bulging eyes, blinding pain fills all my senses, and I shriek so loud that Hanna startles awake.

The broken look in her eyes distracts me, if only for a

few moments.

"It's okay... it's okay," I try to soothe her through gritted teeth.

But the guy brutalizing her seems to get a new lease of life, a horrifying grin on his face, just as tears well in Hanna's eyes.

"Anni..." she whimpers.

"I'm so sorry..."

But she doesn't respond to that, her eyes terrifyingly stuck on my body, to the knife in my thigh.

Can she even feel what's being done to her anymore?

Tears fall freely down my cheeks, my soul in pieces at her plight. I've begged so much for them to take me instead; I'm out of options. I've never felt so powerless... useless. I just want her pain to stop.

Please, make it stop.

"Is that all you want? For me to beg for my life?" I ask, turning my attention back to Bartiste, forcing myself to ignore the pain in my thighs.

But Bartiste's attention has shifted. It's still on me, but as I look between him and Hanna, I realize they're fixed on the same spot—Hanna with horrible fear in her eyes, and Bartiste with newfound power. It hits me then... my hands sit possessively over my belly. Even as I'm bleeding out of one leg, and with a knife in the other, I'm covering my belly.

I can't let go. Not as sickening goosebumps spread all over my skin from the hungry look in his eyes. It's a different type of hunger than I've ever seen before. It's foaming at the mouth and demanding payment in pain and suffering. It's stripping me bare and waiting patiently, because it knows... My time to beg starts now.

"Anni..." Hanna whimpers.

Bartiste slowly wraps his hand around the handle of

the knife, with each finger tightening around it the blade widening the hole in my leg and I have to bite my lip so as not to scream again.

"Could it be?" he almost whispers.

"Kill me. If I start begging, nothing will change. My fate is sealed."

"*When*. When you start begging."

He slides the knife out as I seethe through gritted teeth.

"And *when* you kill me, your plan will have the same effect on me. It's a waste of our time... just do it now." I sound brave, but my insides are shaking.

"Who said that my plan is to kill you?"

He's speaking in the same chilling tone he used when we first met him, and he gave his promises of what would happen to me if we crossed him. I refuse to focus on it because I know I haven't found out yet the true extent of his wrath.

"Don't you get it? I'm using you to my benefit. At this moment, the benefit is my pleasure. Once I'm bored, and I expect it will happen soon, you will be my payment for the trouble you've caused. Now, I haven't decided how many dicks you'll have to take for the debt to be repaid. It could be a few hundred, or... maybe you'll fetch a good price at auction."

A shudder rips through my whole body, but I only seem to feel it in the stab wounds in my thighs. The prickles pure torture in that bloody mess.

"Which brings me to the second part of my pleasure. Considering how protective you appear to be of your belly, you might actually fetch a pretty damn good price. They love the pregnant ones at these events. They especially love those spawns that come out of you. The things they do to those babies, tsk tsk tsk."

Nausea hits me so fast and hard, there's nothing I can do to stop the wave that rushes through me. I vomit on the floor, narrowly missing my legs and his shoes, my stomach spasming even after there's nothing left. There wasn't much in there to begin with, since we haven't exactly been fed three meals a day.

"I'll die before anyone can get their hands on this baby!" I hiss, spitting right in front of his feet, the thoughts he just planted in my brain so vile, I would rather kill myself than let this baby be born in this world.

The asshole laughs. He fucking laughs and more damn tears stream from my eyes, but I'm not even sure why anymore. Too many reasons are thrown at me.

"Wishful thinking, pretty bitch. I think it's time to assess that snatch of yours and see for myself just how much you could fetch at auction. Although... a hole is just a hole, doubt yours will be any different."

No, no, no!

Bartiste steps forward, reaching behind me, and suddenly I'm yanked up, the rope around my throat tightening as I'm forced to my feet. Blinding pain rips through my stab wounds, but the shriek that shreds my lungs is caught in my throat, right behind the rough rope I'm hanging from when my muscles refuse to work and my legs buckle.

I desperately reach up, trying to grab onto the rope to hoist myself, and I'm met with the asshole's harsh grin.

"I don't want you on your knees just yet."

He yanks me up with such force, I have no choice than to rise and grab onto his forearm to keep from falling. There's no option to debate the pain I'm in, not with the cold blade he suddenly pressed onto my cheek. I find whole new ways to fight through it as it tears through my muscles.

"If you cut me," I mutter slowly, "you'll fetch nothing for me."

He cocks his head, then yanks the rope another fraction

of an inch, and I immediately feel the nick of the knife on my skin.

He doesn't give a shit.

"You've seen too many movies, little girl. This is no luxury virgin auction where you end up in some millionaire's mansion. This is the type of auction where only people with very particular tastes attend. There's a world of possibilities for someone in your condition. Their imaginations will run wild, and you'll be lucky if by the time they're done with that progeny of yours, you'll still have all your limbs left, or organs, for that matter. They can't even make horror movies about the people who buy your kind of meat."

My eyes burn with every word he speaks, and I realize that anything... absolutely anything is better than what he just described. Death before it all is an absolute gift I'm ready to receive.

My knees give out, my arms drop, but he still holds me firm by the rope circled around my throat. Only, it's not a rope anymore—it's a noose.

"You're so fucking stupid. You think I'll allow you to die like this and escape your destiny?" I spit at him, but cough frantically when he yanks me up even harder.

It lasts a second more, roughly swallowed when his dirty hand cups the bare center of me, his grip unrelenting.

"Like I said, it's time to assess your snatch," he says as he slides a finger through my slit, and I manage to cry out in anticipation.

"Leave her... the fuck... alone." Hanna's raspy voice sounds from the floor behind Bartiste, almost startling us, but more importantly, distracting him.

She swings backward with vigor I haven't seen in her since we were brought here, the crack of bone resonating through the concrete room as she connects with the man behind her. The rope loosens and I reach for Bartiste's knife, but the asshole turns as I'm about to grab it. All of a sudden, he shouts indecipherable profanity as he looks down, where Hanna claws at his legs, pulling and making him lose his balance.

"You fucking bitch!" He spins, dragging me with him, and in one swift move, he kicks her straight in the belly.

But time slows after this. A sick goddamn joke the universe is playing on us... because my world crumbles as I watch him bend over and slam his knife into her middle.

Twice.

He tugs me back as I scramble to get to her, but the air feels like molasses, slowing my movements as a harrowing shriek bursts my eardrums.

The scene plays in slow motion, a movie I can't wrap my head around, because there's no way anything I'm seeing is real. It must be a nightmare. It has to be. Just like I've had every day since I've been here. That must be it—a nightmare.

"Shut up!" someone yells, just as a deep slam in my ribs takes my breath away, the noose falling limp around my neck.

It's not a nightmare.

"Hanna!" I cry out.

Something scratches my leg as it pulls on me, but I don't care, I'm almost next to her, witnessing the pain slowly dissolve from her eyes.

"Hanna! Please, please, honey, please stay with me!"

There's a commotion around me, urgent exchanges between men, but I can't focus on them. All I see is her.

Metal on metal screeches, then a different light streams in, giving me a better view of the pool of blood gathering underneath the woman who has given me life over the last six years. I don't turn, though. I refuse to break eye contact.

I finally reach her, roll her onto her back, and press my

arms on the bloody mess on her stomach. Breaking eye contact for a moment, I look around the room in a panic, searching for something to wrap around her, to apply pressure. A screeching metallic sound splits the air once more, the dim light all that remains in the space. That, Hanna's staggered breaths, and my whimpers. Nothing else.

We're alone.

"Please, hold on! You're so strong. Between us, you've always been the strongest. A goddamn force to be reckoned with!" I sob as I take in her paling face.

"Anni..." she whispers, grabbing onto my forearm with a shaking hand. Her whole body is trembling.

"No! Don't you dare show weakness now. If anyone can do this, if anyone can survive this, it's you!"

"I love you, Anni. So much..."

Blood begins to spill out of her mouth, a trickle at first, then more with each breath. I lean over and lift her head so she doesn't choke, while trying to apply pressure to her stomach with my other arm.

"Hanna, please, please don't leave me." Pushing through the sting in my eyes, my tears fall onto her body, mixing with her blood.

Yelling and frantic thuds distract me, a whirlwind of crashes and noises coming from beyond this door. *Fighting?* Gunfire sounds a second later, jolting me, confirming. The blood rushes back into me with a welcomed force. *Is it them? Ronan?!*

"We're in here!!!" I scream repeatedly with newfound power, holding Hanna to me. "They're coming for us. Hang on, just a little longer, honey. I'm begging you, just a little longer."

But she's not shaking anymore. She's still, apart from her chest that moves with slow breaths, too much time between each one. And she's smiling.

"Please, please don't leave me."

"We had some fun…" She quirks her lips.

"We'll have some more. Me, you, whoever's growing inside my belly. You can't leave me. I can't do this without you."

She takes a staggered breath, choking silently on the blood that fills her mouth.

"You're so mu—much stronger than you think. And… you'll never be alone again. You'll have everything… you've ever wished for."

"Please, not without you. Please… I love you."

She's too goddamn calm!

"We're in here!" I yell even harder this time, the commotion closer to us now.

"I love you… You better tell your baby all about me."

"Goddamnit, Hanna! Fight! You have to fight! You have to tell them yourself!"

"Tell Finn… tell him I want him to forgive himself. And you… too."

Her breaths are not breaths anymore. Only a wheezing noise that doesn't pass through her throat.

"Hanna?" *No, no, no.* "Hanna?!" There's no light in her eyes… "Hanna!!!"

A desperate cry splinters the air, just as light fills the room. Moments later, warmth envelops me, my throat raw, but I can't stop the onslaught of wails. My lungs are constricted by the grip around me, but I can't stop crying, bellowing, and begging the gods to bring her back. That warmth holds me tighter, wrapping me in a protective shield as all I can do is break.

Someone falls on the other side of her, gripping her beautiful face, swiping the stray hairs back.

Finnigan...

I'm struggling to see, my vision blurry, like I'm underwater with no goggles. Even so, it's impossible not to recognize it in him—agony. It's filling me too right now, the type that burrows inside of you and demands a home. It marks you. Taking away something precious, irreplaceable.

He gathers her in his arms, holding her bloody, broken body to his chest, speaking to her in loving, begging tones.

But she doesn't hear him.

She'll never hear him again.

She'll never hear me... see me... give me her sassy looks with her perfectly trimmed cocked eyebrows. She'll never light up a room again.

She'll never be...

I can't pry my eyes off her, afraid she'll disappear for the final time. I can't... I sit there on the cold floor, crying as Ronan kisses my forehead and whispers things to me that I can't understand. He might as well speak a different language, all of them could. He rips his t-shirt and ties scraps around my bleeding thighs, then wraps me in his jacket. There's silence in my eardrums, my throat sore and scratchy, my eyes dull and burning from all the tears.

I think they ask me questions. Or maybe Ronan does. But speaking just seems... wrong. Blasphemous. Why do we deserve to have a voice when hers was so brutally taken away in an instant?

I'm lifted off the ground completely, watching as Finnigan does the same to the only friend who has ever meant anything to me.

I'm forced to break eye contact as I'm carried out the door. When the smell of rusty metal combines with wet grass, I finally turn to Ronan. I thought there was nothing left of me to break, but his gaze proves me wrong. More of me shatters at the conflict marring his eyes. Gratitude tears him apart, the rips filling to the brim with agonizing guilt.

The same one that begins to drown me.

It's all my fault...

Every broken piece of me sinks with the excruciating weight of this shame.

I'm still here. *We* are here. My body is warm. Alive. Cradled in his arms. We have a chance, a future together. And Hanna has nothing...

How are we supposed to carry on in this unfair universe? How am I supposed to bring a child into this world when my first memories of them in my belly are filled with violence and grief?

"I'm sorry," Ronan whispers.

Me too.

I can't seem to say it, though.

Our lives are forever changed. In such cruel, contradictory ways.

I drop my head to his shoulder and let myself get carried away to wherever this pain can fester in peace.

CHAPTER 16
Ronan

’M THE BIG BROTHER. I’M SUPPOSED TO fix this. I’m supposed to do something, anything, to make this better. No. Better sounds wrong.

It’s been four days since our world crumbled. Annika hasn’t left our bedroom, has barely spoken, barely eaten.

Katya and I started making arrangements. We’ve tried to track down Hanna’s family, but it turns out that Annika is all she had. There are some distant relatives out there, but none who were part of her life—she was adopted. I had no idea...

How could I? I never even fucking bothered to ask her about her life. I don’t even know if Finn was aware; I couldn’t ask him.

He can’t even bear to look at me.

Guilt eats at me every time I head toward my side of the penthouse to check on Annika. I know what he’s thinking, and it's impossible to ignore. When I enter our bedroom, where she lies under the covers, silent, her soft breaths the only sound in the room, her empty, broken gaze tells me that she's thinking the exact same thing too.

Such a cruel twist of fate.

She's been borderline catatonic since she woke up in the hospital after the brief surgery on her sliced thigh muscles. I haven't pushed. I've just taken care of her in silence, giving her what little comfort I have to offer.

I had to fight the hospital staff to tell me of her condition, since I'm not family. Apart from the two stab wounds, she has a broken rib, bruising, and a few cuts. They haven't said if she was sexually assaulted. I don't have the heart to ask her yet. She's broken, no matter what her body shows.

Then there's the thick bruise around her neck... I've built so many scenarios in my head around it and each is worse than the last. I know it's from a rope. I pulled it off of her when I found her in that concrete box, whaling as she held the lifeless body of her best friend. Did they hang her? Was she dying when I burst through that goddamn door? What the fuck was happening in there?! If I would have been a few minutes late... would I be organizing two funerals right now?

That mark around her throat is a constant reminder of how badly I fucked up. I'm a failure... and I don't think there's anything I can do to fix this for her and my brother.

Finn is barely recognizable and he's not transitioning through the stages of grief. I thought he was about to... but then we got Hanna's autopsy report. We saw her body, we thought we knew what to expect written on those papers. We were wrong. Parts of it made bile rise to my throat. We're no angels; we've done some terrible shit in this *career* of ours, but I could never justify this kind of mindless, pointless torture and sexual assault on a person. I tried to keep the report away from Finn. I didn't want him to see what they did to her, but he forced it from me.

I guess he had a right to know, but I would have done anything to protect him from another wave of pain. It piled up on top of everything else that burdens him, like the sense of failure we both share. He read that report with a straight face, but his staggered breathing betrayed that composure. I thought he would break, lash out, but he said nothing. Did nothing. Finn swallowed every devastating feeling, absorbed it all within himself, then he left. I didn't see him until the next day. I have no idea where he went and, even if I asked, he wouldn't have told me anyway.

He'll never look at me the same again.

Not when I have Annika back.

I'm supposed to grieve too. But... she's here. My Annika is still here. The happiness I feel is overwhelming. And sickening.

I still hear that harrowing bellow when I drift off. It shook the basement of that house, where we found them. It made me sick to my stomach, and I almost blacked out as I killed the rest of the men that stood in my way. When we finally burst in, in that dim light, I couldn't tell who was lying on the floor and who was crying over who.

There is no way I'll ever forget how my heart sank. It was at that moment I realized just how much I love her. Just how much my soul depends on her.

Funny... what love does to a person. It alters our chemistry, making us dependent on them like it's the oxygen in the air and we would never be able to breathe without them ever again. Annika is my oxygen, running through my veins, and keeping my heart beating.

When I realized it was Hanna lying there... unmoving, through relief and guilt, I wondered if my brother felt the same about her as I do about Annika.

I never asked... Talking about our feelings in such detail has never been a thing of ours.

Probably because neither of us has ever felt *this.*

Death is not new to us, not in our profession. But violent deaths of the people we love... those we're not familiar with.

I'm standing midway between the door and the bed, hoping for a sparkle from her eyes that seems to look right through me. A hint of recognition. Something... anything.

Nothing comes.

So I do what I've been doing every day since I brought her home—I wash her, help her to the bathroom, re-dress her wounds, brush her hair, and try to feed her, then slide into bed next to her, drifting in a restless sleep. She functions, she walks, she sits, she does everything she's supposed to, but she's just existing here... going through the motions.

I don't push. As much as I crave her comfort... she's the most important thing right now. I'll be here for her, for as long as she needs me.

* * *

I open the door to our bedroom with one hand, carrying a tray in the other, with tea and buttered toast lathered in her favorite plum jam, but I'm stopped dead in my tracks. For the first time since I brought her here six days ago... she turns to me.

It startles me and I stand, dumbfounded, marveling at the beauty of this sight. She's actually looking at me, not through... and she's stunning. Even with pain-stricken eyes, she's everything.

I kneel next to the bed, not even realizing I've put the tray down somewhere, pulling her small hand in a tight grip and holding it to my lips.

She rolls over fully, moving intentionally for the first time since she's been here, and she grabs onto me, pulling me up. I have no idea what's happening, but I let her take me with her as she scoots back in the bed, making me crawl under the covers, and when she doesn't stop me, I scoop her in my arms, enveloping her in my body as she rests her cheek against my chest.

I could fucking scream right now. Her warmth seeps under my skin and suddenly I can breathe again.

My t-shirt dampens, her tears soaking it as soft cries gently vibrate against me. They come in almost silent waves, her arms gathered to her chest, trapped between us, and I could get on my knees and thank the gods for this. Instead, I tighten my hold, pressing soft kisses to the top of her head as I gently rub her back and let her weep.

I don't think she's cried since I brought her here. Maybe when she was alone, but never in my presence. Most definitely not in my arms. I've touched her to clean her, dress her wounds, but she hasn't sought my touch. Maybe it's shallow, or selfish, but it terrified me; the fact that this loss would have such an impact that she might have never allowed herself to carry on... with me. With *us*.

Through the partially open blinds, the sun streams in, shifting slowly as we lie here, entangled in comfort we so desperately need.

"She was being raped, yet she was trying to save... me. I don't know how to live with that. She was murdered because of me."

"No... Annika, she was murdered because a psychopath made the decision to kill her."

"You weren't there... if she hadn't tried to pull him off me, she wouldn't have made him angry, and he wouldn't have stabbed her. You came mere minutes later... we would have both been saved." She pauses, sobbing softly and catching her breath. "I can't stop blaming myself for her death."

"You're not alone, baby. I feel that guilt too. If I made a different decision, if I listened to my gut..."

Fuck!

"Ronan... I'm scared."

I pull away, enough to look into her eyes.

"Little witch, I'm never, ever, letting you out of my sight. I'll protect you with all I have."

"No... I'm scared because I don't know how to be happy without her."

The sadness in her eyes as she speaks those words is heartbreaking. She's lost, and I can't even claim to know how to help her.

"It will take time. It's too soon to think of that now. Eventually, a little voice will pop up inside your head that will sound like her, and she'll bully you into getting your shit together."

"She was very bossy."

I scoff. "In the best ways, really."

"She could have ruled the world," she trails off.

"She would have made a great aunt."

That statement brings a whole other wave of sadness, and I regret saying it. I don't need to add more pain.

"This is really happening..." She touches her belly, and I dare cover her hand with mine.

"It is, little witch."

The hospital did a blood test before the surgery and a scan when she woke up. She's early on, but she's definitely pregnant. With my child. *Mine.*

I thought this moment would scare me. That it would

bring unknown anxiety and doubts about my future. None of that happened. Instead, I felt enormous relief when the doctor told us everything looked good and was developing as expected.

There are no doubts, but the opposite actually. It took no time at all to make a decision about my future— *our* future.

Now I just have to wait for the right time, to see how she feels about it.

Annika

CHIRPING WOKE ME UP. LOUD. SHARP SOMEHOW. Demanding. Breaking through the brain fog that has plagued me for days. I lift my head from the dense pillow and blink the sleep away, but I can't see anything. The blind is down and it's dark in here.

Dark.

Too dark.

A sickening feeling fills my throat, and my body starts to shake from the inside out. It settles in my chest with such terror, I'm somehow choking. I'm suddenly cold, shivers coating my skin, my muscles frozen in place, as panic sets in.

I will my lungs to pump, do something, anything, but my chest only spasms, tiny bursts of air barely passing through my nose. My vision blurs.

Then a scent penetrates the rising blood pressure. It's rich, deep, and comforting. It smells of cedar and jasmine. *It smells of Ronan.* And it breaks through the barrier, my lungs filling with the relief he brings.

You're in his bed.

My fingers twitch against the soft touch of the comforter, pushing me to further focus, rationalize the shadows around me.

It's a different kind of darkness.

But it's darkness nonetheless. A surge of fear-fueled adrenaline passes through my muscles, and I jump out of bed, almost ripping the cord of the blinds as I roll them up. Bright sunshine penetrates Ronan's bedroom, making me take a few steps back while covering my face with my forearm. I'm panting as the sunshine heats my cold skin, making the shivers subside.

Shit.

The last thing I need is an aversion to darkness.

"Aaah, Christ!"

I bend over, gently pressing my palms over the bandaged stab wounds in my thighs, realizing I jumped out of bed far too quick. My muscles will take time to recover, and sprinting like that is not freaking helping. But feeling something, anything, is better than this numbing heartbreak. And I feel a lot... ribs hurt, my lungs seem to ache, my shoulders, neck and back. None compares to my heart.

Nausea hits me like a ton of bricks, and I rush to the bathroom through the pain in my thighs. I drop to my knees, hugging the toilet, and emptying my stomach. There's not much food in there, enough to keep this nugget in my belly growing, but that's it. I haven't had much of an appetite. Luckily, I haven't had too much morning sickness either. Hopefully, this is not the start of it.

That sharp chirping distracts me again. It's not birdsong, it's more like... a call. A long, demanding noise.

Is it coming from inside the penthouse?

I brush my teeth, then go to the bedroom door, opening it for the first time since Ronan brought me back. I wince as I get the first peek through the corridor that leads to the open living area. There is so much sunshine there, it sparkles against the space, and suddenly I hate everything about being here. It's... beautiful. Cheerful.

Nothing deserves to be beautiful right now. Not for a long time.

It's the silence that keeps me from slamming that door closed and crawling back into bed. Silence, apart from that damn bird.

Am I alone?

I've heard voices before. The guys always seem to come here now, probably for their business meetings, since Ronan has been reluctant to leave. Even Ekaterina was here, the only one, apart from a doctor and Ronan, who had stepped into the bedroom. She helped him, helped me.

But I don't think anyone's here, not even Ronan.

I haven't had the power to move, to breathe too hard, to do anything but lie in bed, sleep, or occasionally deal with morning sickness in the en-suite bathroom. I can't find the will to pretend I can carry on. But that's not the only reason I've stayed in Ronan's bedroom. He shares this penthouse with his brother. Finnigan—the man who lost her too.

I'm terrified of facing him. I know he wasn't with her for that long, but if their connection was anything like what mine is with Ronan... fuck.

Does he blame me as much as I blame myself?

I take a tentative step forward. Then another. And by the third one, I still can't hear any sound. So, I go on until I'm in the living area, the floor-to-ceiling windows to my right letting far too much sunshine through those sheer white curtains. But one of the doors that leads out to the terrace is open, one of the curtains dancing slowly in the breeze. The salty scent of the ocean drifts through, and I take a deep breath.

That chirping calls to me again, urging me to move farther. My instinct tugs at me to go back, pull the blinds down, and crawl under the covers until this reality dissipates, because it's all too much. Against my better judgment, I step into the doorway of the terrace, and the view knocks me out. It's offensive... with its calm ocean, blue sky dusted with fluffy clouds, and the source of the incessant chirping darting around—two swifts flying happily.

The birds soar right in front of the terrace in a crazy dance around each other, chirping away like a bickering couple. Then they disappear to the right, yet their peeping remains. I follow the sound, and when I find the source, I'm met with more pain—they have a nest in the corner of the terrace, right under the awning of the roof. I can hear more of them, not as loud... baby swifts.

One of them flies around again, the ocean view its backdrop, before it lands on the railing, only a few feet before me.

When have I stepped out onto the terrace?

The bird cocks its head from one side to the other repeatedly, watching me. I've never been so close to a bird. Especially a swift. They're always on the move, flying so fast, their movements sharp and controlled, so gorgeous with that forked tail and graceful wings. They remind me of Hanna. Elegant, slim, energetic, intelligent.

Slowly, I lift my hand in its direction, then take another step forward. I don't know why. I just do. Then another step. Then another. Then stop, dropping my arm.

I'm fooling myself.

Just like Hanna, this bird will fly away too soon. I'll never touch it... ever. The only difference is that I'll hear that bird sing, but I'll never hear Hanna's voice ever again. I'll see that bird in its flight, moving with such grace in the sky, but I'll never see Hanna move with that grace ever again.

As expected, the bird darts away, but stains my view with its flight, before the other one joins in once more. Queenscove buzzes below. So alive, oblivious to this loss that stopped my world in its tracks.

It's beautiful. Idyllic. That type of view that puts a smile on your face, and makes your day better, makes you happy. It's horrible. The world doesn't deserve to be happy when she's not here to experience it. I don't deserve to be happy when I didn't do everything in my power to save her.

She did everything in hers to save me.

Everything.

She gave her life to protect me.

And soon... soon, she'll be just a pile of ashes.

The breeze hits my face, chilling the tears that fell against my cheeks, and I don't dare wonder if they'll ever stop. I deserve this—the pain. I deserve to have this guilt eat away at my soul until I'm like her... dead. I deserve so much worse than this.

The tears fall faster, whimpers being carried away by the breeze. They're mine.

That contradiction hits me like a brick, the weight of it pushing me to my knees as sobs fall in harsh waves. Because I know that in however many months, I will have at least one reason to be happy. There will be a light in my life that will pull me out of this state, maybe even before the baby growing inside my belly will be born. I know that eventually excitement will fill me. The anticipation of a new soul born out of love in a world that rips it away in an agonizing heartbeat.

I'll be happy... I'll be fucking happy, and nothing feels more horrible, more terrifying than that in this moment. How can I allow myself to be happy when she cannot even *be*?!

Sobs turn to wails, covering the birdsong of the swifts as I sit on my heels, hands braced on the tiled floor, and every tear that falls on the skin of my bare thighs feels like tar.

Someday, when this baby is born, I will have to be strong, for Hanna... She'll want me to be strong and smiling. But today is not that day and it won't be for a while. Even when it comes, it won't erase the guilt that tarnishes my soul.

I don't know how long I sit here crying. This reality hurts... this world that keeps spinning like she wasn't taken away just days ago. It makes no sense.

The breeze sweeps against the back of my neck, but this one feels different... chilling. I whip my head around, and I'm met with cold blue eyes staring at me from the doorway—*Finnigan*.

There's something indescribable passing through his gaze. He's completely still; he doesn't frown, doesn't curl his lips, doesn't even seem to breathe. His eyes fixed on me make mine burn. My soul urges me to run, suddenly in the sight of a predator, but my heart... it shatters all over again. It recognizes the anguish gazing back at me.

I earned the malice he wants to inflict on me. Judging from his expression, death would be it. Only, there's a smugness in those eyes, the message loud and clear—gracing me with the pain of this life will hurt so much more than the ease of death.

Not one muscle moves. Not even in his tightly clenched jaw. He looks at me like I'm wasting the air that fills my lungs. Then he turns and leaves.

"I'm... sorry." I finally whisper.

BEING AWAY FROM HER MAKES MY MUSCLES twitch and I'm fucking struggling to breathe. It's excruciating. I crave to be around her, even if she has been distant lately, colder than the night she hugged me and fell asleep against my chest. It doesn't matter—being in the same space as her is enough. I hate that I had to leave the apartment. It was way too soon.

My stress levels are through the roof, even knowing that the penthouse has become a fortress with all the security stationed not only at the door, but all through the building and its entrance. She had security the day she was taken. What good did that do? It meant nothing against Bartiste's men, his firepower. Lesson fucking learned.

However... Finn is on his way to the penthouse now, and I wish the thought would calm my nerves. The opposite is happening.

I had no choice but to be here. I insisted on it and Finn drew the short end of the stick. We all feared he would kill before extracting information. He's not rational enough right now for this. I'm not sure I am either, but I've been cooped up in the penthouse for so long now, fantasizing about all the horrible ways I want to exact my revenge, that I'm fucking famished for it. But I refuse to be irrational. Not when the man who did this to our women escaped and it's imperative to find him.

"I don't know where he is."

The voice of the men tied to the metal chair bounces off the walls of the concrete room, as he stares up at Vin standing before him. He cocks his head, the act so slow, the guy blinks rapidly, erratically, the growing discomfort palpable.

"I'm... I'm serious," the asshole stutters.

Vin straightens, and the man's eyes flicker to the small knife he is lazily rolling between his fingers, his other hand casually sitting in the pocket of his black trousers.

"Fuck, man! I get it, he took your women, but I had nothing to do with it! I'm not in Bartiste's inner circle. I have no idea where he's gone!"

"I didn't ask," Vin finally replies.

"Then what the fuck do you want from me?"

"To tell me where you think he is."

"Is he for real?" He turns to look at Madds toward the left corner of the room, before his gaze drifts to me, his attitude growing cocky. "I just told you I don't know where he is, man."

The shriek is the first thing we hear, before we even register the swift, fluid movement with which Vincent threw the knife. It pierced the man's inner thigh.

"You seem to have an attention issue. I asked you where you *think* Bartiste is, not if you know his location. Now..." Vin leans in, just enough that he grips the end of the knife handle with the tips of his thumb and middle finger. "You have until I completely pull out this blade from your thigh to answer me with enough detail that Maddox here can imagine every single street, door, and window, so he can fucking paint it afterward. He's not good at painting, you see, so you have to make sure you're very accurate. If you give us everything I want, I'll stick the knife back in and you won't bleed out on our new floor."

"Fuck you!" he spits, but Vincent dips to the left quick enough that it misses him.

His answer is the slow, harrowing pull of the knife as the asshole seethes through clenched teeth.

"It has a very short blade, as you saw, and right now it's the only thing blocking the flow of blood in your femoral artery."

"Like you won't kill me anyway."

"I'm a man of my word. If I tell you I'll stick this knife back in and won't kill you, I mean it. Now... you don't have long. Spill. Oh... sorry, no pun intended." He puts the man in a daze, constantly switching his attention from his words to the blade slowly sliding out from his flesh.

It confuses him, and he *spills*, telling us the details of the two locations he's heard Bartiste talk about. The motherfucker escaped. He was shot—twice, yet he still fucking escaped. He might be dead, but we don't want to take the chance. We need to make sure.

When we're satisfied with the amount of information he offers, I take a few steps forward as Vin slides the knife back in, then steps back. The man lets out a strained sigh, relieved as he looks down at his leg. He might be lying to us, but the information was too specific, and it's better than nothing. Hope shines in his eyes when he meets mine, ready to be released and make good on Vin's word. He wasn't lying. He is indeed a man of his word, and if he says he won't kill him—he won't.

I made no such promise.

The last expression in his eyes before my bullet pierces his lung is of confusion. It paused on his features for a couple of seconds before he realized his blood was replacing the oxygen needed to breathe.

"You said..." he gurgled as blood rose and spilled from his mouth.

"*I* didn't say anything."

His eyes widen and pain fills them with such speed, the realization that he's facing a slow, painful death hitting him far too early. He will suffer. Yet not nearly as much as he deserves.

I don't care if he wasn't one of the culprits who hurt Annika, or Hanna. They all deserve to burn. I would have strung him by his toes to the fucking ceiling if I wasn't on a mission to find the man who needs to pay in blood, flesh, and bones for touching what's mine. He will die.

I turn and look toward Vin, but he speaks before I get to.

"Go. I'll tell Carter."

I nod, head to the door, but stop after I pull it open.

"I have this gut feeling we won't find him," I tell him without looking his way, my lungs heaving with anger and exhaustion.

"In my experience, pieces of shit like him always pay the price of their sins. Eventually, he'll make a mistake and crawl out of his hole, and we'll be there when he does." He's talking about his father.

"At least you sent yours to the hole yourself. You got that satisfaction," I push back.

"One day, he'll come out. Vile men like him can't fathom

bowing down, and it's always their downfall."

For both our sakes, I hope that's true.

"I can't wait as long as you're willing to." I sigh.

"And if you don't have a choice?"

I step into the dark corridor, letting the heavy door slam behind me, refusing to think of that possibility. There's this gnawing pressure building in my head with every step I take. I fucked up... I fucking fucked up! And Bartiste is still out there.

I wipe a hand over my face, trying to pry Vin's words out of my head. *I need the fucking choice!*

He's been through a lot. The only one of us who didn't come from money. He came from poverty, emotional, and physical abuse. I don't know if it shaped him differently, or if

he was always this way, but Vincent Sinclair does not need anything to make people crawl to his feet. He can turn over his pockets and let dust fall from them, and people will still spill all their secrets.

Maybe it's his charm too. Maybe it's the deadly look in his eyes.

Or maybe it's the effect of that one singular moment when he brought his father to the brink of death and kept him there until he agreed to fuck off out of our city. Either way, no one's been missing the man. Especially not Vincent's mom.

I hope I get to witness Bartiste's downfall soon, even though it might not make a difference to the idea that formed in my head, the thoughts surrounding it getting louder every day.

That's not what I want for Bartiste, though. There will be no mercy for the man who dared take Annika away from me and kill my brother's woman. He will not be chased away. No, he will be hunted down and gutted like the scum he is.

Annika

I CAN'T EXPLAIN WHY, BUT THE MOMENT THE bedroom door opened behind me, I pretended to be asleep. I didn't need to turn around to know it was Ronan, even in this room laced with his scent, I could recognize how much stronger it becomes with his presence. It was him. And I just lay here, hugging the comforter to my chest, my back to the door, and my eyes closed.

I stayed like that while he paused next to the bed, listening to his strained breaths like the weight of the world sat on his shoulders. I laid here while he stroked my hair, before he gently lifted the comforter from my legs to check on my bandages, as he's done multiple times a day since he brought me here. I even stayed like this while he went to the bathroom and took a shower.

I didn't even move when I heard a loud thud that rattled the shared bathroom wall and the hiss that followed. I stayed like that as he crawled into bed with me, keeping his distance, yet... extending a touch to me, a gentle one between my shoulder blades. No, he wasn't---isn't keeping his distance—he's giving me space. The two are worlds apart.

But everything feels wrong now and I'm not sure how to make it right.

I can feel the heaviness that weighs down the mattress right along with him as he returns from his shower, the anger, the frustration, the burden of everything else. I want to turn around, soothe him, tell him it will all get better. But I can't move... I can't lie to him.

Eventually, I fall asleep for real, but even in that slumber, I can feel him—I'm safe.

***

I woke up with a start. Multiple voices sounding past the bedroom door, and this goddamn room is dark again. I take a deep breath, praying his scent will ground me yet again. Only I seem to have gotten used to it now. It's not as strong anymore... and it smells like me too. *Like us.*

Jumping out of bed quickly, I'm careful not to force my muscles, and pull the blinds open. I head toward the door and listen, breathing easier when I recognize the voices. There're three of them. One of them is Ronan, one is probably Finn, but I'm not entirely sure who the third is.

I turn around, slowly walking back to the large window, taking in yet another marvelous view of Queenscove and the sea beyond. But today... today I don't seem to hate it as much as I did yesterday.

I can't avoid the world any longer. I can't avoid the arrangements that have to be made for Hanna either.

Although Ronan did dare to ask me some very general questions about her, like her favorite color, music, and her favorite flower. He stopped when my voice began to tremble, on the verge of sobbing.

After brushing my teeth, I pull one of Ronan's shirts on. It's long enough that it covers my ass, but doesn't quite reach the middle of my thighs. It doesn't matter; since those days with Bartiste, my nakedness hasn't felt important.

The voices are louder when I walk into the corridor and near the living area, but when I step into view, the room goes silent. There're more than three people here—Ronan, Finnigan, Vincent, and Ekaterina. All sitting or standing around the kitchen island.

It seems like I interrupted a discussion I'm not supposed to be privy to. But it's not that, is it? I'm the elephant in the room. The woman who got kidnapped along with her best friend, but only she came back.

Ronan rushes to me before I even finish that thought. He wants to comfort me so badly, but I attempt to step around him and toward the fridge.

"Sit down. I'll get you what you need."

"It's okay, I can do it."

"Annika," he warns. "Sit down. Tell me what you want to eat, and I'll do it for you."

I drag my eyes up and look at him briefly before turning my head toward the empty seat. It's between Ekaterina and Vincent. That means I will be facing Finnigan... fuck.

It's okay, I don't have to look at anyone.

I comply and go to sit, mumbling something about wanting fried eggs, bacon, and maple syrup. The reality is that I would also want some French toast, a whole bucket of syrup, maybe some pancakes too, and some hash browns. This pregnancy is starting to mess with my appetite.

I suck in a wince as I attempt to lift myself onto the stool, and before I know it, Ronan is there, hands around my waist, lifting me up and setting me down gently. I didn't expect it... my gaze flashes to Finnigan involuntarily, and I catch him glaring at me. Ekaterina clears her throat, and he suddenly looks away.

I'm still not sure how I feel about her. She's done nothing to me. On the contrary, she's been helping Ronan and I, but I can't figure her out. She gives off a chilling vibe, guarded, like she takes years to warm up to someone, and trust is a privilege she doesn't give freely.

She's in her element amongst these guys, though, comfortable, at ease. I just feel... out of place.

The reason why sits across from me.

A generic conversation begins, but I'm so unfocused, I don't register a thing about what they're saying. They could be speaking to me, but my attention is glued to the man currently pottering around the kitchen, cooking me breakfast. I try really hard not to meet Finnigan's eyes, even as they seem to challenge me. The heat of his gaze is so different to Ronan's. There's no comfort in that warmth; it burns me in the worst kind of way.

Not long after, a plate with two fried eggs and many more slices of streaky bacon is set before me, and I drench it in maple syrup before I begin eating. Finnigan keeps watching me, and once in a while, Ekaterina clears her throat again, making the burn on my skin ease. I don't know how to change this, how to make it better.

Annika.

Hmm?

"Annika?"

I twitch, pulled back into the room, when I realize Ekaterina is trying to get my attention.

"Yes?"

"When you have a minute, would you mind if we have a word?"

Her expression is a shred gentler than usual, but I'm still taken aback by the request. I don't remember ever speaking with her in private.

"Um, sure. Whenever you want."

She spots my apprehension and confusion and continues.

"It's about the ceremony. We just want to make sure we're doing everything right."

About the... what?

"Ceremony?"

"Funeral."

I flinch at Finnigan's cold voice. That one word knocks at an imaginary door inside of me, which holds the raw emotions I'm trying to keep at bay.

"O—Of course." I push the plate away, my appetite gone. "Do you want to go now?"

She nods and slides off the barstool, offering me a hand to help me. If this numbness wasn't so deeply etched inside of me, I would be real sick of being treated like an invalid... but I couldn't give less fucks about it.

"Where do you think you're going?" Ekaterina asks, and I turn to find her looking at Finnigan, who's following us.

"She was mine. I get to be part of this," he warns.

"I don't deny that, but you already know what's happening. Annika should be the one to have the final say in everything and let us know if we're missing anything.

"It's okay..." I say gingerly, trying to diffuse the growing tension.

Ekaterina straightens, her stance shifting in this commanding way that reminds me so much of Hanna.

"No. Finnigan, if we need you, we'll let you know.

Annika was—"

"There when my Hanna drew her last breath?! The reason why she—"

"Careful, brother! You're crossing a line!"

Ronan's at his side now, Carter on the other. Veins bulge in Finnigan's temples.

"What?! You know it, I know it, everyone motherfucking knows it! She fucking died because of you!" He throws his arm out, pointing at me with such anger and disgust, I actually take a step back.

Tears well behind my eyes, heat flashes through me, and it sears through numbness that has plagued me. It turns to fire, walls crumbling at my feet, and before I know it, I've stepped toward him, heaving as I watch Ronan put his hand up to keep me away. But I don't give a shit.

"Fuck you, asshole!" He doesn't have time to react before my hand slaps him across the cheek, snapping his head to the side, but the guys pull him back. "Fuck you! You think I don't fucking blame myself every single goddamn day?! She died in my arms! She died in my fucking arms! I lost her! She was everything to me, the goddamn soul in my body! I am nothing, fucking nothing without that insane aura she projected!"

Carter and Ronan are holding him as he pulls to move closer to me, struggling in their grip.

"Let me go, asshole!" he spits, giving his brother a warning look. "Don't think for a second that I will ever stop blaming you for holding us from going with them on that goddamn island."

I can see Ronan wants to respond, but... he doesn't seem to have a comeback for that.

"I lost her too!" Finn rasps. "She was mine. She was the present and the future and you fucking sent her way back to the past! Yet everyone is treating me like goddamn nothing!"

He turns back to me and bellows, "You let her fucking die!"

"I did nothing! I couldn't do anything! They made me fucking watch, Finnigan! I begged until I lost my voice! She bled on my flesh, she bled with your goddamn name on her lips, and there was nothing I could do to stop the hurt, to stop her from leaving me! Your blame on me pales in comparison! I don't need you to tell me she's fucking gone because of me!" I close the distance between us, my hand flexing, ready to hit him again. "Because I already know that!"

He holds still, defiantly, his eyes on mine. No, not defiantly... but painfully. Harrowing, devastating pain. He's waiting for his punishment. So, I do the one thing I don't want to do, but need to. Because he's the only one who has lost her almost as much as I did.

I wrap my arms around his waist and bury my face in his chest, putting all my emotions in my grip, all the grief, the anger, the sadness. I don't know when the tears started falling, but they're soaking his t-shirt, and his hard body softens. As my grip loosens, and I'm about to pull away, his arms wrap around me, keeping me close, his hot breath hitting the top of my head.

"I should have never left that island," he whispers to me alone.

This is not just about my guilt. I hold him tighter again as I feel his staggered breaths against me. I want to tell him to let go, but I have a feeling he's closing off that part of himself that accepts these kinds of emotions. I know in my gut this will be the first and last moment Finnigan Hennessey opens himself to me.

Nobody speaks a word until we pull away. We both take a step back, looking at each other with different eyes, yet we both know that the blame and the guilt will be with us for a long time. If not forever.

CHAPTER 18
Annika

I'M NOT SURE THERE ARE ACCURATE words for my state of mind since Hanna's death. I laid in bed, but my body was on the concrete floor... next to her. My mind was not here, not in Ronan's bed, not in this penthouse, not in Queenscove. I wasn't here. I was there with her... holding her hand as she shifted further and further into the darkness. Only, that darkness wasn't the absence of light, it was my mind. It was a thick, unforgiving smoke that wouldn't dissipate. It flooded my lungs, and took everything that didn't seem to matter anymore, choking it until it almost died.

There was so much of it, and I didn't want to break through. I deserved it. I needed it to make sure the pain of everything would always be fresh, burn my lungs, and rip me apart from the inside.

Until one day, broken blue eyes penetrated the smoke. I saw them before, a slightly brighter shadow in the smog, but that day they looked... defeated. The light was dim, so dim I wasn't sure if they were simply moving further away. They weren't. The light was dying. I couldn't let something else die because of me... I deserved the agony, the punishment. I deserve it and more. But those blue eyes were paying for my sins, and I couldn't allow it.

So, he became clearer as he knelt next to the bed that felt less like a concrete floor. And when I touched his hand and pulled him to me, such an odd thing happened... those eyes slowly filled with saturation. The more I touched him, the more vivid they became, breaking through the smog, making me crave more of their light.

That was the first day I saw, truly saw with a clearer mind, the weight of me. I wasn't nothing... I was someone to this beautiful person who had scoured this continent to save me. Ronan saved me. I was worth something. In the midst of that smoke, it wasn't what I wanted, because I knew I didn't deserve even an ounce of what he was offering. I wanted to let him go. As horrifying as the impact of his absence would be on my heart, I wanted better for him. But when the color was coming back in his eyes, when I saw the brightness returning, I knew I could do no such thing. He was mine... and I couldn't be the reason something else died. Even if this was a feeling, not a person.

It took little time for him to break further through the barrier of my mind and, slowly, I was seeing just how much everyone, not just him, was doing for me. Memories of the last few days flooded, snippets of conversations, of worry, sadness, and anger. All of them, even Vincent and Carter, were involved. These people, who I was a stranger to mere weeks ago, cared in their own way.

Now, as I watch Ekaterina summarize the decisions we just made during our discussion, I understand it even more. We came into the bedroom after what happened with Finnigan, and had an uncomfortable conversation that needed to happen. But now, Hanna's simple, yet beautiful, ceremony is fully planned out, mainly because most of it was done before I even got involved. Ekaterina is so much different than I thought. Behind that stern, poised exterior, there's a kindness she offers selflessly. She has her own, fairly internalized way of expressing it, and I'm grateful I got to feel it. She even helped me send the rest of Hanna's things to storage, where we shipped everything when we emptied the house we rented here.

But it is done now... Hanna's ceremony is all set. Small, intimate, since she didn't have any close friends, and definitely no family. It's been just us, like sisters, for the best part of six years. Making lasting connections through all the traveling and the shady deals was never an option for us. We had each other.

She adored the sea, which is why our *retirement* homes were on a quiet island, which held only a couple of towns and villages. The houses are close to the sea, with uninterrupted views, and a private beach. So, we're going to hold the ceremony on the edge of a small cliff, above a private cove, then we can scatter her ashes over the rippling waves.

I take a deep breath, urging some composure. I can't pretend this is easy, it's nowhere near that... yet, strangely enough, the outburst Finnigan and I had helped somehow. He and I will never be close, I know that, but I think we helped let out some plaguing demons today. I know that the darkness that had me trapped is dissipating. I hope his will too someday.

"Ekaterina?" I stop before we leave the bedroom and turn

to her.

"Please, just call me Katya. I like my full name, but it is a bit of a mouthful."

"Oh, okay, Katya, it is. I know *this* is not in your job description, so I just want to say thank you. For taking the time to take this on while I was..." I trail off because I have no idea what I want to say. Injured? Grieving? Numb?

She shakes her head gently, her sandy blond braid falling off her shoulder and down her back.

"I've seen enough loss to know that help is usually never requested, but always needed. There's plenty of men in your life now, but if you need a woman... I'm here."

She doesn't reach for me, but her words are like a warm hug. She may look like a hard woman with her stern features, but she's oddly comforting, even from the distance. Maybe that's why the girls who have been working for her and the guys are so keen.

We walk out of the room, heading back to the living area, when I hear an exchange that makes no sense.

"Did Carter find any trace that Bartiste was there recently?"

I stop in the middle of the room, looking at the men who sit around the sofa, staring at a laptop screen, speaking of things that... shouldn't be.

"Did you... did you just say, Bartiste is..." The vase sitting on the table I'm leaning against is rattling on the wood, and my legs seem oddly soft.

Finnigan and Vincent turn to Ronan, while he looks at me with wide eyes.

"Does she not know?!" Katya exclaims, a comforting hand coming to rest on my back.

"What the hell is going on? Is Bartiste still alive?!" I can't seem to control the tone of my voice.

Ronan rises from the sofa, and when he takes a step in my direction, I step backward. I can see the deep fall of his chest as he exhales, weighing his words. But I can already tell there isn't any sort of remorse in his eyes.

"None of you get to judge me, and you"—he nods to me— "you don't get to be mad at this. There wasn't a right time to tell you that the man who did this to you, to Hanna, escaped."

"No, you don't get to decide that, Ronan. It's not your call when is or isn't the right time to tell me something like this."

"That's where you're mistaken, little witch."

I flinch at that term of endearment thrown so casually in a room full of people, Finnigan's gaze burning a damn hole through me at the sound of it.

But Ronan doesn't care as he continues. "After everything you've been through, your healing was the most important thing to me. So yes, I decided that after my mistake, after what Bartiste did to you, to Hanna, after your surgery, through this loss, the last thing you needed was to know the motherfucker was alive. You don't get to be mad at that."

I'm speechless, mouth gaping, shocked at the audacity of this man.

"I had a right to know!" I seethe.

"And now you do. At the right time."

He takes another step, and I have the urge to slap him.

"Right time? I walked into this conversation. If I didn't, when would you have told me?"

"At. The right. Time."

I don't know when he closed the distance between us, but he's too close, brushing his hand up my arm, then my shoulder, and just as he's about to touch my cheek, my eyes flicker to his brother, to the anger and flickering sadness in his eyes. I step out of his orbit, turning on my heel and heading straight to the bathroom.

I attempt to slam the door, but a thud sounds behind me instead. The bastard's scent hits me before the door bangs against the frame and the lock clicks. I turn, ready to kick Ronan out of here, but before I can say a word, he rushes to me, forcing me to step backwards until my shoulders hit the bathroom cabinet. He towers over me, his energy different than before, the gentleness he has been treating me with since bringing me here, long gone.

There's a simmering rage behind the blue of his eyes, like a ruthless storm in the middle of an ocean and I'm about to be caught by one of the waves.

"I can't read your mind, Annika. You're pulling away from me, and I'm trying very, very hard to give you space. But I can only give you so much before I fear you're going to pull away completely."

Fuck.

"I just…"

"Don't say this is about grief."

"It is!"

"Do you not want me anymore?" I can practically taste the fear in his angry voice.

"This is not about you, dammit!"

"Is it not? It's me who you're pulling away from. It's my touch you've been avoiding or rejecting, when I've only ever wanted to comfort you. I'm not imagining this, little witch."

"I need time."

He inhales deeply, pulling his lips into his mouth, but his eyes hold an intensity I want to dive into head on. He's so… everything. He's fucking everything. All kinds of wrong when the world has fallen off its axis because Ronan Hennessey's *comforting* touch is not what I'm supposed to be thinking of right now. Especially since his thoughts are innocent… mine aren't.

"I'm okay with that, as long as you'll still be here when that time's up. But I need to know if it's more than grief that made you shrug away from my touch out there." He points toward the door.

"Are you kidding me?! Is this what this is about? Me rejecting you in front of your *friends*?! What is this, high school?! Get out of my way, please." But there's no politeness in the tone.

His gaze darkens, head tipping down to me so slowly I can practically taste his annoyance.

"You could do it in front of the goddamn king, little witch, I don't give a fuck. I only pointed it out because it was the last time you did it. Now, tell me what's going on," he seethes, but I'm already pissed off.

"No. Get out of my way." I'm deflecting, and I can't seem to stop myself.

But the bastard is like a wall in front of me, refusing to move an inch and I can't bear to have this conversation right now. I slam my hands against his middle in an attempt to shift him away, and the man winces, his body folding ever-so slightly. *What the fuck?* I'm not that strong. I lift my hands to touch him again, but he covers his middle with his forearm before I can reach.

I look up at him, brows furrowed, but not in anger, then pull his arm away and lift his shirt.

"Ronan! Oh my God, you're hurt!" I grab his biceps, turning him around until his back hits the bathroom cabinet, switching places, then touch the mean stitching on the side of his abdomen, not far from his waist.

"What happened? Who did this?! When did this happen?"

It looks similar to the ones marring my thighs. So very similar. I lift his shirt higher and frantically begin to check every inch of his torso, panicking that there might be more.

There are bruises, so many bruises, at various degrees of healing, some darker than they should be, some already in the faint yellow stage.

"Have you been hurt this whole time?! Goddamnit, tell me what happened!"

But the man stands there, pulling his lips between his teeth, and I could have sworn I caught a glimpse of amusement in his eyes. They're... warmer now.

"Answer me!"

And he does... but it's not the reply I was expecting.

He grabs my head in his hands and presses his lips to mine with such fierceness, I grab onto his forearm to steady myself. He kisses me like he's been thirsty for decades and I'm the only lagoon in the middle of a desert. My legs turn to mush and those stab wounds have nothing to do with it. Core tightening, my already sensitive nipples hurt against the graze of the bra.

Fuck... I didn't realize how much I missed this. His lips on mine, his touch, him. All of him.

I let him in, and he doesn't hesitate as he slides his tongue into my mouth, exploring every inch of me with a subdued hunger. There's more of him to give, but it's not that kind of kiss. This kiss is filled with longing... the soul demanding the connection, not the body.

His hand threads into my hair, pulling my head back to deepen the kiss, only I wince into his mouth, and it all stops in a heartbeat.

"Fuck! I'm sorry." He brushes that hand against my head, soothing it immediately.

"It's okay. It's gone. It's just a bit sensitive."

He brushes a palm over his face, and it's like he takes off a mask. The look in his eyes, the color under them, the curl in his lips, they all change into something I want to nurture and nurse back to health. It's pain, fear, and something... something that looks back at me every time I look in a mirror—guilt.

I caress his cheek, wishing I could wipe it all away and make it better. But it doesn't go anywhere.

"Baby," he sighs. "I have to ask. I'm so sorry, I just, I want to try to understand, and learn how to... how to help. Did they *touch* you?"

I'm not sure what I was expecting, but it wasn't this question.

"You don't know?" I'm a tad confused, and he shakes his head. "I thought they would have said something at the hospital when they did the checkup."

"No. It felt... private. Invasive in a way. I asked about everything else, but unless there was something medically necessary, I thought you would tell me when you felt like it. And I stand by that. If you don't want to talk about it now, I'll be here when you do."

"They didn't rape me, Ronan."

The way his chest collapses is like the weight of the whole Earth rolled off of him.

"But... they've touched me enough to leave a mark."

Telling him that might have been a bit of a mistake. If I ever wondered if fury has a face, I don't need to anymore. It's here in front of me, staring into my soul.

"I'm going to hang him by his fucking dick," he seethes between gritted teeth.

"You're going after him?"

"Will we ever have peace if I don't?"

I don't know. But... do I want him to leave me all over again? I don't know that either. The idea of Bartiste being out there scares the shit out of me. However, being away from Ronan again scares me so much more. Not because of me being taken, but because I cannot possibly lose him too. I can't bear that. I already can't bear the way Finnigan looks at me.

"Can't the others go?"

"They can, but that son-of-a-bitch touched you, Annika. What he did to both you and Hanna... he's not getting away from that. If Finnigan doesn't get to him first, I'm gutting him from dick to throat."

"No..." I whisper.

"No?! You're the sweetest person I know, Annika, but even you couldn't possibly tell me that the asshole doesn't deserve it." His brows furrow as he cocks his head.

I rub my eyes, pressing my hands a bit too hard, attempting to erase the conflicting feelings.

"Fuck, Ronan, I'm not saying I don't want him to die a horrible death. I would gut him myself for what he did to Hanna if I had the stomach for it. But... I just can't be away from you again," I finally confess.

His eyes soften, but the expression doesn't last.

"I don't either. I can't take any more guilt. I fucked up, I fucked up so bad. Finn was right, we should have stayed with you. And those days while Bartiste had you... I thought I knew what pain was. I was so wrong. I was so wrong, little witch. It's why I can't let him get away with this."

"Long and hard, I thought about that moment when Hanna told you two that you should go. She and I spoke about it too... while we were *in there*. You didn't see his men on the island, Ronan. They were on a mission, and you and Finnigan wouldn't have stood in their way. You would have died, and there wouldn't have been anyone to save... me."

I almost said *us* for a moment there.

"Maybe you're right. But it doesn't change the fact that he might still be out there, and he doesn't deserve to be."

"Wait. Might?" I ask, confused.

"He didn't escape unscathed. He was shot several times, but we couldn't find him in the vicinity of the building or surrounding area. So we're going on the assumption that he's still alive, but we have no idea where he could be."

"Then, you're not going anywhere for now." I sigh, relieved.

"I was going to go to one of his locations to see if there's any trace of him there. Sloane's territory is close to one of his other locations, and he said no one has been there."

"Wait, who's Sloane?"

"Oh, he's our cousin. He runs an... organization, up in Venator, and he helped us with the rescue and all."

"He was there when..."

"Yes."

"I'm sorry, I don't remember. I don't remember anything from Hanna's death until the drive here from the hospital." I've been trying, but I really can't recall a thing. Maybe it was the anesthesia, or, yeah, I actually don't know.

"I didn't expect you to. It's not like we had time for introductions. He's helping us with Bartiste now, since our numbers are down, but I—"

"I want him dead, Ronan," I interrupt. "But I want you here with me more."

Ronan

WELL, FUCK. WHAT AM I SUPPOSED TO SAY TO THAT? *No, I want to kill the motherfucker who wronged you more?*

The look in her eyes breaks me apart. She begged me once before to come with her... I didn't. Look where it led us. The choice is clear because it isn't even a choice—I'm staying here with her.

But the guys and I, we better start recruiting soon, because I need more people to make sure there're enough eyes on the motherfucker.

I wrap my hands around Annika's waist and hold her there, at enough distance that I can still look at her beautiful face without her craning her neck up to look at me.

"You haven't told me why you're pulling away from me," I deflect.

"Are you staying?"

I pull her to me, kissing her plush lips that seem to taste of peaches. Sweet, soft peaches.

"I'm not letting you out of my sight," I finally reply.

She sighs, an invisible weight coming off her as her body relaxes, and she looks somewhere beyond me.

"It's Finnigan. He looks at me like he's about to wrap a noose around my neck and throw me over the terrace railing. And I can't blame him one bit."

"If you want me to talk to him…"

"No. He's hurting. If anyone understands, it's me. He resents me… and not because he blames me for her death. The displays of us, our love… I feel like I'm rubbing it in his face."

"*We*, little witch, *we*. You are not alone in this." I thought I was paying attention to them. I've been focused on their individual healing, on our interactions. My brain acknowledged but skimmed over my brother's reactions at the sight of Annika, the mention of her name. And us.

"I know, but you're not the one he's livid at," she almost whispers, looking up at me with sad eyes.

"Yeah, I am. He blames me for not staying on the island. But I understand. We'll keep it lighter around him."

"Thank you."

Her small hands slide around my waist until she pulls her whole body against mine. I'm not the first Hennessey she's hugged today, but the first one needed it so much more than me.

I sink into this, into her, reveling in the feel of her, how perfectly she fits wrapped around me. I'm not a believer in fate, but fuck me if she didn't make me one. Even through these horrid circumstances, I found her, and I just can't be mad about that.

I don't want to break this moment, but since she seems to be feeling a bit better, I wonder if she's up for something different.

"Baby, do you, by any chance, fancy a change of scenery?

A breath of fresh air?"

Leaning back slightly, she looks up at me, arms still linked around my neck.

"Umm... I don't know if it's a good idea. I don't really want to see anyone."

"No. I was thinking we could go to the waterfall." Her brows furrow, but I see a little sparkle in her eyes.

"What, in the forest? Where we went to that party."

"The very one. It's usually quiet there, especially during the week."

She ponders the proposition, chewing on her lip as the cogs spin.

"I'm not sure if I'm up for it today. After Finnigan and... Bartiste. And honestly, I could use a bath. I'm sick of just washing myself with a cloth. The doctor said I could take a bath starting today."

I don't know if she can see the slight defeat on my face because she quickly follows up. "How about tomorrow?"

I'm beaming from the inside out. I don't want to get too excited, but... I'm proud. She's making some progress, letting herself heal slowly.

"Sounds good. Tomorrow then. Now, let's go say goodbye to everyone and go get you in a bath."

I begin to pull away when she forces me back to her.

"Not so fast. You still haven't told me why you're stitched up!"

I almost forgot about that. How rude of me, considering it's the discovery of that stab wound that flipped her attitude just minutes ago, from anger and rejection to full-blown concern, all the above dissipating in a matter of seconds. I couldn't suppress my grin when I realized that she definitely did not stop loving me.

I tell her a shortened version of the events leading up to

her kidnapping and I'm sickly enjoying the worry and shock on her face. She's constantly asking me if I'm okay, if it still hurts, how I feel, and so on, like she's not sporting worse wounds in her thighs at the very moment. She worries about me, completely forgetting her own condition. If that's not good mother material, I'm not sure what is.

When we finally leave the bathroom, I catch a glimpse of Finn retiring to his side of the penthouse, and the rest of the space seems silent.

Good, we're alone.

"Bath now?" she asks with a ginger expression.

"Bath now."

But I'm looking forward to tomorrow.

CHAPTER 19
Annika

THE SCENT OF THE FOREST, THE WILDFLOWERS toward the end of their bloom, and the wet ground around the waterfall are a treat to the senses. Last time I was here, on a midsummer night, Hanna and I were playing what seemed like a dangerous game. If only we would have known what was coming... I guess it's better we didn't. We were so free, so happy. It's August now, yet that night seems like it happened much longer ago, in a different life.

Yet Ronan's touch on me, his lips on mine for the first time, they linger. I can't help but fall into that memory. I had a lot of liquid courage, but it wasn't just the alcohol that took me out of my shell, it was the man holding my hand right now. I looked at him and something in me stirred, a sort of animalistic hunger that demanded him. And I let it consume me. I don't think that hunger is gone, just dormant somehow.

We walk around to the right edge of the pool, and he pulls me on top of this large, flat rock.

"We'll sit here for a bit, yeah?"

I nod and lean over to get my shoes off, but his hand on my shoulder stops me. I turn to him, confused, but then he drops on one knee in front of me, picks up my foot, and begins untying my shoelaces. Looking at him in awe, I steady myself on his shoulders.

He's on his freaking knee helping me out of my shoes!

I'm not sure if it's showing on my face, but internally I'm squeaking.

He removes my Converse, giving my bare foot a quick swipe of his thumb, sending a shudder through me. I think I might ask him for a foot massage at some point. He's good with his fingers, so he'll be amazing at that too. He does the same to the other foot, then he rises, and helps me sit on the edge of the rock, my feet submerged in the slightly chilly water.

God, it feels good.

He takes off his own sneakers, rolling up the legs of his sweatpants, his toned, defined calves distracting me before he sits next to me.

We say nothing for a while, enjoying the day, the sounds of the forest, the scent of everything, the sun on our skin. There's something to be said about the ability to sit in silence next to someone and to be so utterly comfortable.

The sun has been high in the sky for some time, the rays making the pool sparkle. It all looks so incredibly different in the light of the day than it looked that night in the middle of that party. It's peaceful, idyllic.

"I wish I could have stopped her from trying to save me that day... One more minute, and your intrusion would have turned Bartiste away from us. Just one more..."

Ronan looks down at me, some stray strands of hair falling over his forehead making his handsome features look more boyish.

"My mother didn't teach me many things herself, but one lesson will always stay with me. As much as I'm not a believer in the mysticism of life, this I tend to believe—if it's meant to be, it's going to be."

"Isn't that usually applied to good things? Lovers reunited and all that?" I ask.

"That's not how she spoke of it. We use it for these hopeful contexts, like when we're trying to make ourselves feel better about a love lost, but like anything else in this world, there is a balance. Tragedies are also meant to be, and when death calls... it's unavoidable. This was her lesson when my grandfather died in an accident. It taught me that hindsight is the death of peace of mind."

I turn my attention back to the waterfall, letting out a heavy breath.

"Your mother chose a harsh lesson."

"She did. We all wish we had done things differently. We regret and are riddled with guilt. But hindsight... it's a whole other type of haunting."

"For a man who doesn't quite believe in the more mystical side of life, or death, for that matter, you sure do have a way with words."

He chuckles low in his chest, and I find him staring straight at me with a slight grin on his lips.

I'm not sure if I'll ever get used to how beautiful this man is. That defined jaw of his, those high cheekbones, and deep blue eyes, are a hypnotizing combination. They stir something low in my belly and make me squeeze my thighs together.

Yet we haven't touched each other since my return. It's not that the attraction isn't there, but... any type of joy feels wrong right now. Out of place. Disrespectful.

"It won't always be like this," he tells me.

"Logically, I know that this will get better. But I can't help but wonder if it will get worse again."

"What do you mean?"

"My world was dangerous, Ronan, but the one you and your organization are part of is so much more than that. I just don't know if I'm ready to take on all this tragedy." I place my hand over my belly, rubbing gently, and his eyes drop there, before turning his gaze toward the waterfall.

I see the irony in my words, considering it wasn't his world that took Hanna away... it was mine. But the connection is there—I know it, and he knows it too.

He's thoughtful in a different way. There's a heaviness weighing him down and I'm not sure how to make it better. What I'm saying is harsh, but I don't want to hide anything from him. Not when it's not just about us.

"The whole world is dangerous, Annika. I don't think there is any way for any of us to escape that." He turns to me, then covers my hand with his, putting a protective pressure on my belly. "But I'll do anything in my power to shield you from it."

The promise is in his eyes, not only in his words. There's a peculiar clarity staring back at me, and I need to be *in* on the secret it holds.

"I made promises to you, and I intend to keep each and every one of them," he says to me.

"Promises? When?"

"On the phone, before Bartiste's men..."

"Oh."

Venator... the mountains... the West Coast, traveling through this whole continent. It feels like eons ago, yet still not far enough.

"You weren't just distracting me."

"Not only, no. I've never thought of doing anything like that, not until you." The blue of his eyes gleams with his words. "I want every experience I can get with you. I want to see you paint in every corner of this country. I want to swim with freaking dolphins. Take all the baby classes. I want... everything. With you."

"You do?"

"I want our great-grandkids to talk about our love the way you talk about the love between your great-grandparents. Only I'll do everything I can to keep you alive until old age takes us both."

I laugh and I swear it sounds foreign. He notices too, that gleam in his eyes growing brighter.

"You have zero control over my death. But... I think I want all of that too."

He doesn't question my choice of words. Maybe deeper inside of me, I don't just think I want it—I know. He probably knows that as well.

"We'll have more photos of each other, though," he says with a smile.

"Yeah, we definitely will. Too bad my grandpa lost great-grandma's locket... I would have had one."

"Locket? Oh, wait. When we met to buy the painting, you said the only photo of her was lost. Was that it?"

He remembers! Oh my God... It was such a small detail. I can't believe he was paying attention to that.

"Y-Yes. She had a beautiful, oval silver locket, not expensive, but special, nonetheless. Inside, there was a photo of great-grandma and great-grandpa. I saw it once when I was very little, and grandpa showed it to me and told me it will be mine one day. He moved houses not long after, and years later, after he died, we realized it was missing. No one really thought about it for years, until we started going through some old boxes. The assumption is that it was probably lost when he moved. Or maybe it got sold. Anyway, it's lost now."

"I'm sorry." He places his hand over mine on the rock and gives it a quick squeeze. "I don't know, important things have a way of coming back to you. Who knows."

I giggle at his optimism.

"Now that would truly be a miracle."

He pauses on me for a moment, a smile I didn't realize I missed so much etched on his features, refusing to let go. It makes me fall deeper into this sensation. We're both smiling... in what seems like forever. It feels like a stolen bit of time we need to protect so it isn't taken away from us.

"Come on, let's go for a dip."

My first instinct is to refuse him. My mouth is open, about to spill the words, when a shrieking birdsong distracts me. Two swifts engaged in an enticing dance as they fly above the pool, before soaring high and beyond the waterfall.

Such a beautiful moment. And it might be my last one here.

"Okay. Just a little dip."

Ronan helps me up, and we walk off the rock and to the edge of the water.

"Little witch, you don't have to go all the way. Keep your underwear on, your bra... I want you to be comfortable."

I stop moving, realizing I'm about to unclasp my bra with no regard whatsoever to my nakedness. I seem to be forgetting that I'm no longer trapped in that basement... with no care about my modesty.

Looking down my body, at the ground where my summer dress lies crumpled on top of the pile of his clothes, I don't know how to proceed. I'm... stuck. What do *I* want? How do *I* feel about it?

Ronan narrows his eyebrows, clearly noticing the shift

in me at the inner-turmoil, and he circles his arms around me, pulling me into his strong, bare chest. *Home.* He feels like home, his skin against mine, his heat warming me, his breath brushing against the top of my head, the pressure of his possessive hold. I'm here... I made it.

I make the decision, drop my hands, and leave my bra on, sinking into his hold.

We saw our baby today, heard the thumping of their little heart, and I let myself fall into the fantasy of having a family with the man who looked at the monitor like it was a miracle captured on screen for the first time. I knew then that I couldn't let myself go... couldn't sink into this sadness and loss of control. No matter how much guilt I feel for having to move forward—I must do it. Hanna would understand. She didn't have one selfish bone in her body, especially when it came to me. She helped me so much over the years to build me up. She took me under her wing when she noticed the will, the need for more in me, for the darker side of the world, for the dangers lurking in the underbelly of society. I wanted a taste, and she gave it to me. Even when she saw I was finally interested in a man for more than a fling, she put a pause on all our plans to get me what I wanted. It was usually easy for her, but not for me. She pushed me, but on my own terms. She would be fucking pissed if she saw me right now, pulling back on everything we both worked for.

It's why I know now, there is no other choice. I will be strong enough to stand on my own, no matter what Ronan decides. I can do this. All of it.

I snake my arms around his middle, running my hands over his slightly damp back, so warm from the sun hitting his soft skin, enjoying how the muscles beneath harden one by one. When he loosens one arm and its heat runs up my skin until it reaches the back of my neck, I look up and I'm met with conflict in his eyes. Such damn gorgeous eyes, a complex blue that sometimes makes you feel like you're lost in the sky in a wingless flight, and other times ruthless waves catching you in the middle of the sea.

I'm distracted once more as his cock hardens between us, and I don't miss the slight guilt in his eyes when it presses against me. He wants me. He's never once even implied anything sexual. He's kept his distance, never pushed more than comfort on me. I don't like that he feels guilty for a natural reaction, the same kind I'm having right now.

I sink into the growing possessiveness of his hand tightening around the back of my neck as he leans in. When his lips finally touch mine, I can't control the soft moan erupting from me just as he can't control the low rumble vibrating in his chest. We kiss under the summer sun and the sound of birdsong and falling water until we're breathless. We kiss until the world looks just a little bit different when I open my eyes. Nothing has changed in it, only my outlook on it, on us, on my future.

"Come." He drops his arms, running his hand down from my shoulder until it forces me to let go of him and snake my fingers between his.

He pulls me into the water, and I jump with a shriek—it's definitely colder than I expected.

"Oh, Ronan, this is... no!"

He lets out a bark of laughter that takes me aback. The asshole is laughing at me!

"You'll be fine, come on. I promise it will get warmer. Our skin is just heated from the sun."

"It's not like I remember it..." I trail off.

He stops for a moment, knowing full well I'm referring to the night that changed my life. Maybe his too.

"Even if this pool was minus ten degrees that night, it

would have still felt like molten lava with you in it."

Holly hell.

My mouth falls open slightly, and he's stuck there for a moment, watching me with a hunger I know he's pushing himself hard to suppress.

Suddenly, the water is not that bad.

We swim for a while, letting the water take away some of the tension from our muscles. I spend most of the time floating on my back, letting the sun warm my body. It's so soothing, my ears beneath the surface, listening to the rush of the waterfall. It's not close to us, this pool is big enough that its waves are light here. But underwater, it's like a different world. One that calms and heals. An odd type of therapy.

I've always known I wanted to live next to water. It's why Hanna and I bought our houses pretty much on the beach, on Falk Isle. I want to do exactly this as much as possible. But... with all that's happening, this baby growing inside of me, everything's muddled in my brain. It's too early for a decision, but even so, is Queenscove the right place for this?

I drop my feet and rise, treading water, the sounds of the forest replacing the loud underwater void, and find Ronan leaning against a large rock, watching me. His strong, long arms are spread wide on either side of him as he braces them against the rock, his head tilted slightly, his gaze filled with need he quickly shadows when he catches my eyes.

"I'm sorry, I kind of lost myself."

He shakes his head, but says nothing in response. I can't take my eyes off of his, the intensity of his stare reaching for me like tentacles through the water, wrapping around me, all of me, snaking through my blood and gripping my flesh from the inside out. My parted lips are suddenly dry, my mouth parched, my soul on fire.

Yet neither of us moves.

My breaths quicken, but treading water has nothing to do with that effort.

I'm not sure I've seen this greedy look in his eyes before. This desire demands more than my body. No, it wants all of me. It wants my soul, my heart, it wants to steal it all and never let go. Ever.

I wouldn't hesitate to give it all to him.

Not when that gaze makes me feel like there could be a harem of attractive women around us, and he wouldn't notice any of them. That need is for me and me alone.

And to think we were almost broken apart. After Hanna was murdered... I was next. There was no doubt about that.

I swipe my hands through the water, moving toward him, when he suddenly breaks the intense silence.

"I think we should go back."

His words startle me. Did I mistake the look in his eyes? The... intention? He swims to shore, and I catch a glimpse of his wet boxers—I most definitely was not mistaken. His erection can barely be contained. Turning his back to me quickly, he sheds the underwear, giving me the most delicious view I could have ever asked for of his taught round ass, before pulling his sweatpants on.

I can't imagine that feels pleasant. His skin is still wet. Why is he in such a hurry?

"Come, little witch." He turns to me, hand outstretched in my direction, as beads of water slide over the ridges of his muscles, over his torso carved of stone, the contour of his shaft far too defined behind the light fabric of his sweatpants.

Parched...

So I go to him, leaving the sanctuary of the water, and place my hand in his. I don't even attempt to mask the way I'm looking at him. He's goddamn magnificent.

We didn't come prepared, no towels, nothing to dry

ourselves with. Luckily, my dress is fairly casual and loose, but I'm still not looking forward to it clinging to my wet body. Only, I don't have a choice and Ronan helps me pull it down over my head, before guiding me to turn, so he can zip the back. He does it fast, too fast, and there's a pang of disappointment in my chest. Then he guides me to turn back around, his hands lingering on my waist, slowly sliding down my hips, and I think there are fireworks going off in my belly. I didn't realize how much I missed his touch, this type of comfort, not the innocent kind, until today.

But that damn worry and guilt flashes in his eyes all over again, and he stops, taking a step back.

Guilt...

For one moment, one beautiful moment in this stunning place, I forgot about those teeth embedded in me.

I thank him anyway.

"For what?" he asks.

"Bringing me here. It helped. I needed it." A little too much.

"Yeah... me too. Come on, little witch, let's get some food, then you have to rest. It's a big day tomorrow."

Just on cue, my stomach makes an embarrassing rumble that earns me a chuckle from Ronan. This pregnancy makes this hunger pop in out of nowhere. I could just see food and suddenly I'm hungry. Even if I just ate. But it seems to fade when I focus on what Ronan said after... tomorrow. It's a big day indeed. The day of all the goodbyes I'm not ready for, of the pain, the finality of it all.

I'm supposed to be strong for her. Watch that casket disappear in the room beyond the curtains, where her body will enter the cruel flames of the furnace that will render her to dust.

My amazing Hanna... she will be nothing but ashes.

Ronan

IT WAS TOO BEAUTIFUL OF A DAY FOR SUCH SORROW. There was nothing I could have done to soothe the pain in either Annika or my brother. They kept their distance from each other the whole day. In the morning, during the ceremony, they sat at opposite ends. They did the same at the restaurant we went to after. They barely even looked at each other when Hanna's ashes were delivered to us and handed to Annika.

Not now, though. At the edge of this small cliff, with the soft breeze brushing against our skin warmed by the afternoon sun in an offensively pleasant way, Finn stands next to Annika. I'm on the other side, Maddox, Vincent, and Carter are right behind us, and some of our men behind them.

Annika hands Finn the container that holds her best friend, signaling for him to wait a moment as she reaches into the pocket of her black blazer. Her body's turned toward my brother and I have no idea what she's holding, but he looks down for a moment, then his gaze quickly jumps to hers. Eyes wide, conflict and pain furrowing his eyebrows, then his shoulders slump and he unscrews the lid. Annika reaches in and I have this urge to step around and see what the hell she's doing.

Instead, I turn to Katya, and she seems to be in on it. There's no shift whatsoever in her compassionate expression as she watches them. I reluctantly stay in my place, watching Annika as she removes her hand, fiddles with something and then reaches in the container yet again. She hands Katya what appears to be a little funnel and a scoop, and I finally catch a glimpse of two small, intricately decorated silver vials, before she slides one in Finn's breast pocket, then in hers.

She looks up at my brother, and they share something unspoken for a few long moments, before he nods. She takes the urn from him, then turns to the glistening calm water before us, and kneels on the ground.

In the faintest of whispers, she says... "I love you," then begins slowly tipping Hanna's ashes, watching the breeze take them away and spread them over the sea. Finn kneels next to her, covering her hands with his when her own begin to shake, and they do it together.

I'm here for comfort, her rock and shoulder to cry on, but this moment... this moment is not mine. It's hers—theirs.

So I watch as the last of the ashes spill, then nod to the men behind us, who turn and walk back down the hill, to the cars. Madds, Vin, and Carter begin to walk away, but stop a few paces from us, giving us space. Katya approaches Finn, while I help Annika close the, now empty, urn and help her up.

Before we move away from the cliff, Annika grabs my hand pulling me to her. I wrap her in my arms as she buries her head in my chest, but she doesn't cry. Her hold tightens around me as she breathes slow and deep through the ache in her heart.

Such a terrible, early end to such an amazing journey. Is this to be all of our ends? Too soon to fully leave? Violent and cruel? Is this what I have to look forward to?

A few months ago, I wouldn't have blinked an eye at it. It always crossed my mind, but it meant nothing. Now, with this delicate, stunning woman wrapped around my body, my baby growing in her belly, I can't even fathom it.

This will not be our end.

Yet I'm not sure my brothers will understand.

CHAPTER 20
Ronan

"F UCKING HELL," I MUTTER TO MYSELF when the first image I see walking down the stairs is Finn getting voluntarily pummeled by Madds in the ring.

I step through the main room of the space that is going to become what Maddox now calls *The Fightclub*. I argued that maybe it requires a classier name, but the reality of it is that it's exactly that—a fight club. It will be savage, bare-knuckle, real, nothing like typical boxing rings with rules that protect the fighters. It will be what Maddox has been craving, a place where the need for pain finds its home. Whether you need to feel it or inflict it.

As I watch Finn now, I'm not sure on what side of that pain my brother found himself in. He's been spending a lot of time here since it started to look like something.

The Fightclub is close to being ready, but not quite there yet as some renovations are still ongoing. On top of that, we're setting up the basis for our money laundering side of things. Fighting is all well and good, but the real money will be in the exchanges, the bets, and it has to work seamlessly.

Madds lands another punch in Finn's gut, and steps back when he falls to the ground, bracing himself on his hands and one knee. He taps once, then twice on the ring floor, and Maddox pulls him up.

In the last month since the funeral, things have started to fall back into some semblance of normal, although my brother appears to have found a new one. All his free time, as little as there is of it, since we've been working hard to consolidate our organization, is spent letting out steam in this ring, or... in bars. He hasn't brought a woman home, but we keep an eye on our own... and our own is out with a different woman almost every night. Sometimes more than one. I'm not asking him about it. He'll just yell at me that I'm not his father. He's done that since we were much younger and our parents were away, as always.

God knows our father had a very interesting lifestyle himself. Always fucking around, never the same woman, no issue whatsoever in having them throw themselves at his feet, considering his looks and bank account. Then our mother came along and, all of a sudden, he forgot other women existed. He and Uncle Preston told us the stories on a drunken night years ago. I can't help but wonder if Finn takes after him? Or was Hanna that woman?

Fuck, he's only twenty-one. There's so much life before him. There has to be more. I take a deep breath and push all those thoughts away.

"Are you guys gonna clean up? The newbies have joined us upstairs," I ask.

"Fucking hell, you're light on your feet." Finn startles slightly. "What time is it?"

"Just passed eight-thirty. Midnight is getting busy tonight."

"Nice! Yeah, give us a few minutes. We'll be right up."

I nod and walk back upstairs and through the corridor that connects to the back entrance to our establishments. I take the door that leads to the back rooms of our speakeasy and debate if I should head to the office to take care of some business or go to the bar.

It's been a hard month. Constantly working, not only here, but home too, making sure our organization is back on stronger feet than before. We lost a lot of men, at least one stream of income, but our reputation seems to be growing by the day. What we did to Bartiste is spoken about in hushed tones through the underground of ours and neighboring cities. I guess taking most of his army down with the few men we had made an impression. At the time, we didn't give a shit; we didn't really see that because the purpose was almost blinding us. If only we had some confirmation of Bartiste's life status...

Fuck it, I deserve a few drinks.

I take the door to the bar and suck in a deep breath as the scents that feel more like home than that penthouse, assault me. Wood, musk, worn leather, basking in the low, warm lights hidden all around the space, in the nooks and crannies, bathing this space in a mysterious aura. The music is a bit louder at this time, deep, southern blues covers the nefarious conversations the patrons are engaged in as they sit in the deep leather chairs, sipping their intricate smoky cocktails or the expensive liquor. This is not the place for just anyone— this is for people like us. Hidden in plain sight and accessible only by memberships or passwords.

This night is one of many to come when we welcome new men within our ranks. These ones in particular came from our cousin, Sloan. He's been really good to us, asking some of his men if they would like to join our ranks. Some of them were happy to climb down the hills of Venator and come to the coast. We couldn't refuse the offer, not when these were men with experience, years under their belt spent in the underbelly of our worlds, reliable, and more importantly, trustworthy.

They took over one of the more private corners of the bar area, happily mingling with some of our men who joined us tonight. I signal to the bartender my order—he already knows my preference; bourbon, on whiskey stones to keep it cool, but not watered down—and join the guys.

It's going well. We discuss, we plan, we share ideas, we talk about life, and drink until I'm feeling a little bit too warm inside. Finn has already bonded with a couple of guys, and they laugh loudly in their corner, talking about God knows what.

Carter observes everyone from a small round table next to us, sipping his absinthe. He joins in the conversation a few times, but the man mainly keeps quiet, as always, taking note of each and every little thing happening around him. Sometimes I wonder how that brain of his works. Does he see numbers that he calculates to figure out what to make of the world and people around him, or is it colors?

Madds sits next to Vin, acting polite to everyone, but that mountain of a man always has an expression that tells you that he might crush you under his brutal grip if you look at him a little bit funny. It's not always intentional, it's just how his features align, with his strong jaw, slightly crooked nose, and low eyebrows that shadow his eyes. The scars marking his skin don't help his brutal aura. Yet sometimes I wonder if he's the softest of all of us. He has a heart under all the muscles, and it seems to beat a bit too hard. Although, much like Carter, he keeps quiet unless he's truly interested in the subject.

Vin's wearing his all-black suit and shirt, as usual, his wide shoulders and lean frame resting against the back of the sofa, as he taps a finger to his glass and explains something to some of our men. He carries himself with such a natural imposing allure, he gets attention without demanding it.

The pits of his eyes flash to me, as if reading my mind and knowing I was thinking of him, and I raise my glass, cocking an eyebrow. He nods and does the same, without interrupting the conversation he was having.

"I've been a bit homesick after moving to Queenscove… but damn, I think I'm about to be cured." One of our new men, Stefan, speaks, both eyebrows raised as he looks somewhere behind me.

"Christ, one more drink, and I'll lay myself at their feet. Especially the shorter one on the left. Fuck me, she looks like she belongs in the old-world atmosphere of this place," Otto, next to him, continues, his eyes glued to the same spot.

Old world? My back warms with something that snakes all over my spine, and when I turn, I'm met with the unmistakable curve of Annika's ass leaning over the bar to speak to the bartender. She's dressed in a form-fitting little number that seems to shine with every movement. A dark sage green satin hugs her body, barely touching the middle of her thighs, and when she turns, I'm fucking parched as I witness the soft curve of her breasts peeking between the plunging neckline.

Suddenly, I want to fucking punch these two, slam their heads together, then throw their limp bodies into all the other men in this place who seem to be sneaking looks in her direction. A few women too. She's here with Katya and Ashley, one of her girls, all dressed to impress, but still tasteful.

"Do you think I have a chance?" Otto asks the other one.

"All you can do is try, brother."

I swear I'm going to pummel him through the goddamn table.

He doesn't know her, Ronan.

It doesn't matter. She's fucking mine either way. Even if he learns the hard way. I'm about to turn back to him and smash my glass on his head, when Annika's steel eyes find mine, distracting me and changing my whole purpose. I think she can tell, because her whole body shifts. I could have sworn I saw her nipples perking up through the thin fabric.

Fuck me.

She looks at me like she's ready to devour me.

It's been so long since I felt her around my cock. I've kept my distance. Tried to be respectful and kind to her situation, to what she's been through, and her best friend's death. But this... her lean, soft legs in those heels are going to drive me fucking crazy.

Does she know what she's doing? Is this fucking intentional?

"Okay, I'm going in." I hear Otto behind me.

But I swing my arm back, pushing my glass into his chest until he takes it, confused, along with the fucking message to stay put.

This one's mine.

I stalk toward her, my steps heavy on the floor, reveling in how her legs seem to squeeze together as she watches me, hands wrapped around that glass as she sucks the orange liquid between her soft lips. By the time I reach her, I'm almost fully hard, my cock strained against my trousers, but she still holds that straw between her lips, doe eyes staring up at me with the same innocence that pulled me to her in the first place. It takes but a moment, and her wickedness takes over, my little witch beaming as she releases the straw and gently places her glass on the bar.

"What do you think you're doing here?" I'm fucking pissed she left the apartment without me, but she's a goddamn vision.

"The bed got cold. All these evenings, plotting to take over the world..."

I lean back a fraction, dragging my gaze down her body, then back up into those steel eyes.

"And you thought it would be smart to come here, amongst all these men, dressed like... you want to be undressed." I'm fucking thirsty. If Midnight wasn't full, I would throw her over the bar and lick her cunt until she quenched this unbearable feeling.

"I just"—she drags her bottom lip into her mouth, unsure of her words—"wanted to make sure you still want to be the one to warm my bed."

What the fuck?

I lean over her, but don't touch her. Close enough that I can smell the orange juice on her lips, feel the heat of her skin, the desire coursing through her pulse. She thinks she can come here dressed like she wants to be fucked, with ridiculous notions that I might not want to warm her bed.

"Little witch, I want to set it on fire."

At those words, her eyes seem to sparkle, before she closes them for a moment as she slowly fills her lungs with air. Her breath brushes against me, the air far too hot, my cock far too hard, her body a glowing vision of need.

"I wasn't sure. After all this time..."

"Don't confuse my patience and respect for lack of hunger. I can barely contain myself, Annika. You look insatiable right now, but you could be wearing a goddamn potato sack and I would still want to rip every inch of it off your body and bury myself in that tight cunt of yours."

She gasps, a cute little gasp that quickens her breaths, her breasts twitching in a way that drives me even more mad. The pregnancy has started to fill her body in all the right ways, and I'm not sure she fully understands how fucking gorgeous she looks in her evolving form.

"You even got our new men mad with lust. They had their eyes on you from the moment you stepped foot in here. One of them almost came here, to this bar, to try to take what's *mine*." A low rumble that sounds more like a growl escapes my throat.

"Yours..." she says on a breathy voice.

"I should introduce you. After all, they need to know who you are and who you belong to."

She doesn't question my words.

"And after that?"

"After that, you can show me exactly how much you and your greedy pussy need me."

She swallows roughly, her skin bursting with goosebumps as a shudder passes through her, and I back up slightly. She breaks eye contact, gets her drink, throws away the straw, and downs half of it, before turning back.

"Okay, let's go. Now."

I can't help the grin. I like the bossy side of her, the needy one.

When I look back in the corner where I left our men, the same two are still stealing glances, while others have joined. Some aren't looking in our direction, but a bit beyond us— Ekaterina and Ashley.

"Katya," I get her attention, "shall I introduce you two?"

She nods, picks up her clear drink that I can guarantee is vodka, and we all walk together toward our men. The two I left there straighten in an instant.

"Gentlemen, may I introduce you to Ashley"—I point to the blonde woman—"one of our valuable employees. She and her colleagues are to be protected and kept an eye on at all times. But Ekaterina"—I glance at the redhead woman who looks like she could eat them all whole—"is the one who will give you all the information you need to know about that side of the business. It operates a bit differently. She's very protective of her girls, and she'll cut you just as easily as she would cut a stranger. What she says goes. Understood?" More men gather before us, and they all nod almost in unison.

Otto and Stefan can barely contain their gaze from flickering to the women standing to my right.

"And finally, this is Annika Backstrom, future Mrs. Hennessey, and mother to my unborn child."

I almost laugh when their faces drop, a sickly color taking over their features.

"Mr—" One begins to speak.

"Now, we're going to leave, but I'll see you boys tomorrow," I interrupt.

"Yes, sir, of course."

I spin on my heel, grabbing Annika's hand and pulling her with me as we head toward the back.

"Oh my God, Ronan, that was harsh. The poor men were mortified." But the sweet tone of her voice is betrayed by the deep flush in her cheeks and sparkle in her eyes.

"Let them be. They have to learn how to speak around people they're just getting to know. Information is becoming our main business, and they have to know how to control it." I push through the back door, thankful the dimly lit corridor is quiet. "Now, where were we?"

Annika

HE PULLS ME THROUGH THE DOOR AND PUSHES ME against the wall, slamming his hand somewhere above me as he leans in so close, my breath catches in my chest.

"Annika..." There's a warning in the rumble of his voice. "Are you sure about this? Because I swear to God, baby, I'm fucking ravenous, and I don't think I can be what you need."

"What do you think I need? Or shall I say, what the *future Mrs. Hennessey* needs?" That introduction made my heart skip a beat. He presented me like a mafia-fucking-queen.

"You need slow, soft, and careful. Since..."

I'm shaking my head before he can finish. "No. That's not what I need, Ronan. I need to *feel*. I need you to remind me of the taste of life, of pleasure and pain, the taste of you."

He grins, a delicious, dark grin that drives me to lick my lips. My tongue doesn't reach the other side of my mouth before his hand is diving under my dress, finding the center of me with a groan.

"Tsk, tsk, tsk, you came here with no panties covering this pussy. *My* pussy." He cups me, two fingers parting my lips, before plunging inside of me, dragging the sweetest of moans up my throat. "So fucking wet and ready, aren't you?"

"Yes..."

How I missed this. I thought memories of the last time I was touched like this, without the pleasure of it all, would cripple me. But they're barely an afterthought. I'll have to thank him later for giving me space... somehow, he knew what I needed better than I did.

He pulls out just enough that when he thrusts back in, it makes me lift on my heels and I have to grab onto his shoulders.

"Such a greedy little cunt, trying to suck me inside of you."

He leans over, the filthy words brushing against my ear, sending shudders all through me as he thrusts inside over and over again, my walls tightening around him.

"But I'm fucking parched, little witch. I need more than this."

Before I take the next breath, he pulls his fingers out of me, drops on one knee, throws my leg over his shoulder, and shoves his face between my legs, dragging the flat of his tongue from the back to the front, sucking my clit as I cry out.

"Ronan! Fuck, someone could come here at any moment!" I shriek, my eyes wide, looking toward the door to my right, but my mind's trapped between my legs, at the quivering mess he's making of me.

He ignores me and doesn't waste any time, his tongue inside of me, lapping at the sensitive flesh like a starved animal. It draws maddening circles against my walls before coming out and teasing my clit. Then relishes every bit of flesh around my pussy, before diving back in. He's ruthless! I'm not even sure if he's doing it for my pleasure or his, as he eats me out like his goddamn life depends on it.

He pulls away for a moment, and I yelp when he slaps my pussy, my mouth gaping at the gesture. Even if my core shakes with pleasure.

"Eyes on me, little witch."

I do as told, and he swallows me whole once more.

But I hear faint voices beyond this damn door... footsteps...

"Fuck. Ronan, there's someone..."

But he doesn't let me go, he doesn't move, he forces my gaze on his as he sucks on my clit, rolling it with his tongue.

"Please..."

What am I begging for?

"You taste so fucking good. Oh... how I missed you."

I'm right there, on the cusp of the most intense orgasm of my life, but he keeps me there... lapping at me until my knee almost gives out.

"Ronan... please!" I beg, the footsteps beyond the door louder, closer.

"What do you want, baby girl?"

"T—to come. Please, make me come!" I plead.

Just like that, fingers replace his tongue, thrusting inside of me as his mouth comes down on my clit, and the whole goddamn world explodes inside of me. My body shudders, and I'm biting on my forearm to keep from screaming so we're not heard, but almost failing as wave after wave consumes me from head to toe. Letting a whimper escape, I'm not sure when his fingers left me and his tongue came back, licking every bit of wetness brought by the orgasm that still has me trembling.

The man is already on his feet, but I can barely hold myself up. I'm giggling as he pulls me after him, out through the back door of the building, and into the private parking lot at the back.

Only it's not that private anymore.

A man we seem to have startled with our presence jumps back away from the door, a screwdriver in one hand and a gun in the other, aimed straight at us. The metal door slams behind me, jolting both me and Ronan.

"Ro—Ronan?"

He steps in front of me, shielding me from the gun. I would run back inside, but it's a secure door, and I can't access the lock.

"Put your fucking gun down." Ronan's tone is frighteningly calm.

"Just the man I was looking for. Well, one of them anyway." The guy says, his tone a mixture of cockiness and anxiousness. We definitely took him by surprise.

"I recognize you. You were there when Bartiste blew up my boat and went after my woman. You ran with him, like a fucking coward."

"I was also there when he shoved his fingers in her cunt."

A distressing laugh charges the atmosphere and a chill runs all through my body. Bile rises, burning its way up to the back of my throat, and I heave instantly.

Ronan reaches behind, finds me, and presses me against his body in a comforting hold, at the same time he pulls a gun out from somewhere under his suit jacket.

"You had a chance to survive this. At least for the next day or two, while we tortured you for information. But you just pulled the rug from under your own feet with that little piece of information. Now... you have to make a decision. You either tell me where the fuck Bartiste is now, or I'll make sure you live for a whole fucking week while Carter carves you like a goddamn Thanksgiving turkey."

"What?" The man sounds confused.

"Where the fuck is Bartiste?!" It's a menacing growl

that vibrates through his whole body, malice dripping off his tongue.

A gun cocks, and I flinch.

"You—wait. You don't have him?"

Ronan leans his head ever-so slightly, and I know what's going through his mind. It's going through mine as well.

"You came here because you thought we have him. So you have no clue where he is or if he's alive, then," he states as a matter of fact.

"Fuck…" That's the last thing the man speaks before a shot splits the night, and I yelp as I grab onto Ronan's jacket. A loud thump sounds next, and I peek to see the man crumbled onto the concrete.

Very much dead.

I step around Ronan and catch a glimpse of the man's face. He looks familiar, but not memorable. If he was there, I don't remember when or why. He's definitely memorable now with that bullet hole in the middle of his forehead.

"Are you okay?" Ronan spins me around to look at him, gripping my face in his hands.

Nodding, I narrow my eyes on his expression. I can't pinpoint it, but his breathing quickens, brows furrowing, and I'm not sure if he's gonna settle on anger or worry.

He releases me quickly, urging me to climb into his car, while he pulls out his phone and makes a call. Moments later, all the guys rush out the back door. They talk for a few minutes before he leaves them and slides into the driver's seat, slamming the door with unneeded force behind him.

"We're leaving?" I ask.

"Yes."

"What about the body?"

"They'll handle it. Buckle your seatbelt, Annika."

Annika… when does he ever call me by my name? What a

clusterfuck this night has turned into.

And isn't it all freaking levels of wrong that I'm still turned on...

* * *

"You just saw me kill a man. A man who was there for the whole trauma you experienced," he says as he captures my wrists in his when I try to get closer to him, in the elevator on the way up to his penthouse.

"And now he's dead. Gone."

He was quiet, tense, throughout the whole car ride back to the building. And yes, I did just witness him kill a man, but... something snapped within me when I watched someone murder my best friend. After that... everything pales in comparison.

"I'm not putting you through this right now. You need to rest."

"No! Ronan... please. I want—I *need* to replace all these shitty things happening in my life with good ones."

"You literally want me to fuck the memories out of your mind," he says, staring at me in disbelief. Though there's a tinge of amusement in his eyes.

The elevator dings, doors opening far too slowly, and he rushes through the penthouse, as I almost run after him.

"Yes! That's right! I know who you are, Ronan! I see you. You protect me, take care of me, keep me safe in a fluffy bubble, and now... I need you to fuck me."

He stops dead in his tracks in the middle of the bedroom, and it halts me in place. His shoulders roll back slowly, his hands curling into tight fists, but other than that, he somehow looks bigger. Stronger.

"Get down on your knees," he says as the bedroom door slams shut behind me.

I don't hesitate. Right there, in the middle of the room, I kneel and watch him with hungry eyes as he walks toward me.

"Good girl." He grips my chin between his thumb and finger, a wicked quirk on his lips only adding to the spell those words put on my pussy. "I'm going to ask you once, are you sure you don't want slow and careful?"

I nod.

"I need you to say it."

"I don't want slow and careful. Make me feel everything, Ronan Hennessey."

Darkness passes through his eyes, and it turns to a shudder when it reaches my flesh.

"Undress."

I rip the garment over my head, and he growls at the sight of me.

"I can't believe you fucking walked out this door with nothing more than that thin slip of a dress on."

He looks furious and, for a moment, I regret that stupid decision. But he doesn't waste another breath as he takes off his belt, unzips his trousers, and pulls his cock out of his boxers.

My throat suddenly feels utterly empty at the sight of him. So damn thick and beautiful, veins adorn his smooth shaft, the head glistening with exactly what I need.

I lean over, mouth open, about to taste it, when suddenly my head is yanked back by the hair, but I'm too stunned to react. I gaze up at him and I'm met with nothing but mischief in those blues that appear black in this dim lighting.

He wraps his hand around his length, running it up and down as he looks at my mouth.

"Tongue out."

I comply, and he comes closer, but not close enough. I try to inch forward, but his grip on my hair holds me in place, and I cry out. Not in pain, but need, and he smiles at the sound of it, a crooked, devious, and delicious smile that makes me squeeze my legs together.

"Hungry, little witch?" He snickers. "Is this what you want? You want my cock in your mouth?"

"Yesss..." I hiss.

"Well, I want it down your throat." And in one thrust, he shoves it past any barrier that stood in his way, making me gag violently.

"Swallow me," he orders.

Tears fill my eyes, struggling through the gagging, the splutter, the noises far too embarrassing, and I'm afraid I'm going to throw up. But his eyes tell me that he doesn't give a shit.

"Relax." He pets my head. "Swallow slowly."

And I do, swallowing the depravity, filling myself with wanton need and the feral look in his eyes that shows a sinful kind of pride.

Just before I think I can't take the lack of air any longer, he pulls out enough to fill my mouth, then pushes down my throat again, saliva spilling from my lips onto my chest. Holding me steady with his hand on the back of my head, he begins a brutal thrusting.

It feels so dirty, so very different from the Ronan I've experienced so far. Sure, he's fucked my mouth before, but it was softer in a way, leaving me time to accommodate. Not now. Not even a little bit. I'm falling down a rabbit hole of pleasure and he's giving it to me, my throat already sore, but between my legs, I'm a sleek mess.

He fucks my mouth through violent gags, smeared tears,

and spit falling constantly from my lips, grunting his ruthless pleasure as I moan my divine pain. And the only thing I regret is that he's still wearing clothes while I'm stark naked. I can't see the ripple of his muscles, his exquisite body as I give him exactly what he wants.

"Jesus Christ, woman. I could fuck this pretty mouth of yours for hours. But it's not where I want to come."

He pulls out from between my lips, steadying me as I gag and splutter, then lifts my head and smiles at me.

"So fucking pretty."

I must have mascara running down my face, saliva falling off my chin, but he doesn't seem to care. He lifts me from under my arms and pushes me face first on the bed.

"Ass up."

Once again, I do as told, and he quickly slides a pillow under my hips. There's no warning after that, his fingers suddenly thrust inside of me, in and out, something between a moan and a sob spilling from my aching throat as I grip the sheets tightly. I hear rustling of clothes behind me, but I have no desire to look and interrupt the pleasure he quite literally stirs inside of me as he swirls his fingers around, before pulling out.

"I'm gonna apologize now, because this is gonna be fast. I've been on the verge for so long... But I'll make it up to you."

"Just fuck me, please! I need you!"

The bed dips on either side of me as he straddles my thighs and the thick head of his cock rubs against my core until it finds my entrance, and in one long thrust, he drives home. I could come right here, right now. The fullness of him is something I almost forgot. There is no more space, nothing as my walls constrict around him.

"Christ... you're exquisite."

Every inch of my skin bursts into tiny electric shocks,

and I'm certain I'm melting into the damn bed. His hand slamming next to me startles me, the other tangling in my hair, pulling my head back until our cheeks touch and I'm forced onto my forearms. He drags his tongue over my skin as his slight movements become torturous inside of me.

"You think I can't feel how you're squeezing my cock? Urging me? This is on my terms, little witch, not yours. Your spells have no power here."

"Oh no?" I slam back, my ass meeting his hips, forcing a groan from the man who dominates every part of me.

So I do it again for good measure, but he growls, releasing my hair and shoving me down. He shifts until he's basically sitting on my thighs, his hands painfully gripping my cheeks and spreading them apart as he slams inside of me with such delightful force, I'm seeing stars.

Each thrust is harder, deeper, each one making me cry out louder, my fingers cramping as I grip the sheets. He rises, and with one hand, he grips my hip and flips me over, and as he rips through me once more, with my ass elevated on the pillow, this time I'm sure... he's reached the end of me. Touching a part of me that makes goosebumps explode over my flesh, shudders rippling through my body until they caress my pussy, my nipples aching.

He snakes his arms under my knees, bringing them up as he falls on top of me and the angle makes my eyes bulge, a few tears sliding from my lashes as he moves in a wild rhythm that crumbles all my walls.

"Don't you fucking dare come, Annika."

What?!

"I can't control it!" I mewl. Does he not know? I can't control this, just like I couldn't control my infatuation for him when I'd only seen him in a picture.

"No!"

"Please, let me..." I'm begging because I know it's coming.

"Not until I tell you," he growls, only that tone is doing things to my body.

"Ronan..."

"Not-fucking-yet, Annika!"

But he keeps thrusting inside of me like I have fucking magical powers. For a moment, I truly think I do, because there's something electric brewing inside of me, rippling beneath my flesh, holding on for dear life.

"Now! Come for me, little witch!"

I hastily reach between us, but I barely touch my clit before those walls shatter and trembling pleasure floods me. Then he does too, filling my pussy as he comes with such force, his jerks send me deeper into this world where nothing but blinding pleasure exists. It carries me through endless shock waves that threaten to render my body completely useless.

When the spasms subside, he begins pulling out of me, but I cry out.

"No." I need him in there... I don't know why, I just need to feel him.

He frowns for a moment before he lets my legs fall around him. Leaning in, he then rolls us over until I'm laid on top of him, my head on his chest, legs on either side of him, and his cock nestled exactly where it belongs.

I fall asleep with his hands stroking my back, my body satisfyingly spent, and my heart full.

CHAPTER 21
Ronan

"WELL, IT'S PRETTY DAMN IMPRESSIVE." I look around the newly renovated space, the fight club looking both rough and somehow luxurious. The ring is in the middle of the vast room with a low ceiling, a few rows of seats surround it on two sides, while the other two have a few small round tables, reminiscent of the speakeasy upstairs.

It lacks decor on its black walls and the only lights in the room are directed toward the ring, everything else bathed in darkness. The lack of windows enhances the privacy of the space, even if it's not really that small. The stairs that lead up to the bar and office are now separated by a wall, and without the right fingerprint you cannot get through the door. On the opposite side, there's a door leading to a couple of locker rooms, toilets, and a gym that looks more like a space where you can take sledgehammers to an old car.

The money laundering business is all set up as well. The club renovations finished a couple of weeks ago, but we gave ourselves more time to make sure the covert side of things will work exactly as it should. It's the start of November now, and it's finally opening night.

"It's perfect." Madds takes one last look around the empty club that's about to fill soon.

We've invited a select few, but word has spread, and even the dark elite of Queenscove wants a piece of the action. There's something about a brutal fight that brings people together.

"I'm still surprised that you don't want to be the first one to fight." I say as I catch a flickering look from Vin. I could have sworn there was a hint of worry in there.

"For a good show I would have to hold back. And I'm not in the mood for that." Madds says flatly.

One could think he's smug, but we've seen him fight—both in the ring and with enemies—he's unforgiving. The act of fighting in itself is not what he's after, but the release it provides, and he doesn't tend to stop until he gets what he needs. Sometimes the brink of death is where he finds it.

But the man is well over six foot, packed with muscles, not really lean, more of a beast with human eyes, yet scarily agile. This makes him a threat to any adversaries and, unfortunately, it rarely takes much effort or time for him to put someone down.

"Yeah, I guess it's wise to let someone else go first."

At least the fights can last longer.

"It's going to be a good show." Vin quirks his lips.

"And we're gonna need that. Two of Katya's girls are bringing their *dates* here tonight. We want them entertained and loose-lipped. One of them is Jonah Holt, and as a favor to The Ghost, we have to get some info out of him," Finn chimes in.

Good. The girls are experts at gathering the precious information we want, leverage to hold on people or to sell, perfect material for negotiation, and maybe a bit of light blackmail. Or heavy ones. Men turn into idiots when they're boozed up or horny, and Katya's training and skill in recruiting is proving invaluable to our operation. Especially since no one knows that the escort service has any business affiliation with us. In Queenscove's hungry eyes, it's only an elite escort service catering to the rich and famous. Definitely not what it actually is.

"What about you?" I turn to Finn.

"What about me?"

"Are you bringing… a date?"

He narrows his eyes before lifting an eyebrow.

"So what if I am? Do you have a problem with that?!"

"It's the excess I have a problem with."

I barely hold myself from rolling my eyes, and Finn scoffs, shaking his head.

"If I wanna fuck a different girl every day of the week, it has nothing to do with you, brother. Mind your own damn business."

"You can do whatever you want with your sex life, I just… you seem to be going down the deep end."

The man turns to me and steps so close, his body almost touches mine, a dark look on his face.

"Like I said, mind your own goddamn business." He holds that stare for a moment longer, then turns and heads to the back rooms.

He's giving me a fucking headache. Madds shrugs and leaves too, although he's probably going to go deal with club business.

"Sometimes I wonder if he would go back to being the Finn I know if we would actually find Bartiste." I say, without turning to Vin.

"I think we've all learned by now that vengeance doesn't change the past. And considering that the guy you killed behind Midnight worked for Bartiste and was looking for him as well, it's safe to say you may never find out if he'll go back to who he was before."

"Shit..."

"He'll be fine, Ronan," Vin says.

"Will he be? Because he's skipped all fucking stages of grief after anger and dove headfirst into pussy. I can't keep track anymore, but every time I see him out, he has a different woman on his arm. I don't even know where he finds them."

"Maybe it's just how he copes."

"Or how he buries his feelings," I say, rubbing my temple.

"There's nothing you can do either way. He's a big boy, he's gonna deal with heartbreak in his own way... He'll learn eventually."

I turn my head, looking into Vin's black gaze.

"Did you learn?"

Those dark pits seem to swallow me as his eyes narrow into slits, The Serpent everyone else knows suddenly making an appearance before me.

"You thought Madds was the only one who knows about your girl?" I ask when he doesn't respond, pushing away the uneasy feeling that gaze fills me with.

"She's in the past," he warns, his tone of voice a low rumble.

"Funny. Could have sworn I caught a glimpse of fiery red hair in some surveillance photos on your phone screen the other day."

Oh, fuck. The look in his eyes turns murderous. Yet I can't seem to stop myself.

"Only... you broke your own heart, didn't you? It wasn't Morri—"

"Careful now," he interrupts. "I'm not your brother, Ronan, and I'll have no issues slitting your throat so you can keep *her* name off your lips."

In the past, my ass.

I put my hands up in surrender, but he doesn't miss the slight quirk of my lips.

"Come on. Let's go upstairs and finalize tonight's preparations."

He holds that gaze on me even after I've turned around to head for the door. I can feel it on the back of my neck. It brings a full-blown smile to my face because I seem to have found the one thing that makes The Serpent twitch—his own *Eve*.

* * *

Today marks one of the last steps in our organization's legacy. The space is booming with cheers and laughter, the ring is splattered with enough blood to paint a whole wall, and the money is rolling in better than we expected. The Fightclub will be a success; there's no doubt about that anymore. Which means that I can move to the next phase of my plan without a guilty conscience. Well... at least with less of one.

When the last patrons finally left, I didn't waste any time. The guys knew I wanted to leave as soon as possible. They urged me to, even as the fights were still happening, but I needed to convince myself. To make sure everything went okay, that it was a triumph.

For almost eleven at night, there was an annoyingly high amount of traffic on the streets of Queenscove, and it made the drive more aggravating than it should have been. But as I step through the door of my penthouse and catch a glimpse of silky light brown hair flowing gently in the breeze, all that annoyance dissipates.

She stands on the terrace, leaning against the railing as she looks toward the sea, the moon lighting a trail across the soft waves. The doors are open, and the sheer curtains flow inside the space on the same rhythm as her hair. Even now, three or so months later, I still can't believe how close I came to losing her. How lucky I am that I get to watch her like this... peaceful, healthy.

I don't know when I started walking again, but I've passed the threshold onto the terrace, and Annika slowly tilts her head to the side. An invitation.

Two more steps, and I've closed the distance between us, slid my arms around her middle, and buried my face in the crook of her neck, inhaling her intoxicating scent. She leans into my hold, laying her forearms on mine.

"So... how did it go?" she asks hesitantly.

"Better than I thought. It's all going to be okay," I say between kisses I dot along her neck.

Her body relaxes against mine, like this whole time I was away, she's been in a constant state of tension. Maybe she was. I think I was too. I slide one hand down, stopping on her belly, where a bump has appeared. She hasn't popped yet, but the slight curve of that belly is unmistakable.

"Let's go to bed," I say, reluctantly pulling away from her neck.

"Can we sit here for a bit? Please?"

I'm not sure why she's asking for my permission.

I pull her with me as I head to one of the outdoor armchairs, sit down, and guide her on my lap. We're still facing the view, the calmness of the sea and quietness of the late hour almost hypnotizing. Although she's the one truly hypnotizing here, because it's her I can't tear my eyes off.

She turns to me when my gaze burns her skin, and I don't get to take the next breath before she captures my face in her soft palms and presses her lips against mine.

I never really enjoyed kissing that much before her. It was always a means to an end, and if I could avoid it, I usually did. But with Annika, it's addictive, her supple lips, the way she nibbles on mine, before she takes me like she wants to eat me alive.

I could kiss her forever.

I could kiss her for the rest of our lives.

"Annika..." I say against her lips.

"Mmm?" She doesn't break the kiss.

"Marry me."

Annika

DID HE JUST ASK ME TO...?

I freeze against his mouth, wide-eyed, as I slowly pull away and break the kiss.

No... he didn't actually ask me.

His blue eyes sparkle with something like hope in the light of this bright moon.

"Are you asking me, or...?"

"I don't think I can give you the choice. I want to marry you, Annika."

"What if I don't want to marry you?"

Something dark flashes in his gaze.

"Don't you?"

"I need to know why."

He narrows his eyes, yet he appears confused.

"Do you want to marry me because I'm pregnant?" I add hesitantly.

The slight quirk on his lips throws me off. I'm uneasy in a

strange kind of way.

"Yes and no," he says, and I'm not sure how I'm supposed to feel about that.

"What does that even mean? And why the hell are you smiling?" I try to pull away from him, but he holds me so tight, my efforts are futile.

"Yes, because I thought the sense of a traditional family was lost on me. I thought I had that modern way of thinking, where families didn't have to be connected by a piece of paper to be just that. But it turns out, I'm more traditional than I thought. By law, our child will have my name, even if double barreled, but I want you to have it too."

I ponder his words, trying to figure out if I agree.

"And no," he continues, "because the idea of marrying you, of making you mine in the most official way I can think of, does something extraordinary to my fucking soul. Don't distract yourself with futile insecurities about your pregnancy, because it doesn't change the fact that you want me as much as I want you." He captures my chin between his fingers, the touch endearing, possessive... loving, "I wanna be yours, Annika."

My lips part in surprise because I'm not sure if I should react to his presumptuousness or the way he called me out on my feelings. Our story started with obsession—mine—after barely seeing him in a photo. Truth is... I'm pretty sure I want him more than he'll ever want me. I want his blue eyes on me, his hands touching every part of me, his lips on my skin sending shivers to my core, and his filthy words in my ears jolting my damn soul. I want to consume him. Every loving caress, every sweet declaration, every little thing he does to take care of me, they all add onto the need, the pure hunger I have for this man.

A wicked grin pulls at my eyes, and then he mirrors it,

before he speaks again.

"Marry me, Annika."

CHAPTER 22
Annika

THIS LAST MONTH SINCE RONAN PROPOSED to me, or... told me to marry him, a fact that made my mom giggle when I told her, has been an absolute whirlwind. Not just because we decided to get married in only a month, but because I had to navigate the treacherous waters that is my former job, Ronan's job, a kidnapping, death, pregnancy, and engagement in the context of my oblivious parents.

They are normal people—well, most might not call my mom normal—but in comparison to the general society, they are. Organized crime, forgeries, dealings on the dark web, kidnapping in a human trafficking ring, and the brutal death of my best friend, are things they only ever read about on the internet or listened about in a true crime podcast. Which meant I had to make sure they didn't hear any of this from us. I did, however, have to offer some sort of explanation regarding my best-friend's death, and a horrible car accident was the most pertinent, realistic option.

They were upset I didn't tell them, because they would have come to the funeral, but they seemed to accept my explanation about being in such shock and upset that I struggled to even plan the thing. In reality, the aftermath of Bartiste's disappearance was still being sorted through, and there was no way I was going to risk exposing them to that.

Nonetheless, my surprise engagement when they weren't even aware of my relationship, was met with mixed feelings. Quite literally. Because my free-spirited mother went mad with joy, singing and jumping around the house on the videocall, while my father looked at me with a scowl bunching his bushy eyebrows, before proceeding to grill me about him and us.

I anticipated this. What he didn't know was that I wrote down potential questions and answers and had them in front of me the whole time. Ronan couldn't stop laughing when he saw me taking notes, telling me he couldn't believe I needed a cheat-sheet to talk to my parents. He quickly shut up and asked for a copy when I reminded him that he has parents too, and he might not want to tell them the real circumstances of our love story. Which meant that our stories had to match.

His parents are not totally oblivious, though. They don't have clean hands, that's for sure, but they deal more in real estate and dicey deals. Or used to, anyway. Either way, they are not in the know about all their kids' activities, which is a choice they made and one that Ronan and Finnigan pushed on them, just for security reasons. So, the cheat-sheet will be very useful for him too.

My father seemed content with my answers, and considering the look on his chubby face right now, as he stands in the doorway of the bedroom, seeing me for the first time in my wedding dress, I would say he's definitely warming up to my situation. He had a long talk with Ronan too, after arriving at the penthouse, and he seemed happy afterwards.

"Oh, Anni." He takes a step in, looking me up and down with such emotion, he's making me emotional too. "You're beautiful. You always are, but... it's the happiness in your eyes that's making you even more beautiful now."

"Thank you, Pappa." I get up from the chair and walk straight into his arms. His hugs always felt like more, like a protective, love-filled cocoon, and as a child, I used to force him to hug me until I fell asleep.

He kisses the top of my head and tightens his hold one last time.

"I don't want to ruin your makeup or your hair," he tells me as he pulls away.

"Don't worry."

I wipe my ring fingers under my eyes, turning back to look in the mirror. I haven't smudged the light mascara. The delicate, simple makeup is very much in place, and the tiny flowers weaved through the loose fishtail braid Katya did for me are still there.

"You look perfect."

I turn back around, smiling at him. I don't know if I do, but I love this dress. It's perfect for our beach ceremony. I'm grateful we live in a subtropical climate, because otherwise I couldn't wear this dress in December. It's long enough that it touches the tops of my wedge sandals, but not too long that I'll drag it through the sand. It's light and flowy, the A-line skirt topped with a few layers of soft tulle, giving it a delicate quality. It will flow beautifully in the sea breeze. I hook my fingers under the thin straps, making sure they're in the right place, drag my fingers over the delicate sparkles lining the top of the bodice, checking that the deep V-neck isn't slipping around, and take one long, deep breath.

If Hanna was here, she would be running around like a busy bee, making sure everything is perfect, in the right place. She would insist on checking my dress herself, retouching my makeup every five minutes. She would be a whirlwind.

Her absence is the reason why I didn't assign the role of maid of honor. It's also why Katya tried hard to refuse the bridesmaid role... knowing full well she would be the only one. She only accepted because she insisted on helping me with the wedding, so she was already doing the *job*. The woman has been everything I never asked for. Whatever free time she had, she used to help me. Granted, we're keeping our wedding very simple and small, so not that many preparations were needed anyway.

Hanna would have insisted on organizing a grand, luxurious affair. Totally out of my comfort zone, as opposed to this twenty-three-person wedding. Which also includes Ronan's parents, who surprised us with their arrival. Although *surprise* is not what I would call Ronan and Finnigan's reactions when they appeared at our door—utter shock was more like it.

"Oooh, my little jellybean, you look incredible!" Mamma suddenly appears and all but runs to me, tears already in her eyes. "Look at you, I just... I can't believe you're going to be a wife. And a mother!" She's fully crying now.

She's been doing this since her arrival, two days ago. I love her, but my pregnancy hormones are barely contained.

"I'm sorry, I'm sorry. I'm a mess." She turns and heads to the vanity, pulling a few tissues out of the box and dabbing her eyes. "Thank God for waterproof mascara. Okay. I'm okay."

Pappa and I look at each other, and a moment later, we burst into laughter. Mamma has this talent of starting a full-blown emotional breakdown and ending it herself within a span of twenty seconds. It's a whole journey, predictable and unpredictable at the same time. It's been worse since I told them I'm also pregnant. The knowledge that she's going to be a grandma has broken through the front she was trying to keep together. I guess it's better than Ronan's mother, who simply said, *"How lovely. Congratulations to you both."* And that was that.

"I don't mean to interrupt." Katya appears in the doorway. "Mr. and Mrs. Backstrom, I believe it's time."

She smiles as she looks at me from head to toe.

"Please—Andrea and Alexander. No need for the formalities," Pappa tells her.

"You heard the woman," I say, trying to usher them out.

"Just one more thing." My father stops us, pulling a velvet box the size of his palm, out of his jacket pocket. "Ronan asked me to give you this before you go out—a gift."

"Oh..." I reach out, catching their knowing looks. Even Katya seems to know what I'm about to see. It's most definitely jewelry and she probably helped him pick it.

Only the smile fades from my face the moment I pop the lid open. I must have blinked ten times before I could even understand what I was looking at.

"This can't..."

"I know," Pappa says, clearly emotional.

"Great-grandma's locket..." I whisper.

"He found it... I don't know how. I can't even imagine the things he must have done in the last three weeks to dig that out."

I run my hand over the delicate flower reliefs that decorate the locket, then pull the necklace out, as Mamma takes the box away.

"But I thought it disappeared when you cleared

granddad's house." I latch my nails in the middle seam, and when it pops open, I can't help but gasp.

There they are... in weathered black and white, my great-grandparents, looking at me with their soft, young features.

"You really do look like her." Mamma smiles.

"I don't understand how their photos are still in here." I'm lost, completely lost. I cannot believe Ronan found this... for me. I can't even fathom where he started, let alone how he found it.

For me...

Tears fill my eyes, and I don't even hesitate as I unclasp the expensive diamond necklace that hangs around my neck, replacing it with the locket.

I press it against my skin and, suddenly, I can't bear to be in this villa anymore. My dad will have to hold me from running down that damn aisle, because I need to go marry Ronan Hennessey.

* * *

It was a miracle I didn't cry for the entire ceremony. Pregnancy hormones were running wild, and the vision of my hot as hell man in that light blue linen suit, waiting for me under that flower arch, made me all kinds of emotional. The walk down the aisle felt like the longest of my life as the world blurred around me to the point that I saw no one but him. The closer I got, the more vivid the wild gaze in his eyes was. I could tell—he wanted to run toward me just as much as I wanted to run toward him.

But that's not what got me emotional. It was how his lips parted the moment I stepped into view. He looked at me like I hung the sun and lit up the moon myself. I didn't miss how he was trying really hard to be tough as he watched me walk to him. In the end, he lost that battle, and I caught him quickly wiping his cheeks the moment I reached him.

I never thought that anyone, let alone Ronan, would have this reaction to me.

There's a different look in his eyes right now, as he watches me from across the room, neither of us paying attention to the people currently talking to us. He glares at me, the hairs on the back of my neck rising, a shiver running down my spine until it wraps around me and makes me squeeze my thighs together.

The corner of his lips quirks, and I'm not sure how, but he seems to know the effect he's having on me.

It's been like this since the moment the wedding reception started. We're in Midnight; I insisted on doing it here, rather than at some typical wedding venue. I wanted it to feel more like home, like us. I asked Finnigan, Vincent, Carter, and Maddox myself, since ultimately, it's their secret locale, and I wouldn't entertain the idea without their approval, but they had no argument since, apart from our parents, everyone in our small party has been here before.

But now, as I catch Ronan's hungry gaze again, the walls seem to be closing in on me. This space is too small, the people around us are a sea of shadows and his bright blue eyes shine amidst them. A trickle of sweat runs down my back, and I constantly feel the need to touch the base of my throat, pressing a bit harder every time to steady myself.

"You still haven't told me, honey, did you plan a honeymoon?" ... "Anni?"

"Huh? Oh, so sorry." The noise of the room explodes in my ears all of a sudden and I turn to find my mom giving me a knowing look. Thank God Pappa isn't here to see me all flustered. "What did you ask, sorry?"

"Honeymoon. Have you planned one?"

"Oh, umm... yes, in a way."

"What does that mean?"

I can't tell her, though. We haven't told anyone, but they'll all find out soon enough.

"We're just not calling it a honeymoon, but yes, we planned something."

She nods, but frowns, and just as she's about to say something else, Pappa shows up, pulling me into a side hug and kissing the top of my head.

"It's a very interesting business that your *husband* and his friends have here. I heard they're involved in other endeavors as well, but it seems the subject has been changed every time I tried to ask what they are."

Oh, Christ.

"It's no time for talking about work." I laugh, trying to push the nervousness down. "I'm sure everyone just wants to unwind and have fun."

I look up at him, and he smiles, seemingly satisfied with my explanation.

Our conversation continues on a safe path, Mamma and Pappa reminiscing about their own wedding, and the moment they begin talking about their honeymoon, I force myself to space out. These people have never been shy enough around me when it comes to the love they share. And while I'm happy for them, I would rather keep all those images out of my head.

An unfamiliar southern tune fills the room as I drag my gaze over the people dancing in the small space we cleared up as a dance floor, and I sense a pull toward a spot at the end of the bar. Ronan's eyes are on me. Darker somehow as he sips the amber liquid from his glass. Maddox and Finnigan are talking around him, and even as he responds, his gaze doesn't shift. Not even for a split second.

A drop of that amber seems to slide down his bottom lip, and when he catches it with his top lip, dragging it slowly, I'm suddenly parched. I swallow the knot that's formed in my throat, but it does nothing to the heat growing in my core.

Our wedding night, our own celebration of our marriage, can't possibly come sooner. Even as we tried to steal some kisses, we still got pulled in some form of cheers, a dance, a drink, a conversation. I need him. I need to feel his hands against my skin, his lips... fuck, this night seems to be never-ending. Only as I look at the time on my phone, I realize it has barely begun. Even if we already had our first dance, and we cut the cake early because my cravings were adamant I needed it then and there, we haven't even been here for two hours.

But now I want him more than cake.

I pull my bottom lip between my teeth as I watch him take another long sip from his glass, and the man cocks his head at me, a wicked grin tugging at his lips.

"We're gonna go get a drink. Do you want something, Anni?"

They're genuinely going to think I'm crazy for constantly spacing out of their conversation with me. But it's better than them knowing I'm just becoming a puddle at the sight of my new husband's feral stare.

"I'm okay. Thank you, Mamma."

They step away, walking toward the bar, at the opposite end from Ronan, and another presence replaces them at my side. I really want a break from people now, but when I look to my left, Carter's chilling gaze is on me.

"Are you enjoying yourself?" I ask, slightly uncomfortable.

"I am, thank you."

"I haven't seen you dance or..."

"I haven't found a partner," he says, smiling politely. "But, if you do me the honor, I would happily steal a dance from the bride."

He extends his hand, waiting for mine, and I look at it for a second too long before I finally accept. I didn't even realize what song was playing until he pulled me onto the makeshift dance floor—it's a slow one. He keeps a polite, comfortable distance between us as he sways us around, holding my hand up in his, the other gently laid on my ribs, just above my waist.

I'm not sure what it is about Carter. He's the most gentlemanly out of all of them, cold, calculated, a bit of a recluse, and I admire his ability to simply walk out of a conversation without remorse when he's no longer interested. But there's this look in his eyes, like everyone around him is simply prey he hasn't chosen to devour yet. It's uneasy, but at the same time, it gives me a privileged feeling because I haven't been chosen—he likes me.

"Could I ask you something?"

He nods.

"Are you actually enjoying yourself tonight?"

He spins me gently, his eyes fixed on me, no expression or emotion in them—yet they're not entirely blank.

"I am, yes."

"It took you a while to respond."

"There's a fine line between enjoying and tolerating. Sometimes I have to think back and figure out which one it is," he tells me with utmost sincerity.

"Doesn't that mean you're at the cusp of toleration?" I ask.

"Close."

"Why?"

He actually narrows his eyes on me for a split second, but they seem to brighten up afterwards.

"If you're wondering if it has to do with the company—it doesn't."

I smile, and he does too. There's a sharp, brutal beauty about this man, and I can't help but wonder what type of person he'll end up with. If any.

"The type of entertainment I enjoy is slightly different from this. But I like this atmosphere, surrounded by people I'm familiar with. Minus your parents, although they seem nice." He turns his head, catching a glimpse of my mother, hands in the air, dancing to a different song in her head. "Although your mother seems... interesting."

I giggle and swallow it when he turns his attention back to me. "Yes, Mamma is quite a character."

He gives me a polite smile, and I know instantly that this thread of conversation is over.

"How are *you* doing?"

He's not asking me about the wedding, the look in his strange blue eyes that seep into hazel is too intense for that.

"Better. Thank you for asking."

"But you're not comfortable here."

"Comfortable?" I cock my head.

"With the unknown about Bartiste. With everything that happened."

If he wasn't leading this dance, I think my feet would stop moving involuntarily.

"Is it bittersweet," he continues, turning his gaze to the room, "knowing that this will be the last—"

"Excuse me," Ronan interrupts, just as my heart falls to my damn feet.

"Of course." Carter stops moving, his gaze back on me, but his unfinished words linger between us as he lets go and steps back. "Thank you for the dance, Mrs. Hennessey."

I take a deep breath, forcing a smile. "My pleasure."

Ronan pulls me against him, my hand in his, while his other presses on my lower back. There is no way I could miss his hard cock against my belly. How the hell has he been walking around with that thing on display?

"Ronan..."

"I think it's time to go," he interrupts, towering over me.

His face is so close to mine, his hot breath tickling my bare skin, and my lips go dry in an instant at his expression.

"We're in the middle of our—"

"Since the moment we stepped into this place, I was forced to watch you from a distance. Every time I tried touching you, you were just out of reach. Every time I tried to feel your lips against mine, someone pulled us apart. Constantly teased by these pretty pink lips I want to see swollen around my cock, that deep, teasing cleavage that I want to rip apart so I can feast my fucking eyes on your perfect tits. I can't stand it anymore, we're going. Now."

The man all but growls at me, his tone of voice low, gravelly, demanding, and my panties are unbelievably soaked by the time he's done talking.

"It would be rude, wouldn't it, to leave now?" I quickly glance around me, various people watching us as we dance to the slow tune, oblivious to our conversation.

"Now, little witch. Or I swear I'll bend you over right here and fuck you where all can see."

I gasp, and he doesn't waste a breath, grabbing my hand and pulling me behind him as he walks toward the back.

We pass through the back door, but this time around, he doesn't stop in the corridor, like he did last time. Instead, he rushes me into the office, slams the door behind me, and turns the lock.

"I can't wait," he grunts.

I'm dripping wet, my delicate lingerie an assault against

my skin, and the last damn thing I want to do is wait. He's on me before I can tell him that I can't either. His lips crash onto mine, his hands hastily lifting the layers of the dress until, finally, I can feel his touch against my skin and my ass hits the edge of the desk. I didn't even realize we were walking.

"Fuck," he growls on my lips as his fingers finally touch the wet mess of my panties.

He doesn't waste a moment, as he pulls them aside and fills me with his fingers as I bite onto his lip to keep the desperate moan as quiet as possible. But he pumps inside of me with desperation, dragging soft mewls of ecstasy from my lips instead, and when the pad of his hand begins rubbing against my clit, I'm beginning to see goddamn stars.

"Nooo!" I cry when he pulls out, just as a surge of pleasure was gathering in my lower belly.

"Shh."

I can't believe it, he freaking shushed me!

In one swift move, he spins me around, folds me over the desk, and throws the skirt of my dress up until my ass is exposed.

"You better hold on."

I yelp when the lace scrapes against my skin, the ripping of fabric. But all air is lost from my lungs when the head of his cock touches my entrance, and in one long, harsh stroke, he drives inside of me.

I grasp the edge of the desk in front of me, as Ronan grips my ass cheeks and fucks me with such fierceness, I'm sinking into the ecstasy of the moment. There's no speed in this assault, but a sheer force that drives me deeper into his oblivion, one hard thrust at a time.

"I couldn't fucking wait anymore, little witch." *Thrust.* "Couldn't wait to bend you over and feel this sweet cunt"— *thrust*—"wrapped around me." *Thrust.* "Begging me for every"—*thrust*—"thick"—*thrust*—"hard"—*thrust*—"inch of my cock."

"Ahh... goddamnit, Ronan..."

"Tell me what you want."

"I... please..."

"Tell me what you want!"

"Come! I want to come!"

My head is yanked back by my braid in a rough pull, and his hot breath brushes my ear as whispers, "Beg me, baby."

The shudder that shakes my body takes control, my nerve endings flying high.

"Please, Ronan, please make me come," I mewl with desperation.

I'm lying here, desperate, hopeful, waiting patiently for the powerful thrusts that will send me to that magical place I've begged him to send me to. But emptiness meets me instead. Cold emptiness as he pulls his cock out of me.

It only lasts a moment. His mouth covers my pussy, his tongue running over every bit of me, licking, pressing, sucking at me until I'm biting onto my arm to keep myself from screaming. I'm almost there, so close but not close enough, as I'm rolling my hips against his face, and when he suddenly pushes his fingers inside of me, curling them to reach that one spot that only he seems to know where it is, my legs shake and spasm, and I whimper through the waves of the orgasm taking over.

Ronan is on his feet in the next second, and I'm still riding through the shocks of pleasure when his cock fills me again. He uses my crying, shaking body as he gets himself off, and I'm not sure I've ever felt so thoroughly satisfied, so full, so fucking happy.

This is my future.

This man who goes down on his knees to give me what

I want. This man who runs headfirst into danger to save me. This man who will give everything up... for us. He's my future.

He falls over me with the last threads of his release jerking inside of me, as he peppers kisses on the bare skin of my back.

"Don't move," he says as he pulls out and moves away.

But I don't think I could have, even if he told me to do it. A moment later, he returns, and a warm, wet cloth is on me as he gently wipes my skin clean.

"I don't think I'll ever stop finding this a little embarrassing."

"What? Me cleaning you?" he asks, surprised.

"Yes... it's like... trickling out of me. Sometimes for ages."

He just laughs and heat flushes my cheeks. I'm about to protest, when he continues.

"I could lick you clean if you want."

I think I forget how to breathe. I think even my heart stops. No. *I know* my heart stops. And another trickle flows out when the walls of my pussy tighten at the thought of him... licking me clean of his cum.

Fuck. Me.

He chuckles behind me, amused at my reaction, and my cheeks are flaming when I finally peel myself off the desk and get up to face him.

"Some other time, then."

When he smirks, I think my heart skips a beat this time. I swear this muscle inside my chest can't catch a break around this man.

My husband.

"Come on, Mrs. Hennessey. Let's make up some excuse and go home." He takes my hand in his and leads us out of the office, but I stop him before we go through the door.

"Ronan, I think Carter knows."

ALL MY WORK, THE EFFORTS, THE PLANNING from the last three-four months since Annika and I talked after our trip to the waterfall, have come to this. Our wedding was only two days ago, but this moment will undoubtedly bring ruin and anger... and also happiness. Happiness for us two. I would hope for the others as well, but I doubt it.

"We already know you're pregnant, so why are we all *gathered* here?" Finn looks around from his spot, standing behind the sofa. Everyone's here—Vincent, Carter, Maddox, and Katya. All waiting for us to speak.

There's no reason to drag this out.

"Annika and I... we're leaving." Silence descends.

Finn's mouth falls open in a mixture of shock and disgust, Vin raises an eyebrow, cocking his head slightly, Madds scrunches his eyebrows, a tinge of anger settling in those creases, Katya is unreadable, and Carter... looks exactly as he did when he walked in. There's no change in his expression.

The bastard does know.

"You're not leaving, brother. You're running," Finn seethes, his fingers digging into the upholstery of the couch.

"If I was running, I would have been gone months ago. I'm not running. I'm making a decision for the future of my wife, my family."

He scoffs, stalking around the furniture and stopping a few feet away from me.

"Family?! She's taking you away from us!" He angrily points at Annika, and I'm going to chop that finger off if he doesn't calculate his next words. "From me! I... we are your goddamn family, Ronan!"

"Watch your words, brother! You know her well enough by now, or at least you fucking should, to be aware that she is not the type of person you accuse her of. Annika is the love of my fucking life and she's carrying my unborn baby, your niece or nephew. I will protect them and make sure they are comfortable until I take my last goddamn breath. Maybe even after."

"She's ripping you away from your life!" he shouts, and I swear he hasn't heard a word I've said.

Annika's hand wraps around my bicep, but I'm not sure if it's because she wants to hold me back in case I jump him or because she needs the support.

"No, Finn. I decided this. I proposed this. I planned every single fucking detail of this. Me, brother, not her! I've been through fucking hell when she was taken. Out of all the people in this room, *you* should be the one to understand why I cannot risk that kind of danger again. I have to do this for them, for us, for me... and don't think for a fucking second that this was an easy decision."

The veins in his temples and throat are bulging, and I'm not entirely sure if he's going to blow. I can't quite blame him. But he takes a deep breath, and it's then I see what that anger shields—pain.

I look at him, remembering the little bundle Mom and Dad put in my lap when Grandpa brought me to the hospital where she gave birth. He was swaddled tightly in a soft fabric, and I saw the ringlets of wild gold peeking out before I focused on his mushy baby face. He opened his eyes, and huge blue irises stared at me with a kind of recognition only blood can understand. I fell for him at that moment. He was mine before he was my parents'. I was barely six, but it didn't make a difference. He was mine to love and protect.

The only thing he needs protection from now is me. He's broken... and I'm not going to be here to fix him. He thinks it doesn't hurt. But explaining my pain to him is futile. It won't change a goddamn thing. I don't want to lose him, but he's pushing me away and I don't know how to make it better. All these months, I wracked my brain trying to think of a solution for this situation... I found none.

"When?" Vin asks, suddenly pushing air back into the room.

"Today."

Annika did say she feels terrible to do this a few weeks before Christmas, but I'm looking forward to our first tradition together.

"You mean now." He gives me that look that tells me he needs the real answer, and I sigh.

"Not right now... but I guess it depends on how this conversation goes."

Finn scoffs again, turns and goes back to stand behind the sofa. It fucking hurts, seeing that look in his eyes.

"One day, you will understand, little brother."

The day will come when his heart heals. It's Vin who speaks when it's clear Finn is done talking.

"You're leaving everything behind, this syndicate, all you've built..."

"Is all yours now." I finish his sentence.

"That's why you didn't leave earlier," Carter states, matter of fact. "The business."

"Not just, but you knew that already, didn't you? I needed time for myself, time with you... and yes, I needed to make sure I left when I was no longer needed."

"You'll always be needed." Madds rises from the armchair, his anger seemingly gone as he approaches me. He wraps his large hands around my shoulders and looks down at me with a tinge of questioning, but he shakes it away and pulls me into a hug. "You'll be missed, *brother*."

I smile, and it finally hits me... I'm leaving. We're leaving... These are our goodbyes. It's not like it took me by surprise— we planned this—but there was no way to plan for the feelings that would come.

"You'll be missed too, Anni." Maddox turns to her and pulls her small body and growing belly into him. "That little one too."

"Please visit. You'll have to meet him or her. You just have to," she begs, sadness in her eyes.

"We will," he agrees, but I'm not sure how true that is.

He tightens his hold around her one more time, then steps away.

Carter comes before me.

"I'm not going to pretend that I understand this... love, this need that all but plagues you, but I understand the need to protect your own, to create a different, better environment for them."

"One day, your world will turn upside down, and you'll flip right around with it. You'll understand then, you'll see that it's actually the right way around."

A crooked smile pulls at the corner of his lips, a rare sight. It's even rarer for it to touch his eyes too.

"That sort of thing happens in fantasy only, Hennessey. I'll see you soon."

I nod and shake his hand. This one is not much of a hugger, and I respect that, but he still holds my hand in his for a bit longer than necessary. I'm not sure how Carter and I got close. Maybe because we're almost complete opposites, maybe because we balanced each other. Maybe because I see a bit of me in him. Somewhere deep in there.

He moves to Annika, and she looks at him, a bit unsure.

"It was... bittersweet," she says, but I have no idea what she's talking about. Carter nods—he seems to know.

"I'm glad you stayed as long as you did," he tells her.

"How long have you known we were planning to leave?"

"Five weeks and three days."

That's specific.

"Five weeks?!"

Finn makes all our heads turn. He mutters something under his breath and shakes his head.

"It was not my secret to tell. I saw no benefit in it. It would not have changed the outcome."

"At least I would have known," Finn seethes.

"I needed time with you, brother..." I tell him, and his stern look pierces me.

He knows as well as I do that he would have been too angry or stopped talking to me. I wanted this period of time to be... normal.

Vin steps in front of me, gives my shoulder a squeeze, and shakes my hand. "We could have protected you here.

She would have been safe. Plenty of people have a family in this underworld."

"I don't doubt that, but this is my responsibility, not yours. I know there are other solutions, but... sometimes these things, love and the mind, they defy logic."

"I like logic."

I tighten the handshake and pull him to me, whispering in his ear.

"Someday, that girl with hair made of fire will come back into your life, and all logic will disappear."

His fingers dig into my shoulder bone, and when he relaxes, and I pull away, the black of his eyes is an entire abyss. There's nothing there but darkness, no hope, no shining light... but there's a slither of red that cuts through.

Katya follows. I brought her into this when she was running a tiny business all on her own. I offered her protection, a home, and it feels like I'm abandoning a child, even if she is older than me.

"Take care of him," I whisper as I pull her into a hug.

She pulls away slightly and looks at me.

"You should have told me, Ronan. I had a right to know. I could have..."

"Done nothing to change my mind."

She puffs and shakes her head. "I know. But this feels so extreme."

"It feels right to me. We'll be on an island, a house on the beach... a tiny town. Paradise."

"So that's it, then. Just like that... it feels more like abandonment."

"Only if you stop talking to me." I kiss her cheek, and she smiles.

"We'll see, I guess. Take care of her, and I want photos and updates."

"Done."

She goes to Annika, and they hug for a while, talking to each other and making promises I'm not sure they'll be able to keep.

"Finn..." I turn to him, but he's unmoving. It fucking breaks my heart. "I'm not removing myself from your life, just from the business, from *this* life."

"Sure, Ronan. My words don't have any pull on you anymore, so I'll keep them to myself."

"It doesn't have to be this way."

"But it is. You chose this."

"Even if I'm not here, this"—I point to everyone—"will always be our own sanctum. I'm not choosing to leave you, I'm choosing to go away with her. It's different. I fucking love you, and I love her and the life growing inside of her. My blood... *our* blood, Finn."

"No, brother. This"—Finn points a circle between everyone but Annika and I—"is *The Sanctum*. You are choosing to leave it, run without even attempting to find what you or Annika need, here. You are leaving... us."

He means him—that I'm leaving him. He thinks it doesn't fucking hurt, that it's easy to go after all we've been through—what he's been through. Although the constant stream of women warming his bed makes me believe he's doing much better than I think. Annika, though, she can't heal here, and I cannot leave her; it would hurt so much more. It's a different kind of love, the kind that will leave you lifeless if it's ripped away, and one day... he will understand. Because I have a feeling that Hanna was not his end game.

"You can't return. If you leave, that's it."

There's such coldness in his words, they don't sound like they came from the same kid who used to follow me around like a lost puppy after he learned how to walk. It cuts deep, too deep. Even though the plan is to stay away for a long while, just in case Bartiste is still alive, to avoid revealing our location, knowing my own brother is basically exiling me is a whole different kind of pain.

"You don't mean that."

"If you're out, you're out." He speaks with such indifference, I wonder if he ripped some pages out of Vin's book, or even Carter's.

"I love you, brother," I say in a calmer tone, sadness so goddamn clear in it.

But he says nothing. A few seconds pass, and he turns and heads to the front door.

"Finnigan!" Annika calls after him, and he stops but doesn't turn. "I am so sorry. I never intended any of this. I hope... please, remove me from your life, but not him, not your brother."

He lingers for a moment, then rips the door open and disappears through, letting it slam behind him, the impact of it like an earthquake aftershock.

He's my baby brother and I have no clue how to fix this.

One by one, everyone else leaves the penthouse and Annika and I are left licking our wounds. Yet with all this sadness, there is so much light, so much to look forward to. This world... it never was really mine. It was always meant to be theirs—Vincent's, Finnigan's, Carter's, and Maddox's.

I wrap my arms around Annika and revel in how she buries her face in my chest, the feel of her against my body, faint heartbeats against my flesh, little kicks in the belly pressed against me, her warmth. This is my world—she is it.

"I think it's time to go, little witch. Away to our own sanctuary."

But too many moments pass, and she seems to be holding me tighter.

"I fear that you will end up resenting me, that you will regret leaving everything behind, regret being with me," she almost whispers.

"*You* are the only one I would ever regret leaving behind. I choose you because I cannot make sense of this world without you in it." I tilt her head, forcing her steel eyes on me. "You are not regret, Annika. You are the guiding light in a sea of it, and I'll always make sure that brightness never fades."

EPILOGUE
Ronan

Nine months later

LILAC FILLS MY SENSES WHEN I OPEN THE door to Annika's studio. She has at least a dozen clusters of candles of that scent dotted around the bright space. When she first started burning the candles, I argued that open flames around all this paint, paper, and canvases might not be the best idea. Especially since she started painting again, she's been losing herself to it, totally oblivious to her surroundings. Her solution was to fill the space with enough of them that she could smell it even if she only burns one. I laughed, but the sparkles in her eyes made me drop it immediately.

She's in that state now... lost in the brush strokes as she swipes the wide brush over the canvas. She's turned the easel away from the door, because she hates it when anyone looks at her paintings before she's ready, so I don't know what she's painting over there. But I know for a fact that the canvas on that easel is the same one she placed there at least a month ago. She's been spending a long time on it, and even if I'm curious, I don't want to pry.

"Little witch, it's time to go soon."

She jumps, and the most stunning of smiles crinkles the corners of her eyes when she sees me.

Jesus, she's the most incredible thing in this world, and she fucking belongs in this room filled with works of art. She even dared to fall back into copying the works of the greats... just for our eyes this time. Even so, she's still the most beautiful work of art in this space... in any space.

I take a step into the room, needing to feel her in my arms, like I haven't had her already this morning, waking her up with my tongue between her sweet thighs.

"No. Stop right there!"

"But I—"

"No, mister. It's almost finished, but not quite yet."

I shake my head, but I stop where I am, smiling.

"Then you better move that sweet ass quicker, because we're gonna be late."

She's flushed now, the color on her cheeks prettier than any of the ones in her palette. She starts washing her paintbrushes, cleaning with delicate movements, her eyes flickering at me from under her thick eyebrows.

"Is Aaro still sleeping?"

"Yeah, he's out. He'll probably wake up after we leave, but Rosa arrived a couple of hours ago."

"A couple? My God, I've lost track of time. Wait, when do we have to leave?"

"Fifteen minutes."

"Oh shit! I thought—" She throws the paintbrushes down, a couple scattering on the floor, but she waves them off and darts toward the door.

I catch her just before she's about to rush past me, pressing her against my body and crushing my mouth to hers. She falls into the kiss, moaning into my mouth, and my dick is already half hard. *Shit... we'll never leave this house.*

Annika breaks us apart and gently swats my arms away.

"I have to clean up and change. Come on, baby, let me go."

"Mmm.... Fine," I concede, place a kiss on her forehead, and release her.

She's so quick nowadays, since she's been losing the baby weight. Lucky for me, it's been a slow and steady process, because I'm kind of missing that thick softness, sinking into her, kneading her flesh... her full hips. I've been enjoying her changing body, constantly finding something new to love about her.

I shake my head and pull at the fabric that now grinds tightly against my cock, readjusting and muttering to myself.

"Jesus Christ... that woman's gonna be the death of me."

I'm about to turn around and leave, but I spot the brushes she dropped on the floor, and I go to at least pick them up and place them on the table for her.

I tried, I really tried not to look to my left, to the canvas she's been working on for so long. But the vivid shades of lilac caught my attention, and I couldn't stop myself.

"Hanna..." I whisper as I look at the woman who's been gone out of my wife's life for far too long now. It was a year and two months ago. She's smiling, dressed in a lilac garment that wraps like a thin veil around her form, looking down at the chubbiest, cutest baby cradled in her arms. My baby... our boy. I could recognize him anywhere. The painting is not finished, but fuck me... the emotion in it is more vivid than the colors that form this image, because its beauty lies well behind this canvas.

It's perfect...

"Baby?" she calls for me from somewhere in the house. I drop the paintbrushes before she can come and catch me snooping.

Closing the door behind me, I walk through the bright corridor that holds a wall of windows overlooking our wild garden, and head toward the entryway. When I get upstairs, I find her rushing from one side of the bedroom to the other, one shoe in hand, one on her foot, her sundress unzipped at the back, ponytail whipping around in a whirlwind.

"Baby girl, easy... we'll get there in time."

"Yes, yes. I couldn't find the other shoe, but I got it now."

I can't help it, and I start laughing when she holds the sandal up, victorious.

"Zip me up, please." She turns around, bending over and sliding the shoe on, but she's flustered in her rush.

"Come here." I pull her up, then spin her around, and drop to one knee.

She calms instantly when my hands are on her leg, and I pull her foot up to rest on my bent knee, then slowly close the strap around her ankle. I can't help but linger, my hands trailing up her leg, past her knee, a shiver running through me as goosebumps cover the skin I'm touching.

"Ronan..." She speaks with an enticing, breathy voice that makes me want to flip her over and fuck her right now.

I look up just as she visibly swallows, and she's about to say something, when we hear footsteps out in the corridor. Considering I left the bedroom door open, it would be wise for our son's lovely nanny not to catch us fucking on the bedroom floor.

"Are you in here, Mrs. Hennessey?"

I drop my wife's foot and reluctantly rise, adjusting my erection before I turn.

"Yes, Rosa."

The middle-aged woman appears in the doorway, her plump cheeks flushed from the heat. She's our son's nanny, but she loves baking, so she's been in the kitchen for the last hour, filling the house with a sweet aroma that makes my mouth water.

"Can you please call me Annika? You've been with us for months now, Rosa."

I know she's not going to do it. Her expression already says it all. The woman is old school, and if she won't call her Mrs. Hennessey, she'll probably end up calling her Mrs. Annika instead. Which is funny, because she's been acting more like a mother with us, always making sure we're fed and happy. I reckon she would either be best friends or mortal enemies with Mamaw June, Vin's mother. They're quite alike.

I walk behind Annika and zip up her dress before dropping a kiss on her shoulder.

"You're gonna be late, you two, go on."

"Yes, all done here. I'll go check on Aaro one more time."

I follow her out of the room, thanking Rosa on the way, and enter the nursery, where our son is sleeping in his cot. It's dark here, with the exception of the faint lights projected on the ceiling, of constellations and galaxies.

Aaro lies in his bed, sleeping soundly, and probably dreaming, considering how he moves his little, chubby fingers.

"I can't believe he's almost six months old. Am I going to blink and he'll be on his first day of school?" she whispers.

"Time's our worst enemy... but we're gonna make the most of it."

I reach over, rolling one of his blond curls in my fingers.

It's bittersweet, how much he looks like him... even if he inherited my hair color, a darker shade of blond, those are my brother's curls.

Annika sighs next to me, and I pull her to my side.

"Do you think Finnigan will ever get to meet him?"

I swear this woman can read my mind.

"I hope so... at the moment, I can't even get him to meet me."

About three months ago, we went back to Queenscove for a visit. We kept a low profile and stayed at my parents' house, since they came home for a couple of days and wanted to meet their grandson. Everyone else came to see us. Everyone... except Finn.

He was *busy*.

I wanted to hunt him down and put some sense into him, but I've been told by more than one person to let him be. Death and loss change a person... and, unfortunately, I'm guilty of the former. I did this to him... I can't force him back to me.

"How long can he really hold on to the anger?"

"He's always been stubborn, so probably for a long time, but this is more than anger—it's betrayal. He'll probably hold on to that for much longer."

"I just... I want Aaro to have an uncle."

"I guess time will tell, baby girl."

I kiss the top of her head and pull her with me as I walk out of the nursery. We say goodbye to Rosa, then Adam and Taylor, the men we hired as security who actually live with us. Ten minutes later, we're driving down the narrow roads of our small town on Falk Isle. A slow song fills the car as the night slowly descends.

"Our life now is such a contrast to how it was. I was a nomad, and you were one of the leaders of a criminal organization—The Sanctum, as they now call it. Do you miss it?" she asks me, her hand on my thigh as I make my way through town.

"Sometimes. The art and contraband deals I started the business with weren't really about the money. It brought us a pretty penny, but I wouldn't have kept at it if it wasn't for the excitement, the adrenaline. But even surrounded by all those people, people I loved and cared for, it was... lonely. What about you, do you miss it?"

I place my hand over hers.

"Same. I miss it sometimes for the same reasons. The thrill of a new business deal was quite something. I would never go back, though. I'm sure I can find another way to get that... excitement."

I glance at her, and her cheeky smile makes me want to stop the car in the middle of the road and make her show me exactly what type of excitement she's thinking about.

"Eyes on the road, mister."

But my dick wants something else entirely.

"I wonder if the guys will hate me forever for taking you out of the business." She changes the subject.

"They don't hate you, Annika."

"One certainly does," she mutters.

"Don't worry, they'll understand. Maybe not right now, but they will when love eventually hits them out of nowhere, just like it hit me."

She chuckles, and it fills my chest with warmth.

"Who do you think will be next?"

"I don't know. They're not ready yet, that's for sure. Power and money are their priority," I reply.

"It won't be Finn, that's for sure."

"No..."

She's not referring just to what happened to Hanna, but

to the new habits he's been developing. My brother, with his tall, fit build, blond curls, and baby blues, has always been popular, with girls in school and women after. Only, now he's been fully embracing those opportunities.

"Carter?" She asks.

"Only if he finds the spawn of Satan…"

"Or the complete opposite?" Annika says, giggling. "Maddox?"

"Possible, but I think it might be Vin."

"The Serpent, of all people?!"

I nod. "He was in love once, not that long ago. He thinks he hides it well, but he's been keeping tabs on her. Not stalking, but once in a while, he makes sure… she's okay."

"And no one else knows?"

"Maddox does. The others weren't even here when Vin was with her."

"Oh… Did he keep her away from them?"

"Not really. I think they knew of her, but Finn and Carter were away at university when Vin got with her, and it was… intense. He was possessive, protective, and she was almost forbidden. She comes from a different world than the one he is from—the high society of Queenscove. It looked like he tried hard to stay away from her at first. Once they started, he was reluctant to flaunt her, not only because of her family, but because she was his weakness, and he didn't want that to put her in danger."

"What happened?"

"I'm not sure. He just broke up with her one day, out of nowhere. The guys were still at university, so I doubt they even knew about them. Madds seems to have been sworn to secrecy for some reason. Either way, I have a feeling we haven't seen the last of Morrigan O'Rourke."

* * *

We're about forty minutes into the movie playing on the big screen of the outdoor cinema. I know because I've been looking at the time every five-fucking-minutes. Not because I'm not enjoying watching Casablanca, but because I've had a constant semi since I went to get her from the studio.

I can't seem to calm myself.

"Fun fact, I chose my last identity because of her," Annika whispers. "I was in love with the old movies when I was a kid, and Ingrid Bergman was stunning. I wanted to be like her."

When I finally think I'm over it, her melodic giggle fills me, and my cock responds all over again. Then she gives me those pretty steel-blue eyes, looking more steel than blue in this light, and I can't help but imagine them painted with ecstasy.

What is wrong with me today?!

The movie moves into a flashback of Rick and Ilsa riding happily on the streets of Paris, their connection suddenly explained, when Annika whispers she's just going to the ladies' room, before she gives me a quick peck on the cheek.

She rises from the blanket and moves carefully around the ones of the other people watching the movie, heading to the edge of the clearing of the small forest. I watch her as she disappears through the door of the bathroom set up at the far end of the area, luckily not that far away, as we didn't want to be in the middle of the crowd. But Bergman and Bogart distract me when the man himself speaks one of the most iconic lines in cinematic history.

I've seen this movie before, but Annika was so excited when she heard that not only was there an outdoor cinema in our small town, but it was playing Casablanca today as well, that I knew I had no choice but to watch it all over again. If only just to see the giddiness in her eyes.

The flashback scene ends, but my wife is not back yet.

I turn and look toward the bathrooms—no movement, no sign of her. As I drag my gaze over the area, I spot her, walking alongside the edge of the forest. She stops halfway, turning to me when she sees me watching her.

Just like that, my world flips on its axis all over again when the woman gives me her most wicked smile, and there's no denying my cock anymore. Then her dress becomes a fluttering whirlwind as she whips around and disappears through the trees.

You wanted excitement, little witch... let's see how much of it you can take.

Annika

I THOUGHT I WOULD HIDE BEHIND A TREE AND WAIT to make sure he saw me, that he was on my trail. But I seem to have underestimated the man who is stalking toward me with a fierce gaze promising something so wicked, my feet burn with the need to run.

So I do.

I take off through the forest, the soft ground kind to my feet as I jump over small obstacles made of branches and rocks.

Humphrey Bogart's voice is a faint echo, the trees far enough apart that the light of the film flashes between them, and my feet seem to be moving in a strange slow motion. Goosebumps scatter over my skin, Ronan's feral gaze burning my flesh, my pussy slick with his silent promises as my thighs rub together.

Each heavy thump of his footsteps sends shivers up my spine, wrapping around my neck, tightening like his hand is there instead.

"Is this what you want, little witch? For me to chase you? Fuck that little cunt of yours and make you come with my name on your lips?" His tone is lower, harsher, a surreal echo through the woods. "Well, you better fucking work for it, because you don't seem to want it hard enough."

His voice is suddenly closer, the rustling of leaves and thumping of footsteps nearer, and with a yelp, I pick up the pace, a surge of adrenaline rippling through me.

I change direction, falling into the darkness of a thicket of trees, and I catch my breath in their shelter. He stops too, but not near me.

He doesn't see me.

"Come out, come out wherever you are..." he taunts, walking in my direction, as he looks all around.

A smile pulls at my lips—I can play with him. Only, that thought is squashed in an instant when he sprints right toward me, and leaps between the trees. I yelp and dart out of the way, but one arm wraps around my middle, pulling me into his body. Grabbing his forearm, I push it away, squirming and kicking. He pulls me harder, my back against him, so I dig my heels into the ground and push back. But he's a mountain, barely moving at all.

When he chuckles at my feeble attempt, I give it one last shove. He loses his footing slightly, enough that his grip loosens just enough. I screech and take off into a sprint in the opposite direction, a raging roar splitting the soundwaves, making my wetness drip down my thighs.

The light of the film is brighter, but I can't tell if I'm running toward the clearing where the cinema is, or alongside it. I can't focus on it when this adrenaline burns so sweet.

"You're gonna fucking pay for that, witch!" His grunts send shivers through my body because, yes, please...

"Make me!" I shout.

I turn my head to the side, trying to catch a glimpse behind me as I skip over the fallen branches, and see the man himself, so much closer than I thought he was.

Instinctively, I shriek, a strange sort of fear infused exhilaration breaking apart inside of me. When my foot catches onto something, I snap my head back to look in front of me and manage to fix my balance, the much brighter lights of the movie helping me find my feet.

Only, it lasts but a moment, before I'm slammed forward, all the air whooshing out of me as his hard body crashes me against the harsh bark of a tree. His hand protects my head, before it tangles in my hair, yanking it back. I shriek as if the man behind me is not my husband. But logic works differently in moments like this because my pussy wants something else entirely.

"You thought you fooled me," he growls, and I'm about to snap back when his hand rushes down between my ass cheeks, pushing my panties to the side, and his fingers rip through me. I scream as my back arches, involuntarily pushing into him. He thrusts his fingers into my pussy, slow and hard, my core tightening around him.

"Is that what you want? My fingers spreading this wet cunt?"

He yanks my head back harder when I don't respond, but my mouth seems full of moans, devoid of words.

"Aaah!" I yelp as he tugs me hard against him and away from the tree.

"Careful, baby girl," he whispers against my ear, "someone might hear you."

My eyes flick toward the lights, realizing I ran almost to the edge of the clearing. The voices and music of Casablanca are all that covers my shrieks because there aren't many trees between us and the first people laid in the blankets in the clearing.

"Ronan, I——"

But before I can continue, he covers my mouth.

"Don't you fucking dare," he warns.

I squirm in his grip, pushing away, but failing miserably and falling on the ground. I rush to push myself up, and yelp when his hand wraps around my ankle, yanking me back a few feet. Reaching forward, I try to grab onto something, my dress riding up, exposing my whole lower half.

"We're too close. Someone will see us, someone..."

His hand smacks my ass, the burn reaching my pussy, quieting me with a shudder.

"Stop pretending this doesn't make you wet." He slams down onto his elbow next to my face, his other hand pulling at my panties until they rip, then his fingers find my pussy once again, sinking inside as my whole body lurches forward.

He's right... it does make me wet.

He rolls those digits inside of me, rubbing against everything that makes my body sing. But the song is not loud enough, I need more.

"Look at them, laying quietly on their picnic blankets, sipping their wine, oblivious to the strong pulses of your walls around my fingers, begging for more."

My gaze snaps up and I see them all. A surreal, calm image as the man who lays on top of me thrusts in and out of me harshly, spreading his fingers as he pulls out, rolling them over and over, hitting that spot that makes me see stars, but not lingering long enough to make them explode behind my eyes.

A heat takes over my body, one that begs to fucking burst into flames, but he doesn't add the goddamn fuel. I want it, I need it...

"Please..." My inner thoughts break out, my voice surprisingly pained.

But he keeps teasing that spot, a ghost of a touch hitting my clit, making my back arch, my hips pushing against him, begging.

"I want... please, Ronan... I need..." I mewl, unable to form the sentence.

"I know *exactly* what you need," he growls, and before my next inhale, his cock impales me in one deep stroke. I cry out in both pleasure and pain, watching, horrified, when one of the people on the blankets turns their head.

Ronan doesn't stop, fiercely slamming inside of me, the slapping of our skin barely masked by the sounds of the music, the buckle of his belt scratching me, but it feels so goddamn good. He wraps his arm around my hip until his fingers reach that nub of flesh, and when he presses two against the top of it and rolls them in small, fast circles... those stars finally explode.

My toes curl, my body shakes, all my nerve endings sing all at once, and I swear I'm seeing all the fucking colors of the rainbow as I bite into Ronan's forearm to keep from screaming. He really did know exactly what I needed.

I think I'm done, but Ronan is harsher than before, fucking me like a wild beast, pressing me harder into the forest floor. His fingers rub against my clit again, but my orgasm has barely dissipated.

"Oh God, baby..." I moan, silently pleading for him to stop because I'm too sensitive. Far too sensitive. But his thrusts are relentless, and his digits drive me to the point of insanity.

"Come for me *again!*" he orders.

"I can't..." I cry out, writhing against his body that uses mine like I'm his to do as he pleases.

Oh, but I am... fuck, he can do anything... everything. He

smacks my clit with his fingers, and I throw my head back as I'm starting to see those stars again. Catching my hair, he pulls my head down and presses the side of my face on the ground, leaning in.

"Annika..." he groans. "I said come for me!"

He presses onto my clit and, *my God,* can I?!

"I can't..." But I think I'm lying.

He pinches it before he rubs in a motion that makes my body shake uncontrollably, my pussy clamping down on his cock, feeling him fill me so utterly well, rubbing against that spot that makes my eyes roll into the back of my head. All of a sudden, all those stars explode into goddamn galaxies and I'm coming with such force, I have tears in my eyes. And even through my cries and his grunts as he spills inside of me, I couldn't care less if anyone sees us here, between the trees, getting fucked by this beautiful man on the dirty ground.

"Jesus Christ..." I pant. "That was insane."

"I had fantasies like this." He catches his breath as he slowly pulls out of me. "But who would have thought that the little shy, delicate girl would be the one to fulfill them."

"Yeah... I wouldn't have thought that in a million years. I guess... you bring it out of me."

"Good." He kisses my cheek and rolls me over, lifting me until I'm on his lap and he's wrapped around me in a comforting hold. I sink into him, my head snuggled under his chin, listening to his quick pulse. I'm still panting, but he strokes my hair, and everything seems to calm.

"Life is funny that way. I never wanted it all, but somehow, I seem to have got it."

"All?" he asks.

"The amazing husband, love, a baby, beautiful house, comfortable life, incredible sex-life... I don't think I deserve any of this," I confess.

"Sometimes I look at you and us and I think I'm gonna blink and you'll go away. Like it was a beautiful dream, because this sort of happiness feels impossible."

It's strange how we seem to share our fears. I smile, pulling away slightly so I can look at him and wrap my arms around his neck.

"Well, darling husband, here's to an impossible life together."

Then I press my lips to his and we sink into the forest floor once more, embracing all that we thought could never be.

* * *

Thank you for reading Annika and Ronan's story.
Reckless Covenant is up next. Scan the QR code below to Pre-Order and see if Vincent "The Serpent" Sinclair finds his way back to the girl with hair made of fire.

Looking for more on Annika and Ronan?
Read the Bonus Epilogue Now to get a glimpse around 7 years into their future, about the same time as Vincent's story in Reckless Covenant.

ACKNOWLEDGEMENTS

I have to start by thanking you, my readers, because you have been incredibly good to me—caring and understanding, even when it takes me so long to write and publish books. Your patience, kindness, and constant encouragement are what keep me going, especially when I'm struggling to find time for books amidst my day job. From the bottom of my heart, thank you.

I hate mentioning names, because I would feel horrible accidentally leaving someone out. So I'm going to refrain from doing so. However, there have been a few people this year, both readers and authors, who have been my absolute rocks. It's been a tough year for me, and your incredible support has meant the world. Even when you didn't know you were helping me, listening to my rants about the most random things was exactly what I needed.

Jess, I do have to mention you, because this book would have never happened if you didn't bring me down from the countless cliffs I so eagerly climbed on. I would have not been here, still sane, without your friendship. I have so much love for you, and big dreams about the South of Ireland.

Thank you to the amazing team of people who have helped me bring this book to my readers. Kenzie, for your mad editing skills; Michele, for not only proofreading, but loving this story; May, for always being happy to read my words and make them better; and Savannah at Peachy Keen Author Services, for helping me spread the word.

Thank you to all of you who took a chance on me and read this book. I appreciate you.

And last, but never least—my husband. You drive me crazy, but I will never stop being thankful for how incredibly supportive you have been when the world felt like it was crashing around me. Thank you for taking over when I'm lost in words, anxiety attacks, or just frozen. I appreciate you so much, even knowing that you'll probably never read this. I love you.

Love,

Lilith

ABOUT THE AUTHOR

Lilith Roman is a romance author who lives with her husband and fluffy bear-dog in the UK, where she writes stories laced with a little danger, intense passion, and dark themes, always ending in a Happily Ever After.

She's an introvert with an addiction for pretty hardbacks she never reads. A lover of anything with chocolate, cursing, and steamy books. And her love for horror movies convinced her without a shadow of a doubt that... even the monster under the bed needs a love story.

For exclusive insights, join her Newsletter, or
Lilith Roman's Corrupted Souls Facebook group.

scan the QR code

ALSO BY THE AUTHOR

Reckless Covenant, a Second Chance Mafia Romance
(The Sanctum Syndicate #2)

Manacled Hearts, an Age Gap Mafia Romance
(The Sanctum Syndicate #3)

Carved Obsession, a Dark Mafia Romance
(The Sanctum Syndicate #4)

My Kind of Monster, a Dark Contemporary Romance

Even in Death, a Romantic Horror Novella

Blissful Perdition, a Lesbian Romance Short Story

9 781739 480318